House of Shadows

Iris Gower

House of Shadows

CANELO

First published in the United Kingdom in 2010 by Severn House Publishers
Ltd

This edition published in the United Kingdom in 2020 by

Canelo Digital Publishing Limited
Third Floor, 20 Mortimer Street
London W1T 3JW
United Kingdom

A CIP catalogue record for this book is available from the British Library.

Print ISBN 978 1 78863 956 9
Ebook ISBN 978 1 78863 886 9

Look for more great books at www.canelo.co

Printed and bound in Great Britain by Clays Ltd, Elcograf S.p.A.

Chapter One

The house should have had a haunted air, but on this fine late-spring day the stonework radiated warmth, the glass in the windows seemed to reflect golden light and there was no mist hanging over the chimney pots. It seemed a fine, normal country mansion, and it was one I coveted. One day I would take out my paints and make a picture of it – my very own Aberglasney. It had an air of peace about it, and I could have hugged it to me – my very own house.

And yet five young girls had died in this house more than twenty years ago, killed, though whether accidentally or intentionally no one knew, for the mystery of their deaths had never been really solved.

Murder was one theory, lead poisoning another, but Edwin Mansel-Atherton, the accused, had killed himself before the trial, so nothing was ever proved one way or another.

I walked in through the open door and stood in the large dusty hall and stared around, wondering where I was supposed to meet Mrs Mansel-Atherton.

And then, drawing me from my reverie, she was there standing before me.

'Are you sure you want to take the old house on, dear Miss Evans?' she said without preamble.

The old lady was odd, dressed in what looked like Victorian-style clothing, with a little lace cap hanging from the back of her head like pictures of Queen Victoria, and she was wearing a warm woollen shawl because, I suspected, the house was so cold. It was hard to believe she was only about seventy years old.

'I'll show you around, shall I?' She was clearly eccentric, but lovely in an old-fashioned way. She smiled sweetly and waved her delicate, ladylike fingers towards the interior of the house.

She took me on a tour of the house. 'This,' she said with a hint of bitterness, 'is the room where the supposed murders took place.'

I looked round the huge bedroom, painted blue halfway up the wall, the top part whitewashed with cracking paint. It was sparsely furnished with a bed and a plain wardrobe and a wash stand – although the room was big enough to fit three or four times as much furniture, I thought – and it was cold. It wasn't a very prepossessing start to my tour of the house, but a sense of excitement washed through me. I wanted Aberglasney.

'I'm sure I want the house, Mrs Mansel-Atherton—' my tone was positive '—and call me Riana. I'd much prefer it.' I gazed around, imagining it as it would be: a grand house, refurbished, parts of it rebuilt, restored. The grounds were huge, so a nature park, a flower garden, a hotel with swimming pool... the possibilities were endless.

'How much do you want for it?' I asked at last, my throat dry. I had very little money; enough, perhaps, for a deposit. The rest would have to come from loans and, hopefully, investments by patrons who liked my rather florid painting style. But I would have it. Aberglasney.

'Well, Mrs Mansel-Atherton?'

She turned her head on one side, peering at me almost coquettishly. 'Beatrice, please. To you, dear Miss Evans, the sum will be what they call derisory, providing I can be here as often as I want.' She showed me a bill of sale – what some people would call a contract – and I gasped at the cheapness of the price of the house.

'"Be here." What do you mean by that?' I asked.

'Just to visit, dear, that's all. I know this will be a good buy for you, but there's a great deal of restoration needed. I want the old place looked after by someone who cares. I have no living relatives, you see, dear; no heirs to take over from me. And remember the American servicemen are still here, which makes selling difficult, but I'm sure they'll soon go home now the war is over. Until those men go away and take their Nissan huts with them the house is not very saleable, you understand?'

I stared at this frail old lady, her skin soft as a rose petal but her eyes shadowed. She had her sad memories; I could see it in those expressive eyes.

'But Mrs Mansel— Beatrice, the price is ridiculously cheap, even so.'

She held up her hand. 'No buts. I know what I want. My solicitor drew up the deeds some time ago. All we have to do is get you to sign them.' The paper was on the desk; she gestured to me to look at it. 'It's all in order, legal and binding. Once you sign it, Aberglasney is yours. Can you live with the ghosts, dear?'

I smiled, humouring the old lady. 'Oh, I can live with ghosts. Don't you worry about me.'

'Then all we need is your signature.'

I took up the pen she offered me, dipped it into the ink pot and signed quickly in case she changed her mind. I could afford the old ruin, but the restoration... well, that would be a problem, but one I was sure I could overcome.

Mrs Mansel-Atherton had already signed the bill of sale, even before I had agreed to her conditions. Her signature was bold and flourishing, as if she was young and strong.

'See you soon, dear,' she said cheerily, handing me the paperwork. 'Take it to my solicitor and the house will be legally yours.'

I left Aberglasney reluctantly and climbed into my waiting van – an old ambulance, battered but sound and strong – and as I drove away from my house I wondered if I'd been taken for a fool. The hall, run down though it might be, was such a bargain... perhaps too much of a bargain to be true.

And the eccentric old lady wanted to visit when she liked. But still, there was no harm in that. She probably loved the old place, but found it was crumbling away around her. I'd do anything to keep the hall, and I would soon find out if the bill of sale was legally binding when I went to see the solicitor in town later on today.

The solicitor, Mr Jeremy of Jeremy Bevan and Brown, wore a long coat and small glasses. He peered at me, and then at the paper, suspiciously. 'You are rather young, Miss...?'

'Evans,' I prompted.

'Ah yes, Miss Evans.' His tone suggested I needed confirmation of who I was. 'Mrs Mansel-Atherton signed this document in my presence,' he said, 'and now you must do the same if this—' he waved the document '—is to be legally binding.'

'Of course.' I signed again where he indicated and sat back in my chair.

'Right, Miss Evans,' he said. 'You are now the owner of the Mansel-Athertons' house.'

I left the small dusty offices on a cloud and stood in the street watching, without seeing, the big dray horse plod past, the load of beer barrels on the cart rattling ominously.

I put the crisp deeds into my bag and snapped the clasp shut with a firm click; I was now the proud owner of a ruin called Aberglasney and, I giggled to myself, the ghosts of the past.

Chapter Two

The builders were taking over my house; plasterboards, white-overalled men and ladders seemed to proliferate in the large rooms. Summer had arrived: the sun was shining, the birds were singing in the overgrown gardens and my heart was light.

I was now in debt, it was true, and Mrs Mansel-Atherton – who insisted I called her Beatrice – showed no signs of leaving. When I broached the subject she laughed a delicate laugh with her tiny hand over her mouth. I said no more. Perhaps she thought it was part of the deal that she stayed, but she was quiet, unobtrusive, and I never saw her unless I wandered into the blue room. It wasn't her room, but she seemed drawn to it by some mysterious bond, though it was empty and cheerless at the moment. 'But not for long,' I said aloud. It would be decorated and furnished, and one day it would make a lovely guest room.

Occasionally, I saw lights flickering across the landings, and I wondered in amusement if the ghosts of the five maids were at their nightly haunting. Heavens! If I turned the place into a hotel, what a draw the 'ghosts' would be. I'd never seen any maids flitting around in voluminous nightgowns, but then I was a sceptic and didn't expect to see anything of the sort.

Gradually, I learned the story of Beatrice's life. She had married her husband when she was only twenty-one. She had one son who had gone to war and never returned, killed in action. 'So you see, my dear—' she never called me by name '—I'm just a lost old widow without a soul in the world to care if I'm alive or dead.'

I changed the subject. 'What about the five maids who died, Mrs… Beatrice?'

Her small white hands fluttered. 'Oh dear, I thought you might ask about that.' She bent her head and her veil hid her face.

'The story was they were murdered by my husband, Edwin.' She paused. 'It's a lie, of course. Edwin never went near the maids, and to kill all five of them in one night would have taken a more cunning man than my Edwin.' She twisted her fingers together. 'He was to be hanged, you know. So unjust, an innocent man to be hanged for a murder that wasn't even proved to be a murder, but unable to bear the disgrace and the injustice, he shot himself. I'll never rest until his innocence is proved. I always insisted the maids died because of the paint.'

'The paint? Surely that was just a rumour?'

'So they say, but the paint, it always smelled funny to me.' She looked up at me, her eyes brimming with tears. 'I'm sure a smart girl like you could find out for me… find out about paint and fumes and things.'

'I don't—' I stopped speaking when I saw the pleading look in Beatrice's eyes. 'Perhaps I could go to the library in Swansea or something,' I said lamely.

She stood up. 'I realise petrol is still in short supply,' she said, 'but there's a good train, you know, into Swansea.' She stood up. 'I think I'll take a turn in the garden, stroll under the yews, sit down for a while and take the air.' She smiled her charming smile. 'I might go away for a few days, dear, so don't worry if you don't see me for a while.'

Strangely enough, I missed her. Not that she ever intruded into my life in any way, but she was always there – sitting in her room or in the blue room where the maids had died.

Curiosity drove me to the library later that week. I'd been to the bank and convinced my manager that I had another sale: one of my paintings was wanted by a rich family in the area. It was only half true; the lady in question had shown an interest in a half-finished painting of Aberglasney. Mr Pruedone, the under manager, sorted out more money, though his mouth was pinched and disapproving of 'lady artists' – who, to his mind, were no better than dilettantes in a man's world – and then, with a sigh of relief, I went out into the noisy street and then into the library.

In the welcome silence of the reading room, I took off my hat and settled to leaf through old newspapers. I was getting bored, until I found the story of the death of the five young girls.

The evidence against Mr Mansel-Atherton was circumstantial. The housekeeper, a Mrs Ward, had seen him outside the blue room that night with something, she knew not what, in his hand. She went on to the landing later and heard gasping and groaning noises. Later still she went into the bedroom to find the maids all dead. Each one of them had their hands against their breasts, nightgowns awry, hair loose and tangled.

Mrs Ward was found to be a woman of impeccable honesty, an ardent churchgoing Christian who would never swear an oath on the Holy Bible unless it was the truth. On this fragile evidence Mr Mansel-Atherton was arrested – and then released on bail because Beatrice Mansel-Atherton had sworn he'd never left her bed that night.

Questions buzzed in my mind, such as: was a doctor called to investigate the scene? Was there medical evidence that the girls had been interfered with? I determined to broach the subject with Beatrice, even though intimacy was a very sensitive issue.

I made some notes and then left the library. Outside, the streets were busy and sunny, and the black thought of murder drifted from my mind as I strolled around Swansea, looking into shops for fabrics for curtains and cushion covers. Gradually, I forgot the ghosts of my house and concentrated on the thrill of plans to restore my mansion.

It was late in the evening when I arrived home. The train journey from Swansea had been a swift one, but the station was a long way from Aberglasney. I had arranged for a car to pick me up, but the road outside the station was empty.

I waited a while and then began to walk, because there was nothing else I could do.

A car passed me, stopped, and then backed rapidly towards me. I thought at first that the car I'd ordered had caught up with me, and I sighed in gratitude. Already, my feet were aching in my new shoes that pinched like the devil.

The dark shape of the car screeched towards me at an alarming speed, the black heavy wheels bearing down at me, the car bonnet – shiny and black in the rain – looking large and menacing as it hurtled towards me. Whoever was driving the car was trying to hit me!

I took a flying leap and landed in the ditch at the side of the road. Another car was coming towards me, its headlights picking out my startled face in the gloom. The black car zoomed away into the distance, gears grating, wheels spinning.

'Sorry I'm late, madam—' the driver leaned forward from his seat '—but I seem to have arrived in the nick of time.'

His voice was strangely accented: a trace of American, or Canadian perhaps. Not what I was expecting from a driver of a hired cab. I tried to dust down my skirt; a button had come off my coat and the front bagged out unbecomingly. I'd lost my hat, and I was horrified and puzzled by what had happened.

'Who are you?' I asked suspiciously.

'You hired the car service from the Frazer Car Firm for six thirty outside the station. They phoned the office where I work and said they couldn't make it, so I came instead.'

'And who are you and…?'

'I'm Tom Maybury, and I'm working at the air force camp stationed at Aberglasney.'

'Show me some identification,' I demanded, still suspicious.

'Here are my dog tags, miss.'

'My name and destination?'

'Miss Evans, and your address is Aberglasney mansion. Do you want me to open the door for you or not?'

I jerked the door open myself, climbed into the car and sank back thankfully on the creaking leather seat. I was shaken. Who on earth would want to harm me? I had no enemies in the small village; no one knew I was here except for the Americans who were stationed near the perimeter of the grounds.

I breathed a sigh of relief as the car pulled to a halt outside my front door. The thought of the attack still gave me a thrill.

The driver opened the door for me, and I realised I had lost my bag. 'If you'll wait here, I'll go and get some money to pay you.' I realised I was still shaking.

He stood. He was tall and handsome; his hair was unfashionably cut; his clothes, casual as they were, suited him. He seemed to be wearing a worn flying jacket and a scarf.

He smiled. 'It's all right. Just ask for Tom when you next want a ride.' He didn't wait, just added, 'Be safe.' His voice sounded caring, warm and somehow familiar, though where would I have met an American serviceman before?

I sighed and went inside my house. The gas lamps shimmered and popped; the first thing I must do, I thought, is to install electricity. I smiled as the warmth of my house closed around me. I was home and safe.

Chapter Three

Beatrice was still away or I would have talked to her about my mystery attacker. She might have some answers for me. Did someone else want Aberglasney? It hit me then like a deluge of cold water: I'd lost my bag and the deeds were inside. What would be my rights now? Would I still be the owner of the mansion? There had to be a copy at the solicitor's office, I realised. Reassured, I made some tea and sat in the only comfortable room in the house, my bedroom.

As I sat in front of the mirror tying up my hair, I heard strange sounds coming from the blue room. Putting on my dressing gown, I went to find out what it was.

I heard muffled gasps and small cries – the sounds of rape or murder? Trembling, I flung open the door. The room was empty. The window banged open and shut, and intermittently the branches of the just-blossoming cherry tree outside scratched the glass.

I gave a shaky laugh and closed the window. I was beginning to imagine things; I was being foolish, hysterical. I didn't believe in ghosts, did I? I had read the papers in the library, but I'd lost my notes along with my bag and my precious documents when I fell into the ditch. Still, I remembered the account of the five maids being killed, and I shivered.

I went back to bed and closed my ears to any strange sounds I heard, telling myself it was only the wind in the branches.

The next day I walked back to the ditch where I'd fallen. It was a long walk, and I was hot and panting by the time I got there. It took a while to find the spot where I'd dived from the road, and miraculously my bag was there – stuck in the muddy bed of the ditch.

The papers inside were wet but intact, although the signatures had run. Still, my deeds were safe, and I clutched them to me as I made my way back home.

She was there, Beatrice, sitting in the blue room with the door open, her small hands holding a piece of delicate lace she seemed to be fashioning into a collar. 'They won't bother you now, dear,' she said with a smile. 'I'm back. They always keep away when I'm here.'

I didn't take much notice of what she said. My thoughts were too full of the things that had happened since I'd arrived, and anyway, I didn't really know what she was talking about.

'I went to the library in Swansea the other day,' I said without preliminary. 'I read some of the old newspapers.'

'Not very a convincing story, was it?'

'No.' I knew she was talking about the evidence against her husband. 'It was all circumstantial; not a shred of proof.'

'Except for the bodies, dear. There were the bodies of the five young girls who died.' She looked up at me briefly. 'Go about your business, now; put your plans into action. I can't wait to see what you're going to do to the old place.'

'I'll install electricity next.' I spoke eagerly. 'These gas lights are eerie and inefficient.'

'I'd have the chimneys swept if I were you.' Her voice was mild. 'Clear the house of smells.' Her eyes met mine briefly. 'We don't want you dying off with poisoning, do we?'

She had a point, in view of her suspicions about the paint, by which she probably meant fumes. Sweeping the chimneys should be a priority, but that small item would have to wait until vital changes had been made. I meant to install proper heating and not rely on messy coal. So in the end I just had the main chimney swept – for effect, more than anything – so that the hall, library and sitting room could be used.

I slept well that night: no sounds from the blue room, no branches tapping on the windowpanes. Probably, there was no wind; it was a calm moonlit night. In the early dawn I woke abruptly. There was no sound, and when I drew the curtains the dawn was shedding a rosy light on the untamed gardens.

Dimly, a figure of a man became visible. He was staring up at the house – at my window! – and I drew back quickly. Who was he? Why was he spying on me? I hid behind the curtain, but when I cautiously looked out again the overgrown lawn was empty.

Perhaps I was imagining things. The dawn light was still full of grey shadows, the trees only now beginning to be washed with colour.

I dressed and then went to see Beatrice. She was up already. It was as though she never moved from her chair and never put down her lacework. There was an antiquated bathroom nearby and a tiny staff kitchen, both of which I assume she used though I never ever saw her walking about.

'I'm going to Swansea again,' I said. 'I want to look up some reference books, see what else I can find out about the murders.'

'Not murders, dear,' Beatrice said firmly, 'just deaths by mysterious causes. Please look up the construction of the paint.'

It irritated me the way she went on about the paint. No one died a sudden death because of paint!

'I will,' I said, more to please her than anything.

As I left the grounds I saw one of the American officers smiling at me. I recognised him at once. 'Tom, you're being an officer today then, not a driver?'

He put his finger to his lips. 'That's hush hush. The driving, I mean.' He smiled, and his teeth looked very white against his tanned skin. Tom, I decided, was a very handsome man. 'How are the ghosts behaving?' He winked.

'How do you know about them?'

'Everyone knows about the poor maids who died all on the same night, and everyone knows about the old lady who keeps them in order.'

I shrugged. 'I don't believe in any of it myself. Don't say you do?'

'What was it that Shakespeare guy said about more things in heaven and earth than this world knows of?'

'Not quite correctly quoted, but I get the gist.'

'And?'

'And I've got a train to catch.'

'Going to Swansea? I'll give you a ride if you like.'

I hesitated and then shook my head. 'Thank you, Tom, but I can't afford to pay for a car. That's why I'm walking to the station.'

'Who's talking about paying? I'm going that way so jump in. It's gratis. Free. I'll be glad of the company, for Swansea's a good way off.'

Thankfully, I climbed into the big jeep. What a treat, being driven all the way to Swansea. The rough road to the station was bad enough to manoeuvre, especially with the danger of erratic car drivers on the lanes.

'Were you looking up at the house in the early light, Tom?' I asked as he did some trick with the clutch and the gears and set off through the lanes at an alarming speed.

'Now, why would I want to do that?'

'Any of your soldiers interested in ghosts then? Because some man was standing in the garden staring up at my window, just at dawn it was.'

'I'll check on that,' he said, 'but you know my soldiers are dark skinned Americans. Was this man dark skinned?'

I was confused for a moment. 'No, definitely not. His face was illuminated by the dawn. He was fair, just like you.' I heard the accusing note in my voice and instantly regretted it. 'I'm sorry, I wasn't implying—' I stopped speaking, not knowing how to go on.

'That I was a sort of peeping Tom?' He grinned. 'Excuse the levity.'

'Tom, forget I said anything. It was too dark to see, really. I was probably imagining things.'

'Like ghostly figures carrying lights along the landing in the middle of the night?'

'You've seen them?' I stared at him, and he took my hand. It felt warm and strong and very nice.

'There aren't any ghosts if you don't believe in them.' He lifted my hand to his lips and kissed it, and a shiver ran through me.

I drew my hand away. 'Concentrate on your driving,' I chided, but I was somehow touched by his gesture.

The sun came out, and I relaxed and secretly watched Tom – his foot deftly double-declutching the gears, his strong hands steering the car – and I felt happy and safe. I was quite sorry when at last the jeep stopped outside the library in Swansea.

I found myself longing to kiss Tom on the cheek, but familiarities that had been acceptable during the war were not acceptable now. I jumped out of the jeep, waved an airy hand and quickly walked up the steps into the solemn silence of the library.

Chapter Four

I was engrossed in my painting of the mansion when I felt a touch on my arm. I had a thrill of excitement and a smile grew on my face, as I thought it must be Tom. Distantly, I'd heard the sounds of shouted orders and the heavy roll of vehicles, and I'd wondered if the troops were moving out. The thought somehow disturbed me.

I turned slowly, my paintbrush arched in my hand... the garden around me was empty. I was frightened and shivery for a moment, but then I shrugged. I must have imagined it.

I gazed up at the sun, and a cloud seemed to obscure my vision. I felt my hand move into the paint and on to the canvas in swift, sure strokes. It was like a dream. I painted swiftly, my brush strokes sure, and yet my mind seemed blank, as if I were asleep. And then Tom was there, shaking me.

'Riana, are you all right? Speak to me, honey, speak to me, it's Tom. Are you dreaming? I wanted to tell you I'm going to stay here for a few weeks, although most of my troops are pulling out.'

I came awake and blinked at Tom, seeing the concern in his face. He touched my cheek briefly, and I remembered he'd called me 'honey', but then didn't Americans call everyone honey?

'You were in a dream,' he said, drawing me to a garden bench warmed by the sun. I sat beside him, and he held my hand. I didn't draw away. I felt strange, as though I *had* been asleep.

'Is that what an artist does when they paint?' His voice was gently teasing. 'Have I disturbed some creative mood?'

'No, not at all.' I shook my head. I looked at him and he was so familiar somehow, so warm, so concerned. 'I don't know what came over me. It was as if I'd fallen asleep or something.' I didn't mention the touch on my arm; I must have been too occupied with my work.

'Come to my hut and have a nice hot cup of coffee,' Tom said. 'I've got the pot on the stove.' He smiled as I hesitated. 'I promise not to ravish you.'

'I'm not coming for coffee then,' I said and laughed. Now, what on earth had possessed me to say such a thing? 'I'm joking, of course,' I added hastily.

'Of course.'

I'd never been as far at the huts before. They stood on the perimeter of the gardens, the grass cut now by the soldiers. Great mounds of dug-over earth formed a sort of street between the buildings.

Tom took me into his office, which was in the same makeshift sort of transient building the other huts were.

'No special luxury for the officers then?' I made an effort to laugh. 'Rough it like the privates – is that what Americans believe in?'

'I'm afraid not. We were billeted in the house until it was claimed back. We're not here for long now. As you can see, most of the men have moved out. There are only two left: Flight Officer Dave Smith and Airman Carl Jenkins. They'll stay until I am ready to leave.'

'And when will that be?' I was aware my voice was shaking. I sat in one of the comfortable armchairs in the room and watched Tom pour coffee into enamel mugs.

'I can't be sure. The three of us will pack up any leftover documents, any stray personal belongings, that sort of thing. We'll probably continue to fly on a few missions, but you could say our work here is almost done.'

I tried to think practically. 'And when will the huts be taken away?'

Tom shrugged. 'Don't know that either, sorry. Why? Are they a nuisance to you?'

'I want to begin on the gardens. Would you like to come and see the cloisters? I've made a start there myself.'

'Drink your coffee first and talk to me. Tell me about yourself, Riana Evans, I want to know all about you.'

I felt a warm glow. 'I'd like to know about you too, Tom,' I said, trying not to sound wistful, 'but soon you'll be going away, remember?'

'Go on,' he said, 'you begin.'

'I'm an only child. My mum is very old and lives in a nursing home now.' I was sad thinking of my mother; she didn't even know me now. 'My father died in the war. He was a doctor. A bomb hit the hospital where he was working and that was it.' I felt tears blur my eyes.

'I was an art student. I loved it all: the big room, the paints, the linseed oil, the seats we used, each with an easel attached – we students called them donkeys. I loved it all. The war changed everything for me, Tom, did you know that?'

'Go on,' he said gently. 'What made you want Aberglasney?'

'I don't really know.' I was thoughtful. 'When I saw the house it felt like coming home. I sold up the family house; it's never been the same without my mother. With the money from the sale of the house, my savings, and the little money I made from my paintings, I had enough to buy me Aberglasney.'

I wondered why I was telling him all my business. I looked up at him. 'I will make a go of it, you know.'

'I believe you.' Tom touched my hand briefly. 'I've seen your work, remember. You're very good, very original. I'm not surprised folk want to buy from such a gifted artist.'

He moved about the small room. He was slim, lithe and very handsome in his officer's uniform. He turned and looked at me, and I wanted him so badly I felt almost ill.

I got up abruptly. 'Come and see the start I've made on the gardens,' I said softly.

Tom followed me from the hut and across the stretch of overgrown gardens to where the cloisters stood out from the surrounding greenery.

'See the arches?' I said. 'Aren't they graceful? They were built in Jacobean times. Isn't that incredible? And there's a walkway above them from where you can see the rest of the grounds.' I walked towards the cloisters and impotently tried to push aside a strong leafed bush. 'These are too difficult for me to cut,' I said, 'but one day I'll be able to afford a gardener, or at least a handyman, and then the arches will be cleared.'

Tom smiled and took my hand. 'I'm quite handy.' He looked down into my eyes; he was very tall.

'I couldn't impose.' He was kissing my hand again. I resisted the urge to rest my hand on his cheek. I wished he would call me honey again because I loved the way he said it, soft and warm and golden like honey itself.

–

The next morning I heard a noise in the garden, and when I went out I saw that Tom was there with the men left behind from the exodus and they were cutting a swathe through the bushes covering the cloisters.

'Gosh, you've been busy.' I knew I sounded full of admiration, and it was genuine.

'Surprising what a good team of men can do in a few hours.' He winked at me, and I felt a warm silly glow as I watched his strong, bare arms wield the saw.

'You left your painting out all night,' he remarked. 'Lucky it didn't rain, though I think the morning dew has affected the oils a little bit.'

I put my hand over my mouth to stifle the not-too-ladylike expletive I'd been about to give voice to. 'I'd best go and see.'

I hurried through the grass to where I'd left my easel, and at first the painting looked jumbled. In among the windows I could see figures, young girls in mob caps and ribbon-trimmed linen gowns. Behind them was an older figure wearing a blouse with overblown sleeves, such as Beatrice wore. Carefully, I counted the figures: five girls and an older woman. Ghosts?

'Don't be stupid,' I said to myself out loud. I sat down on a tree stump and closed my eyes, but when I opened them the painting was just the same: the figures were still there. I remembered then how vague I'd been for a time when I was painting. It was almost as though I'd drifted off to sleep or gone into a trance. I must have been daydreaming, drawing unconsciously, I decided.

The sun was hot above my head. I looked up at the windows of my house, my beloved mansion. The windows were blank. No one was there, no shadows, no strange lights.

I felt a touch on my arm and was almost afraid to turn round, but this time Tom was bending over me. 'Daydreaming again?' he asked.

'Yes, that's exactly what I've been doing.' I smiled. 'Daydreaming.'

Chapter Five

I sold my painting, including ghosts, to a London gallery, and as I walked out into the war-torn streets of the big city I felt a glow of achievement. This was the first time I'd had a painting taken by anyone other than a provincial gallery.

The owner, Mr Readings, had a buyer who liked old mansions and also liked the idea of hauntings, and the painting was just what he was looking for.

It was Aberglasney, it was bringing me luck. No, it was bringing out my real creativity, I told myself sensibly. Everyone made their *own* luck. As for the ghosts, they existed only in my imagination.

As I was in London, I took the opportunity to go to the library and look through the old newspapers. The mystery had made the London papers, and I found several articles on Aberglasney, on the deaths of the five maids who slept in the blue room. Most stories took the line that the girls were murdered; only one cast doubt on the story, citing the evidence as 'circumstantial', lacking in substance, and without a shred of proof to verify the police findings. It made no difference in the end. Beatrice's husband had been blamed for the deaths and had killed himself before he could be charged – all on the evidence of Mrs Ward.

I wanted to know more about this Mrs Ward – upholder of the truth, a paragon of virtue – was anyone that holy and good? I knew there would be very little about her in London, though. My search would have to be carried out in the little village where my house was built. Eventually, I grew tired of the big city and caught a train home.

To my surprise, Tom was waiting for me at Swansea Station. He smiled, and I felt a sharp tug at my heart. I smiled back at him, and he took my hand and led me to the staff car, equipped with a driver.

'Congratulations!' he said as he helped me into the car.

'How did you know I sold a painting?' I settled myself against the warm leather with a sigh of content. Tom sat close to me as the car pulled away along High Street.

'What makes you think I'm talking about a painting?' He was teasing.

'Come on, tell me.'

'I've bought it,' he said softly. 'A piece of you.'

I didn't know what to say. I studied his face, wondering exactly what he meant. He was such a handsome man, a lovely man. Did he like me, desire me, what? I didn't dare ask. In his flying jacket and thick boots, he seemed very official.

I was very aware of his arm close to mine. 'How could you afford to buy my painting? It was very expensive, judging by the money I received from the gallery owner.'

'As an officer in the United States Army Air Forces, I'm well paid. I have no wife, no family to keep, and I wanted the picture.' He touched my hair briefly. 'I saw your painting before it went away to be sold, remember?'

I looked down at my hands, aware of the intimacy of the car. We were close together, and for the first time in my life I felt desire for a man, real desire that burned in me. What was wrong with me? I hardly knew Tom, he was from America, and soon he would return home and I would be alone again. Best not to become too involved. In any case, I had Aberglasney to think about and, of course, the ghosts.

'Thank you for buying my painting,' I said primly and moved slightly away from him. 'The money will be a great help.'

'What's wrong?' Tom asked. 'Didn't you want me to have the painting?'

He seemed to look right into my head. I shrugged.

'I know the gallery wants more of them,' he said. 'I spoke to the owner. I'd like more myself, but the one I already have is wonderful.'

'I'm flattered you like it, but I didn't know you had any interest in the mansion except as a stopover while you did your service in the forces.'

'Some of my folks are from this area.' Tom's voice was cool. 'I'm interested in finding out about them, but if I'm presuming too much, intruding into your life, I can only apologise.'

'No, no.' I sounded weak. I shut up and sank back into the seat. It seemed *I* was presuming too much; Tom wasn't interested in me, just in his Welsh heritage. He only wanted the painting because it was a bit of background for him. I'd been flattering myself that he liked me.

'What's wrong, honey?' His gentle voice penetrated my thoughts. 'You've gone away from me. Now you're somewhere I can't reach.'

'It's nothing. I was just wondering where your family were from.'

'Around here somewhere,' he said. 'I asked to be posted here when I knew I was coming abroad on service.' He sighed. 'I love this old house. It seems familiar to me now, as if I've always known it.' I could hear the smile in his voice when he spoke again. 'We officers were billeted here before you bought the house.'

'And Beatrice, was she here too?'

'Beatrice? No one was here – except the ghosts, of course.'

'You believe in ghosts?' I was surprised and it showed.

'Oh yes, I believe in ghosts… if it's only the ghosts from our past. Ghosts of people we've loved, lived with or never known. A bit of our past is always with us in the colour of our hair, the way we walk, or the turn of the head or the way we talk. Oh yes, the past lives on in all of us, so yes, we live with the ghosts of memory every day.'

'I didn't quite mean anything so profound by my painting, so why did I paint those figures in when I didn't actually see them?'

'I suppose they call that creativity.' His voice was smooth, golden, and I knew I would miss the sound of his voice when he went away.

'When will you be leaving here?' My question was blunt, but suddenly the answer was very important to me.

'Are you that anxious to get rid of me?' His voice was teasing.

I smiled. 'Not at all. I'll miss you when you go, that's all.' I turned to look at him, and then his lips were on mine, briefly but so sweetly. I hid my surprise very well, but I was warm and full of emotion. I was acting like a girl, a girl kissed for the very first time, and that's exactly how I felt.

The car pulled up outside the mansion and Tom hurried round to open the car door for me.

'Tom, would you like to come up this evening for a drink and perhaps look at some of my other paintings?' It sounded like an old line from a film actress, *come up and see me sometime*. I waved my hand. 'I'm sure you're far too busy.'

'I am, I'm sorry. An air force briefing, that sort of thing.'

I felt silly, then, and inept; too anxious for his company. 'Of course. Another time then.' I hurried indoors and closed myself inside the hall. My face was burning.

'My dear, what on earth is wrong?' Beatrice was coming towards me. Her clothes, as usual, were immaculately pressed and starched. How on earth did she manage it?

'Nothing, I've just made an ass of myself.'

'My dear, what an inelegant expression. I suppose you are talking about making a fool of yourself over a man?'

'I just offered an invitation, and I was turned down.'

'Come and tell me all about it, Riana.' Beatrice floated up the stairs, and I followed her, knowing she was only comfortable in her own room. She settled into her chair, as dainty as a butterfly landing on a flower. 'Now, talk to Beatrice,' she coaxed. 'Perhaps I can be of some help.'

'It's the American officer Tom. I clumsily invited him in, and he said he was busy. I've really shown myself to be too eager, haven't I?'

'Tom,' Beatrice said softly. 'Tom. I've seen him around, haven't I? He helped clear the area round the cloisters.'

'That's right, but I thought you were away then.'

'I'm never far from Aberglasney, my dear. Look, this Tom, he's a colonial, not of our race, dear. You'll meet some fine gentleman who will be a worthy master of Aberglasney, I'm sure of it.'

I swallowed my anger. I didn't want a 'master'. I was 'mistress' of the mansion, it was mine, and I didn't want to share it with any man. Except, perhaps, Tom, a little voice said inside my head. I brushed the thought away.

'I've decided,' I said abruptly, 'that I'll take some paintings up to London tomorrow. Just one or two small ones I can carry on the train, and if the gallery is interested they can send someone down to see the bigger pieces.'

'But, my dear, why rely on that sort of difficult venture? You are a clever, modern educated lady. Think of some sound business venture that will raise money. I know you can do it, otherwise I wouldn't have let you have the house.'

I nodded thoughtfully. Beatrice was right. Painting was slow and chancy work. It did bring in good money when a work sold, but it wasn't a solid income. I would have to think of something else.

'I'll go away and think,' I said. 'I had imagined making it into a superior country hotel.' At the door, I turned to look at the tiny lady sitting calmly in her chair.

'What about ghost weekends?' She smiled wickedly. 'I'm sure I could persuade some ghosts to show themselves.'

'That's a very good idea, Beatrice. Or perhaps I could teach painting and drawing,' I said, 'but that's not really art, is it?'

'Children are too messy, and there are all sorts of rules and regulations regarding housing children, aren't there?'

'I suppose so. I'll think about it, the ghost idea, Beatrice. It would be good to have adult company, more amusing and more stimulating. I would have to make the bedrooms liveable in first though.'

I went downstairs to the kitchen and put the kettle on the stove. I could really do with a cup of tea, I thought, and a chance to sit down and work out some figures. Perhaps I could do up some of the bedrooms with the money from my paintings? So far I'd only concentrated on the downstairs rooms.

I drunk the hot tea gratefully and sat at the scrubbed wooden table to make some notes. People were short of money in these difficult times, food was still rationed and Beatrice was right; her ghost idea was beginning to grow on me. I dipped my pen into the ink and began to write.

Chapter Six

London was bustling as usual, with rag and bone carts mingled with army vehicles and the latest sleek modern cars. There was money about, I decided, but how to attract the well-off to Aberglasney was the problem.

The gallery was busy, and I stood awkwardly with my canvases waiting for Mr Readings to come to speak to me. At last, he did. He smiled and took my painting with an apology for the delay. He placed my paintings on an easel and stood back, his fingers stroking his chin.

Meanwhile, I spotted all the faults I should have seen before: the angle of the roof, the colour of the grass.

Mr Readings spoke. 'Not bad, dear Miss Evans, but I think there's something lacking. Ah—!' he clicked his fingers '—the ghostliness is missing, the mysterious figures wrapped in mist. That was what made your other painting special.'

'But a friend bought my other painting. He knew Aberglasney, knew about the ghosts, knew about everything.'

'Ghosts! We must have them, dear. Come back to me with ghosts and we'll talk.' He turned away to another customer.

Disappointed, I took my paintings back on the train with me. It had been a fruitless journey. I'd just wasted money going to London, and now I had nothing to help my plans along: no ideas, no money and two useless paintings.

At home, I lit the fire in the little sitting room and sat there alone, trying to think. After a while, my thoughts became jumbled. I realised I was hungry and made some tea and toast, which made me feel a little less lethargic.

Later, I wandered into my studio – an airy room, half walls and half glass – and stared at my pictures helplessly. I had no idea how to change them.

There was a knock on the front door, and my heart began to beat faster. It surely must be Tom. No one else knew or cared that I now lived in Aberglasney. To my disappointment, the caller was one of Tom's men. He was very handsome, with dark skin and curly hair, and had the same soft American accent as Tom. Though the weather was mild, he wore a stout pilot's jacket of leather and fur.

He handed me a bottle covered in dust. 'My senior officer sent this for you, Miss Evans.' He bowed politely.

I took the bottle and saw it was a fifty-year-old brandy. 'Thank you, and please thank… your officer.' I realised I didn't know Tom's surname. 'Is he calling on me tonight?'

The pilot raised his cap. 'That I don't know, ma'am. Goodnight to you.'

I felt embarrassed as I closed the door. How cheap I must seem, hopeful, almost desperate. I decided I'd go to bed early and take a tot of the brandy with me.

It was cosy in bed with the oil light flickering and the thick quilt pulled up to my shoulders. I sipped the brandy, sweetened with honey, and consoled myself with the knowledge that Tom had at least thought of me.

Eventually, I put out the lamp and settled down to sleep, feeling light-headed and warmed by the liquor, but much as I wrestled with the problems of money and the paintings during the night, I didn't come up with any answers. And all night the ghosts plagued me.

The sounds from the blue room were abominable: strangled cries, bangs, thumps, and the opening and shutting of doors. In the end, I jumped out of bed and went to the bedroom. There was no sign of Beatrice; goodness knows where she'd gone.

'Will you shut up and be quiet!' I shouted in exasperation. 'If you don't keep quiet, I'll call in an exorcist!'

The noise subsided.

'That's it!' I said out loud, excitement bubbling inside me. 'That's it, Beatrice was right! I'll organise ghost hunts. Put people up for the night and charge them exorbitant fees.' I smiled round the room. 'Thanks, girls.'

I thought I heard a giggle as I closed the door and went to my studio. My poor old imagination had gone into overdrive.

I squeezed out some oils and began to paint in the shadowy figures: five girls in simple cotton nightgowns, with floating hair. I brushed in a mist behind them that blotted out part of the house, but the haze of greyish fog surrounding them was somehow effective.

At last, without bothering to clear up, I went back to bed, but I couldn't sleep. I kept thinking of the farms I could visit to buy eggs and butter and chickens and potatoes, and perhaps I could name the whole thing a 'ghost-hunting' or even a 'ghost-haunting' weekend. I was jubilant, and I didn't fall asleep until dawn was poking rosy fingers through the curtains.

The painting sold the next day. Mr Readings of the London gallery was greatly impressed.

'My dear Miss Evans, this is your signature. Your ghostly paintings give you an individuality other artists do not have.' He paused, examining the painting in the light from the window. 'Your strength is the spirit world, my dear. Did you know that?'

I didn't mention that the 'spirit world' had kept me awake all night – or was it the brandy?

I smiled. 'I'm so glad you like the work. Shall I paint some more?'

'Larger, my dear, you must have a larger canvas. Go inside the house. Paint the landings, flickering lights, that sort of thing. Be more... what shall we say? Misty, that's the word! Chilling. You are the artist; use your wonderful imagination.'

He came with me to the door.

'I shall expect another canvas in a week or two, Miss Evans.'

With money in my hand, quite a large sum of money, I went to a coffee house. I was lucky to find one that wasn't flattened to the ground by the war, and I sat alone with thoughts racing through my head. A few more paintings and I could refurbish some of the bedrooms, put in another bathroom on the second landing. Soon, very soon, I could begin to really work at my plans.

I would have to advertise my weekends in the local newspapers at first and then further afield – Cardiff, Bristol, even London. I drank my coffee; there was no sugar and the milk was slightly tangy, but it tasted like nectar to me as I played happily with my ideas.

After coffee, I walked back along the street, past the gallery, and to my surprise my painting was already in the window. The price made me gasp; it was about time I negotiated a better payment from Mr Readings for my work.

I went home on the train, and when I arrived at Swansea I felt disappointed that Tom wasn't there to meet me. But why should he be? He didn't even know I'd been to London.

All at once my elation vanished. Tom was keeping away from me and it hurt.

Chapter Seven

I tried all week to paint the blue room, but somehow the essence of it escaped me. Beatrice fluttered around the landings like a ghost herself, scarcely making any noise but grumping as she looked at my futile attempts at painting.

At last I put down my brush in exasperation. 'What on earth is it, Beatrice? You sound like one of the bulls in the farmer's field! What are you hanging around me for?'

'You're not doing it right,' she said, her hands on her tiny hips, her chin lifted and her ballooning sleeves making patterns against the light from the windows.

Seized by a sudden inspiration I began to paint Beatrice. Her outline against the light was hazy, her lifted chin a proud silhouette. I etched her face like a cameo, the only distinct feature in the painting. Behind her I painted in a misty, indistinct room with blue walls and the outline of five beds with wraithlike figures sitting, standing and reclining on them.

I don't know how long I stood painting, but at last, with the daylight fading, I dropped my brush. 'Oh, dear lord Beatrice, have you put a spell on me?'

'You've forgotten the pot-bellied stove,' she said, her voice weak, and I realised she, too, must be very tired.

'Stove?' I looked into the blue room, trying to imagine how it must have been years ago. I picked up my brush and dipped it into the paint and picked up grey, white and deep blue oils. I drew a faint outline of a stove in the corner of the room. I stood back then. 'You're a genius, Beatrice! It's just what the painting needed.'

But Beatrice was at the door of the blue room, and I could see it as it really was: refurbished, bright but still blue, with only one bed in the room now, and old but smart Regency striped curtains and covers. The door to the blue room closed, and I carefully carried my canvas to the studio and set it against the wall to dry.

That night when I walked in the garden I smiled. Tom and his men had made a good job of clearing the long grass and bushes under the cloisters.

In the shadow of one of the cloister arches I found a bench smelling of newly carved pine and guessed that one of Tom's men had made it for me. I sat down, and then I saw his familiar figure walking towards me, illuminated now by a bright moon. My pulse quickened.

Tom sat beside me, and it was thrilling and comforting to have his arm next to mine.

'Evening, Tom.' My voice was low, throaty.

'Tired, honey? Been working hard?'

'I finished work about an hour ago.'

'Just as well my men made you a seat then.'

'It's lovely,' I said, feeling the warmth of him next to me and revelling in it. Tom had such a lovely voice, a golden syrup sort of voice, smooth and devastating.

'This work you spoke of. Does it involve painting?' He sat beside me, still and quiet, his voice lowered, blending in with the subdued sounds of the night.

'It does, as it happens,' I said equally softly.

'What is it about?'

'Would you like to come and see?' I offered the invitation and immediately regretted it; now he'd think me fast.

'I'd love to.' He stood up and held his hand out to me. I let him lead me to the house, wondering how I could tell him that the invitation was simply that – a few minutes to view my latest work. 'I'd like your opinion,' I said breathlessly. 'The gallery man suggested an indoor painting on a large canvas. I wasn't sure at first and then—'

He stopped my nervous flow. 'It's all right,' he said. 'I'd love to see the painting. I won't stay long. I don't want to... What is the word you English use? "Compromise" you, that's it. I wouldn't sully your reputation, not for anything.'

I felt myself blush, and I left the front door open as I went into the house. My studio was at the top of the building. As we passed the blue room all was silent; I guessed Beatrice had gone to bed. I was relieved, for I didn't know what she'd make of me leading a man upstairs in the dead of night, like some wanton hussy.

Tom stood in silence staring at my painting, and even I was amazed and moved by the power in what I had done. The figure of Beatrice seemed to move against the backdrop of hazy light. Behind her, the stove, softly sketched in, threw out a remarkable glow of light, and the ghostly figures merged like real ghosts into the darkness at the rear of the blue room.

Tom took a sharp breath. 'That's brilliant, Riana.' It was the first time he'd been so familiar. 'You're really talented.'

I was flushed and happy with his praise. 'I think it's the house,' I said. 'Aberglasney has done something to me, given me peace, I don't know what it is.'

He took me in his arms then and kissed me, a real kiss, his mouth lingering on mine. I stood there like a lifeless doll. I'd never been in love. I'd never really kissed any man except my father. I'd played 'kiss chase' when we were children and when kissing the boys had been more of a laugh than anything, but this was different. It was as if I'd been brought alight; a glow filled me, colouring the world just like the flames from the imagined stove coloured my painting. *My painting*. Had *I* really done that?

I stood in the shelter of Tom's arms, and we both stared at the painting and then at each other.

'I think I'm falling in love with you, Riana,' he said softly.

'I hardly dare believe you.'

He sighed heavily. 'I really mean it, honey.'

I sensed a hesitation in his voice. 'Then what's wrong?'

'It can't come to anything.'

He released me, and I stood back away from him. 'Did you lie to me, Tom? Are you married after all?'

He shook his head, and a shock of hair fell over his forehead. 'It's not that… but you have a bright future here in England, while I… Well, I have my life in America and I'll have to go home soon, we both know that.'

His reference to America as 'home' upset me, but he was right – there was no future for us together. He was a pilot, he had his career to think of, and I… Well, I had Aberglasney. It would take all my strength and ingenuity to bring it back to its former glory.

I wanted the house and I wanted to succeed at my painting. There was no way I could abandon everything and go away with Tom, even if he asked me to – and he hadn't.

I led the way down the stairs and into the vast, half restored kitchen, gestured for Tom to sit down, and then made us both a cup of coffee. I made it hot and strong and black, just as I knew Tom liked it.

'You are so talented, Riana.' Tom smiled and my heart melted. I wanted to fling myself at him, tell him to love me, make love to me, but young ladies didn't do anything as forward as throw themselves at a man. The war was over; those days when young people grasped at life in case there was no tomorrow had gone. Times had changed now, and women were more circumspect.

I had seen the sad results of abandoned love affairs. Men gone back to their respectable lives after the danger of war was over. Weeping British girls left behind, sometimes with child, when their American and Canadian lovers went home.

'Drink up,' I said, unintentionally brisk. 'It's about time I got myself to bed. I've got a long day tomorrow.'

Tom stood. 'Going to London?'

'I might,' I prevaricated. 'I'll have to do a small study of the painting to show the gallery owner, I suppose. I can hardly transport a large canvas all that way without the certainty of a sale.' I led the way to the door. 'Night, Tom.'

I stood watching his tall figure stride away along the drive towards the barracks, and then I slowly climbed the stairs with tears running down my face, not knowing what I was crying for.

Chapter Eight

The morning sun slanted across the gallery from the big window; the light was why I'd chosen this room for my studio. A sheet hung across the large canvas, and I frowned when I noticed it. I didn't remember putting it there; for all I knew the paint was still tacky.

Carefully, I lifted the cloth and stood back with a cry of dismay. The canvas had been slashed from edge to edge so that a gaping hole hung in the middle of the painting, completely destroying the ghostly mist and the faint image of the dead girls.

I sat on my little stool near the window and stared out at the garden without seeing the cloisters, cleared now of bushes, or the garden, made neat by the Americans, or the clear sky. All I felt was despair and the pain of loss.

I had put my heart into that painting. I could almost say I'd been inspired. I could try to paint it again for I had the little study I'd done, but I knew it would never be the same work; it would never have the same ghostly atmosphere of the original.

I went to look for Tom. It seemed the natural thing to do because Tom would know a little of how I was feeling.

Tom wasn't there, he was flying, and my heart missed a beat. I knew Tom was still a working American airman, but I'd never thought of him facing danger – not now the war was over.

'It's only a training mission,' his second in command, Carl Jenkins, assured me. Disconsolately, I walked back to the mansion. *I must get to work*, I thought. *I need paintings to make more money if I intend to get my ghost weekends under way.*

I squeezed out the paints on to the palette, but for once I had no idea what to paint. The sunlight streamed into the room, hurting my eyes. I looked at the unused mounds of oil and knew they would dry and harden and be wasted and I couldn't afford to waste anything.

I began to paint, but nothing was going right. In my frustration, I threw down my brush. I wandered out into the garden again and sat in the shadow of the cloisters. I closed my eyes, dazzled by the sunlight that suddenly burst into my little nest beneath the arch. I think I slept, because next thing I knew Tom was sitting at my side.

'You were looking for me?' His honey-sweet voice washed over me like a balm. He was safely home from flying, and suddenly I wanted to hug him. Instead, I told him about the painting.

'Show me,' he said. He took my hand and led me upstairs; he knew the house as well as I did. It was shady now in the gallery, the sun slanting away to the west where it would sink behind the hills and illuminate them with brushes of gold.

I lifted the cloth over the canvas and stared in disbelief. The painting was intact, no terrible slashes, no holes in the fabric... Was I dreaming?

'What's this, Riana?' Tom asked. 'If you're trying to lure me upstairs there's no need for dramas.'

'The painting was cut to pieces!' I was indignant, chagrin making me blush to the roots of my hair.

'A trick of the light,' Tom said soothingly, but I could see he didn't believe me. I didn't blame him. I couldn't believe the evidence of my own eyes. Wonderingly, I touched the painting. It was nearly dry.

'It's one of your best,' Tom said. 'You were sleeping in the garden there; it must have all been a dream, the cuts in the canvas. A horrible dream, that's all.'

'No, Tom, I could feel the slashes in the painting. I touched it, it wasn't a dream.'

'A nightmare then.' Tom smiled. 'A daytime nightmare, that's all it was, Riana. Who is here to do such a thing? Who would *want* to destroy your work?'

'Someone who doesn't want the house done up,' I suggested.

'That would hold water if the painting was really damaged, but it's not, Riana. The whole thing doesn't make any sense.'

I capitulated. 'I know. Let's go and get a drink. A stiff gin or something.'

We took our drinks out into the garden while I tried to fathom the whole thing out. The work on the easel was mine all right, so the cut-up canvas was a fake. But who would go to all that trouble and why? I wished now I'd looked closer at the destroyed canvas, but I'd been too horrified and baffled to examine it properly.

'Penny for them? Isn't that what you British folk say?'

I shook my head, not wanting to seem more foolish than I was. 'My thoughts are just a jumble, Tom. Someone tried to run me off the road when I first came here, and

43

now this. What am I supposed to make of it all – except that someone doesn't want me here?'

'The ghosts?'

'Are you mocking me?'

'Trying to lighten the gloom a bit, Riana. Forget all this. Enjoy the warmth and the drink and, hopefully, the company.'

I looked at him as I sipped my drink. Could he be doing all this to get me out? Was he my enemy, not my friend? But why would he do such a thing? What could he hope to gain?

It was as if he read my thoughts. 'I wouldn't hurt you for the world, Riana. I hope you know that, honey.'

He took my glass out of my hand and put it on the floor, then he deliberately kissed me. My arms crept around him, my dear safe Tom. He was the one who had rescued me on the roadway; what was I thinking of being suspicious of the only friend I had in the world?

I pulled away just before I became swamped with passion, for I didn't want a lover, not just now. In any case, Tom's life was in America. What was the point in getting involved with him?

'I'll going indoors now, it's getting dark—' I shivered '—and chilly. Goodnight, Tom, and thanks for being a friend.'

He stood up straight away and strode into the darkness. I supposed I'd offended him, but that was just too bad. I could do without an involvement of any kind I had a living to make and a career to forge and a grand scheme to work out. My house would be ready for visitors any day now.

Chapter Nine

It was the end of July, and it was my opening night in more ways than one. My paintings had gone on display in the London gallery – just a small selection – and my house was open for the first 'ghost-haunting' night.

The local newspaper reporter had turned up with a camera and with an assistant who impressed me by writing shorthand when she interviewed me. 'This story will be circulated around the press all over Britain,' the assistant said proudly.

Granger, the chief reporter, pushed his way towards me. 'You have a good crowd, Miss Evans. About forty, would you say?'

I nodded, pleased and yet alarmed at the crowd of noisy people sitting round the big dining table in the newly refurbished dining room. Still, I didn't have to do all the work myself. I'd brought Rosie and her mother, Mrs Ward – the same Mrs Ward who had spoken up against Mr Edwin at the time of the murder. But she was the only one who would agree to work for me. The rest of the villagers were too superstitious about the ghosts.

Mrs Ward turned out to be a first-class cook, and she and Rosie would serve and wait on table and I had to be very grateful to them both. Supper and breakfast was all a part of the ghost night, and already on this first event I could tell the weekend was going to not only pay for itself but also make me a good profit.

The female guests were to stay in the bedrooms I'd already turned into dormitories. I could fit the sixteen women of various ages in three of the dorms. I expected the men, being men, wouldn't mind roughing it a bit and would prefer to ghost hunt all night rather than sleep. Indeed, even as they filed out of the dining room they looked around as if expecting to see apparitions floating around the house.

I had my sketch book at the ready and unobtrusively began to draw. One gentleman was an old army man, Colonel Fred, and he hugged his bottle of brandy close to him like a baby. He was affable and keen, with shrewd eyes and a sun-wrinkled face, and I liked him on sight.

'I mean to spend the whole night in the house,' he said. 'I'll sleep in the hall if I have to.'

'So will I,' Jim from Aberdeen said firmly. 'I'm determined to see this ghost of yours.'

'That won't be necessary,' I said, quickly amending my plan. 'You men can have the rooms at the back of the house on the ground floor.'

Tom appeared at my side. Startled, I stared at him. 'I didn't hear you coming in,' I whispered.

'Perhaps I'm a ghost too!' He put his arm around my shoulders and hugged me, and I laughed at him.

'You're a bit solid to be a ghost.' I had my arm around his slim waist, and I could feel the rough material of his uniform under my hand. 'Thank goodness,' I added with a mischievous wink.

'Hey, don't get fast with me, honey.' He playfully kissed my cheek, and then I noticed the guests were spreading out examining the rooms, some carrying glasses of wine or spirits they'd brought along to the 'party' themselves. Next time I would include the drinks in the price, I decided. A little 'cheer' would help things along nicely.

Later, as Tom and I walked in the garden, we could hear the ghost hunters singing some sort of chant which they all seemed to know. I smiled up at Tom. 'Something's keeping them happy.'

'It's the spirits,' Tom said, laughing. 'The ones in the bottles.'

I leaned against him, weak with laughter, and then I froze as I heard a blood-curdling scream from the hallway of the house.

I was running then, across the lawn with Tom just ahead of me. In the hall, everyone was on their feet, their white faces turned up to the top of the stairs. One of the younger girls was pointing, her hand shaking.

'Betty—' I touched her shoulder '—don't be scared. It's only—' I broke off as Tom caught my arm and made a shushing noise.

'Young lady—' his voice was stern '—pull yourself together. It's exactly what you came to see, wasn't it? A ghost from the past.'

Betty nodded her blonde head. 'I know, but this is the first time I've seen anything supernatural at one of these weekends! Usually, it's just a laugh and a drink and the chance to meet—' She stopped and looked around at the faces of the other guests.

'Come along now, dearie.' Colonel Fred shook his head reprovingly. 'This is not a dating club. This is a serious ghost hunt. She's gone now, frightened off by all that screaming. You've spoilt the night for us all, so please don't come here again.'

I started up the stairs. *Beatrice must be frightened and confused by all the noise*, I thought. *I must reassure her.* I got almost to the top before I realised the ghost hunters were following me.

One young gent stopped me and held out his hand. 'I'm William,' he said. 'And I'd like to use the description of your ghost in my report to *Spirit News*, the magazine for believers, if that's all right.' He shook my nerveless hand. 'This is the first time the whole thing hasn't been a charade, a set-up, an act! Your ghost is real enough, for my sensors picked up something strange, some unfamiliar vibrations, and I will certainly book your next weekend of ghost hunting,' he said, gesturing to the other silent guests, 'and so will most of the people here, I feel sure.'

The others surged around me, and then I felt a push and I was falling downwards, hitting stair after stair, landing in a heap in the hall. My head narrowly missed hitting the huge sideboard that stood near the foot of the stairs.

Tom picked me up and held me gently in his arms. 'Riana, are you all right?' His face was pale, anxious.

I puffed out my breath and rested against him for a minute. 'I'm just winded that's all.' I tried to smile though I knew I'd have some bruises in the morning.

Betty brought me a cup of tea and, though she was fluffy and flirtatious, she was very concerned and very kind.

Young William, his camera swinging around his neck, enquired anxiously after my health, and when he had assured himself I wasn't really hurt he smiled. 'Dear Miss Evans, you will have to furnish other rooms because your fame will grow once this news gets out.' He leaned closer, smelling of brandy. 'Your ghost must have become irritated with the disturbance and used her force to project you back down the stairs. Tell me, Miss Evans, what do you call her? Your ghost, I mean.'

Weak and wanting to laugh hysterically, but restrained by Tom's warning hand on my shoulder, I told him, 'Well, we just call her Beatrice.'

'And,' Tom added, 'you are privileged to see her. She rarely comes out of her room. It is the blue room, the one that's haunted.'

I dug him in the side with my elbow.

'And are we likely to see the five maidens who died there so mysteriously?' the colonel asked.

I had no time to reply, which was just as well.

A young business-suited man stood in front of me. 'Jack Winford.' He held out his hand and I took it. Suddenly, I was surrounded by enthusiastic ghost hunters, each determined to ask questions concerning the murder story and the haunting and how often the ghosts were seen and my head was filled with the babble of voices.

Tom rescued me, taking me outside into the cool air of the cloisters. 'I don't think I can stand too much of this,' I said, sitting down abruptly in the shadows.

Tom sat beside me, his body warm as he rested his arm around my shoulder. 'You can and will put up with it until you make enough money to refurbish the entire house,' he said firmly, 'and then you can bring in a manager to run the ghost hunts and hide yourself away and do your wonderful painting.'

I remembered then how my painting, or what I thought was my painting, was slashed to shreds, and as I listened to the voices of my guests from inside the house I shivered. What was I doing having strangers in my house, and who had pushed me down the stairs? Because I had been pushed by a human hand, not moved by some supernatural force. I shivered, suddenly scared.

'Can you sleep with me?' I asked before I realised what I'd said.

Tom understood me, however and kissed me lightly on the cheek. 'Yes, if that's what you want. I'll come and stay in your house. There are plenty of rooms and several comfortable sofas.'

'Thank you, Tom.' I felt myself blush, and I bent so that my hair covered my face.

Tom took my arm and led me inside to the comparative quiet of the library. The ghost hunters were all in the hall, watching the stairs, with Brownie cameras at the ready and flashlight and sensors and all sorts of equipment I didn't begin to understand.

Tom and I drank some wine and then fell asleep alongside each other on the sofa. I woke to find his arms around me. He had taken off his jacket and my face was against the smooth material of his shirt. I pretended to sleep a little while longer enjoying the closeness and warmth of him, but at last he stirred, and I sat up, rubbing my eyes.

There was a bustling noise in the hallway and the ghost hunters were coming back to life. I heard Mrs Ward in the kitchen, the smell of bacon permeated the air and I breathed a sigh of relief; after breakfast I would have the place to myself again. I could start to paint more pictures, work on the sketches I'd drawn last night.

William – 'young William' as the other guests called him – seemed to have formed a truce with Betty, who in spite of her plumpness was very pretty, and together they went outside to wait for the taxi taking them into town.

'Perhaps I should arrange a bus,' I murmured, and Tom, who had come outside after me, rested a friendly arm on my shoulder.

'I think that would be a very good idea. It would mean the visitors would have to keep to a time schedule and leave promptly at whatever time you decided.'

'I'd have to charge a small fee, or put up the price of the visit by a few shillings, otherwise I'd lose out,' I said and burst out laughing. 'I'm becoming quite mercenary, aren't I?'

'Businesslike, that's what you are becoming, and just as well if you mean to turn this old heap back into a liveable, pleasurable house with a show garden.'

'Oh, I never thought of showing the gardens.' I hesitated. 'I suppose the cloisters are worth seeing, and the yew-tree arch, and even the entrance flooring is as old as... well, very old.' I decided that I would have to research the history of Aberglasney very thoroughly. I would ask Beatrice where the original plans were and see if I could find out anything more about the house at the library in town.

At last, all the visitors had departed, and Mrs Ward was kind enough to provide us all with a roast for lunch. We sat down together: me and Tom, Mrs Ward and her daughter.

'Thank you so much, Mrs Ward.' I cut a juicy piece of beef and popped it into my mouth.

Rosie smirked. 'It was me who cooked the dinner, Miss Evans,' she said. 'My mam taught me. I've known how to cook since I was a little girl.'

'The gravy is a delight,' I said, feeling slightly reproved.

51

'Mam made that, miss. She's good at gravy is our mam.'

'Well, you are both invaluable to me.' I hoped I was being tactful. 'Perhaps we can make this a regular arrangement. Do you both think you can bear to come and work for me, say once a month?'

Mrs Ward nodded, her mouth full, and it was Rosie who spoke up. 'That would be very handy, miss, what with Dad lost in the war, but all this screaming about ghosts shakes me up, mind.'

'This ghost business is a lot of nonsense.' Mrs Ward tightened the knot on her wraparound apron and adjusted her turban, tucking in a stray curl of permed hair. 'Hysterical people see what they want to see.'

'There's a lot of truth in that, Mrs Ward, but it seems to be paying, and if I earn money I can put the old house right and afford full-time help before too long.'

Mrs Ward brightened up. 'Well, as long as I don't have to speak to them townies. I'll stay in the kitchen and mind my own, and you, Rosie, will do the same thing.'

'I will that, Mam,' Rosie said meekly, but her eyes were on Tom. 'Mr Tom, sir, I hear the soldiers are having another party tonight with some of the village girls. Can I come along, sir?'

Mrs Ward bristled. 'Don't be so forward! In any case, remember that those soldiers are… are not from this country,' she added, looking flustered.

'They are black Americans, Mrs Ward. They are getting together from all over Wales,' Tom said easily, though I could tell he was offended. 'They are good brave men, and if the enemy had come here they would have defended the people of this village – including you and Rosie – with their lives.'

Mrs Ward lowered her eyes. 'I got to agree with that, sir,' she mumbled. 'I suppose you can go, Rosie, so long as you keep yourself tidy.'

We all knew what she meant, and I met Tom's eyes, trying not to laugh. Rosie was ecstatic.

'You'd be welcome,' Tom said. 'And perhaps Miss Evans would kindly come along as well?'

I could hardly say no in the circumstances. 'That would be very nice,' I mumbled.

At last I was alone in the house. Tom had gone, and there wasn't even a sign of Beatrice; she must have been frightened off by the crowds. The quiet was a little unnerving after all the excitement, but I looked forward to seeing Tom at the social evening he'd arranged for the remaining black airmen.

For the rest of the afternoon I painted as if I was possessed. I was so involved in my colours and what was appearing on the canvas I forgot to eat the sandwiches Mrs Ward had left for me for my supper; I only remembered them when I realised I badly needed a drink.

I sat outside, fed the sandwiches to one of the feral cats that wandered the estate looking for mice, and drank a hot cup of tea. Then I went back to the studio to catch the last of the light.

The painting was of the house; the weather-worn exterior was a lovely mellow golden, heavy with shadows where the light didn't touch it. In one window was a dim figure that I didn't even remember painting, but it looked good, very good, and my heart lightened. I felt in my bones that the canvas would be bought and put in the London gallery.

It was only when I heard music and laughter from the perimeter of the gardens that I remembered the party. Hastily, I washed and dressed in a clean full skirt and a white collared blouse. I couldn't find suitable shoes so I walked across the grounds barefoot, enjoying the cool feel of the grass.

Tom's men had cleared the lecture room, moving the tables to one side and leaving a good space for dancing. Rosie was looking very pretty in a demure blue dress and blue sandals, her hair loose around her flushed face. I hoped she wasn't drinking too much.

One of the Americans bowed and asked me to dance. I took his hand and he held me at a discreet distance, holding me lightly around the waist. 'I'm Billie,' he said in his soft drawl, 'but the men, they call me the black bomber, miss, because of the colour of my skin and—' He hesitated, and Tom appeared at my side.

'And because this man is a wonderful bomb-aimer,' he said. 'Now, may I cut in here and dance with Miss Evans?'

Before I knew it I had been swept into Tom's arms and we were whirling around the floor to the tunes of the Glen Miller orchestra. I felt my hair fly around my face and my cheeks flush with pleasure as we danced and laughed. After a while, breathless, I begged for a drink, and Tom brought me a glass full of amber liquid.

'Here's a scotch and rye, Riana. Drink it up! It will do you good.'

The liquor wove its way in a spiral of fire down my throat and into my bloodstream, and instantly I felt light headed. The music changed to a slow waltz, and Tom took my hand and led me to the dance floor. He drew me close, and – almost without thinking – I put my head on his shoulder. Gently, he rested his cheek against my hair, and I'd never felt more happy and more comfortable with a man in my life.

I reminded myself that he would have to leave for America before long; I didn't really know when the last of the airmen would go. I supposed it would be wise to ask Tom rather than go on wondering when I would be alone again.

We had the last dance together, and then Tom took my arm. 'I'll walk you to the door, honey,' he said softly. He took my hand, and we left the heat and the cigarette smoke of the mess room and went out into the night.

The moon was full casting an eerie light over Aberglasney. As we drew nearer the doorway I thought I could hear voices. 'Tom, have the visitors made a mistake and come back to the house, do you think?'

'What do you mean, honey?' He sounded puzzled.

'Don't you hear the voices?'

'All I can hear is the pounding of my heart when I feel your hand in mine, honey.' He turned me to him and kissed me, a real kiss, deep and passionate. I warmed against him, the alcohol dancing in my blood, and the sounds of voices faded. I was drunk on Tom's Scotch – and what's more, I at last admitted it to myself, I was intoxicated with Tom. His hands gently moved over my shoulders, down my arms and on to my waist as he pulled me closer.

To my great disappointment, Tom released me at the door. 'See you tomorrow, Riana,' he said softly, and then he was gone into the shadows.

Being alone was such an anticlimax. I didn't know what I imagined would have happened if Tom had come in with me. Would I have allowed him into my bedroom, into my bed? On the other hand, how could he have walked away from me? I was his for the taking, wasn't I?

I sat at the kitchen table and rubbed my eyes wearily. I had been saved from making a fool of myself by Tom's good sense; he was an American officer and he would never take advantage of a drunken friend.

When I opened my eyes again, Beatrice was sitting opposite me. 'What were all those strange people doing here?' she asked.

'Oh—' I pulled my senses together as much as I could after drinking all evening '—they were visitors, looking for ghosts. Remember your suggestion? Well, I thought about it and decided ghost hunting was a very good idea.'

'I presume they were paying good money to stay here then?'

'Yes, I suppose they were, but they all enjoyed themselves and intend to come again.' I was a little on the defensive.

'Well, don't let the old house down, and don't forget your vow to solve the murders, my dear. I would like my late husband's name cleared.'

'I didn't know I had actually *made* a vow,' I said, puzzled.

'Well, you did.' She smiled a beautiful and somehow old-fashioned smile. 'In spirit, anyway.'

I began to laugh. Everything seemed so funny suddenly: Tom, me, my ghost nights, and my struggle to build up a crumbling old house. I was a painter – what was I doing trying to be a businesswoman?

'Go to bed, dear,' Beatrice said reprovingly. 'You're a little bit the worse for wear, I believe.'

Like a child, I obeyed and went meekly to bed.

Chapter Ten

I didn't see Tom the next day. I deliberately stayed in my bright studio, working on my painting of Aberglasney. At one point I stood back a little way and thought that the light and shade I had added worked well and that the shadowy figure in an upper window looked rather like Beatrice. I smiled fondly. She was becoming a good friend, a companion, soothing me when my nerves were frayed.

Mrs Ward called early afternoon and I beckoned her into the kitchen. I lit the stove and set out two cups. 'Do you take milk Mrs Ward?' I asked cheerfully.

She nodded and put a basket on the table. 'I've brought you some eggs, Miss Evans.' Her voice was hoarse from her continuous smoking, and as she sat down she lit up another Woodbine. 'My Rosie didn't come home last night, Miss Evans. She told me she stayed with you.' She was narrowing her eyes against the smoke and scrutinising my face.

I poured the tea to give myself time to think. The last I'd seen of Rosie was her dancing with a handsome American airman. 'Well, there's plenty of room here,' I prevaricated. 'And I was a little bit... tired myself, so everything is a bit blurred, but I'm sure if that's what Rosie says that's what she did.'

'I see, miss.'

I was sure she did: right through me. I hadn't the heart to let Rosie down, but I meant to have a word with her when I next saw her. How dare she use me as an alibi when she had obviously been up to no good?

'When will you want me and Rosie again, miss?' Mrs Ward's voice broke into my thoughts. I looked at her and saw her brows were drawn into a frown. She knew I was lying, and she was displeased with me.

'In a month's time, Mrs Ward,' I said flatly. She was being paid to help me, not to question me. 'If you have the time to come and work for me at Aberglasney, that is.'

'Yes, I want to come. I need the money, and anyway, I like cooking and waiting on town folks and foreign folks alike. But—' her eyes narrowed '—I don't like them dark-skinned airmen down at the barracks. Up to no good, they are. Chasing after respectable girls like my daughter.'

'Thank you for the eggs, Mrs Ward,' I said, hastily changing the subject. 'How much do I owe you?'

She told me, and I counted out a shilling and then took the eggs from the basket to put on the cold slab in the pantry. They were brown and fresh with bits of feather sticking to the shells, and my mouth watered. I realised I hadn't had anything to eat that morning, and it was well past lunchtime.

When Mrs Ward had gone, I made some poached eggs on toast and ate hungrily. When I had finished, I glanced out of the kitchen window and decided I'd do another hour or so's painting while there was still plenty of light.

I worked until my back was aching and it was almost dark, but finally the painting was finished and all I needed to do was to let it dry. I opened the big window in the gallery – and then, on second thoughts, shut it again. I didn't want anything happening to this painting. I'd worked too long and hard on it.

I put on the gas lights and heard the pop and saw the widening of the light. One day I would be able to afford electricity in more of the rooms, but for now, the gas worked very well – at least it was most atmospheric for my guests on the ghost nights.

I helped myself to a glass of sherry and then, just when I felt relaxed and sleepy, there was a knock on the front door. My heart almost stopped as I imagined Tom's big figure waiting for me outside, but when I opened the door it was Rosie who was waiting for me.

'Just the person I wanted to see,' I said in a hard voice. 'Will you please keep me out of your private life in future? I won't be your alibi again.'

'I'm sorry, but it wasn't what you think,' Rosie said quickly. 'I was helping Carl with a letter he was writing home to his mother, that's all.'

'And for that you had to stay out all night, is that it?' My tone was steeped in sarcasm, which Rosie missed completely.

'Well, no, not *all* night, but then I fell asleep on the sofa – in the communal sitting room, mind – and Carl left me there while he went to the barracks' dorm, as he calls it.'

'I'll believe you, though not many would,' I said. 'Just don't tell your mother you stayed with me again, hear me?'

'I hear you, miss,' Rosie said meekly and made a quick exit.

Alone again, I tried to fall back into the relaxed state I had been in before she'd come, but somehow the mood was gone. I wanted to be with Tom. Almost without thinking, I went outside and stood in the garden and saw my seat, a patch of light wood, under the arches of the cloisters. I walked towards the seat, and as I came close I heard a scraping sound above my head.

I glanced up in time to see a huge stone object falling towards my head. I darted under the cloister just in time as the stone crashed down, throwing up dust and fragments that shot like bullets towards me.

When I caught my breath, I saw one of the stone dragons had fallen – or been *pushed* – from the walkway above the cloister. It now lay shattered and broken at my feet.

One huge wing stuck up from the ground – embedded in the earth like a giant, curving scythe. If the statue had fallen on me I'd have had very little chance of survival.

I scrambled up the steps, too incensed to be frightened. Someone was trying to kill me, or to destroy my mind! I stood there in the darkness… and, of course, I was alone. I stared out at the shadowed land around me. Why would anyone want to hurt me? Was it because I was trying, in a feeble way, to solve the deaths of the five young maids? Or was it because I was the new owner of Aberglasney?

Shivering, suddenly apprehensive, I returned to the house, curled up in my chair and helped myself to another glass of sherry. Soon I felt more relaxed. It had all been an unfortunate accident, I told myself, but before I went to bed I switched on some lights and made sure all the doors and windows were locked against the outside world.

Chapter Eleven

In the morning, my painting of Aberglasney was almost dry. The colours seemed to blend in harmony, and the whole house had the mysterious air I'd been trying for. The figure, who looked a little like Beatrice with a dim glow of warmth behind her, gave the painting a piquancy that took it from a cold stone building to a lived-in house.

It was a great pity the ornate portico was missing from round the front door, I thought. It had been sold some time before I'd bought Aberglasney, but I vowed that one day, when I had enough money, I would get it back.

There was no sign of Tom, and feeling restless, I decided to take a train into town. I would go to the library, read up on the house and delve more into local reports of the deaths of the young maids.

The train journey was enlivened by the antics of a young girl and her brother, who were shut in the same small carriage as myself. At last, tired of the exuberance of the children, I wandered into the corridor for a little respite. Enclosed in the carriage behind me I could hear them play and fight, and then the girl began to cry, and by the time I arrived in Swansea I had a thumping headache.

Miss Grist, the woman behind the counter, helped another librarian carry the huge book of newspapers without so much as a smile and placed it on the table for me.

'Be careful with the papers, Miss Evans,' she said. 'You know how careless some folk are. They lick fingers and touch the old newspaper, and it doesn't do it any good at all.' She suddenly sat down beside me. She wasn't the typical type of librarian you see on the stage in a theatre: no glasses, no bun, but heavy lidded eyes and a full, drooping mouth.

True, her eyes had lines around them and the skin of her jaw was rather loose, but she would be a very good subject for a painting. I could see her in a Pre-Raphaelite gown of bright gold with her hair hanging loose against the silk. I realised I was staring and picked up my pencil.

'You are the lady who bought the old house, Aberglasney, aren't you?'

'That's right.' I carefully opened a newspaper, aware of her watching eyes.

'I hear there was quite a stir there last weekend. The ghost hunters actually found a ghost, I believe?'

'It seems so.' I tried to keep my voice steady and I took a deep breath. This was the sort of publicity I wanted, needed... so why did I feel such a cheat? 'Of course, I didn't see a ghost myself,' I added, absolving myself of some responsibility.

'And you living there. Isn't that strange?' She watched me with shrewd eyes. 'But there are some eerie goings-on there, I know that.'

My attention was caught; I turned to look at Miss Grist. 'How do you know?' I spoke gently, not wanting to frighten her away.

'I did some collating of books for the owners some time ago,' she volunteered. 'The library was extensive in those days, so I was told. I don't know what it's like now, of course.'

'Did you know Mr Mansel-Atherton?'

'Not personally. I'm a little too young for that.' Her tone was sharp, and I tried not to giggle. 'It's all very suspicious, if you ask me.'

'You think the maids were murdered then?'

'All I know is that they died in strange circumstances,' Miss Grist said briskly, as if *I* was prying into the past when it was *she* who had brought it up.

'Why are you so interested?' I looked at her suspiciously. She had sensible black shoes and even black thick stockings, like a nurse, perhaps... or a policeman.

'Just a feeling,' she snapped. Evidently, talking about Mr Mansel-Atherton was touching a raw nerve for Miss Grist. 'So, what have you found out about the strange things that happened *before* the girls died?' Miss Grist said after a moment's silence. She asked with more interest than a mere librarian would, I thought.

'Accidents,' I said. 'I read there were strange accidents, but not since Mr Mansel-Atherton died.' Just then someone came to hover at Miss Grist's side, and with an apologetic look at me she departed to help the other librarian.

I tried to concentrate on the papers and made notes about Aberglasney, the maids, and the accusations against poor Edwin. There were brief reports in most papers, and one lurid headline in a Sunday paper about 'Murder at the Manor'. No new details, though – just the suggestion of sexual misdemeanours, written for sensationalism.

I found nothing new or helpful in any of the reports. I would have to talk to the locals and read church records to try to find the background to it all. But I decided, as I hauled the book of papers back to the desk, that I would certainly talk to Miss Grist again when I had the opportunity.

It came sooner than I expected. I was sitting in a small tea room just minutes after I had left the library, admiring the pristine white tablecloths and the aprons of the waitresses, when a shadow fell over me.

'Could I join you, Miss Evans? I feel the need of a cup of tea.' She had a hat squashed over her hair and a black sober coat, straight-hemmed and with huge buttons.

'Please.' I indicated the chair beside me. 'I would love some company.'

I waved to one of the waitresses, and she came and took our order for a new pot of tea and some scones with jam and cream — a real treat after the wartime shortages. The cream was synthetic, but the jam was home-made and tasty. Miss Grist looked doubtful when they arrived.

'My treat,' I said breezily. 'Have you got the afternoon off, Miss Grist?'

'No, this is just my lunch hour, but I had to talk to you.' She leaned forward. 'I have to advise you to vacate that house before harm comes to you.'

'Do you mean the malign spirits, Miss Grist?' I hoped my scepticism didn't show in my voice.

'The threat is real enough,' Miss Grist said. 'I don't know who or why, but you are in danger from something — or someone — if you go prying into the past.'

'Were you in danger when you were collating the books at the house?' I heard the scepticism in my voice – but Miss Grist, apparently, didn't.

'A few nasty accidents happened.' She didn't look at me. 'A huge stone statue from the roof fell and nearly killed me.'

'Was it a dragon?' I asked suspiciously. She seemed to be echoing my own experiences, not her own.

'And then there were other things,' she said, as if I hadn't spoken. 'Someone came into my room in the night. I could hear footsteps, stealthy movements, but I never saw anything. Except, that is, an eccentric old lady.'

'Ah, Beatrice.'

'She was all right until Edwin had an illegitimate son,' Miss Grist said, almost absently, 'and then she became strange, almost – one would say – possessed.'

I hid my surprise. Beatrice was the most sane, practical woman I'd ever met. I didn't know anything about her having a child – only the grown-up son who was killed in the war.

'What child?'

'Edwin had a child, it wasn't Beatrice's. The child disappeared one night, never to be seen again. Apparently, he was the child of one of the five maids who died, you see.'

The news was a shock to me. I'd not heard of another child – not even from Beatrice. She'd talked about her lost son, of course, but nothing about the other boy. She must have been cut to the quick at her husband's infidelity. 'The child, he would be a man – grown, by now, of course. I wonder what happened to him.'

'Unless he was killed as well.' Miss Grist's tone was sombre.

'Why do you say that?'

'Because there's been no sign of the child for years.'

'He couldn't have just vanished. Wasn't there talk at the time? A search, police enquiries, something?'

Miss Grist looked at me thoughtfully. 'Why are you probing into the past, if I might ask?'

'You started all this, remember? Anyway, I'm curious because I own the mansion now. The house is mine, and I want to know all about it. Do you disapprove?'

'I disapprove of a lot of things, Miss Evans, but mostly I feel it best to let sleeping dogs lie, as they say.'

I took a deep breath to argue and then thought better of it. 'Well, I'd better be getting back,' I said instead. 'I have to pick up some brown paper and string first though. I have paintings to pack up, ready for London.'

Miss Grist brightened. 'Going to London? How exciting! Will you go on the train?'

'I can't travel by train tomorrow, not really. I'll have to take my old van to carry the paintings. I hate driving all that way, but I have no choice.'

Miss Grist wiped her chin with a nice blue-edged handkerchief, and I thought again what a strange woman she was. She must have been a voluptuous beauty once – still was in a mature way – but her ways were those of a spinster lady with nothing but dry books to keep her occupied.

I left her at the door of the little tea shop and walked along the High Street to the ironmongers. I made my way past zinc buckets and boxes of nails to the counter and bought my string and brown paper. Paper was still in short supply, but the owner of the shop knew me by now and sold me what he had in his cellar.

A few minutes later, I climbed into an empty carriage on the train and sank back appreciatively, hearing the *puff puff* of the steam and the clank of the wheels against the rails. I was on my way home from Swansea to Aberglasney.

Chapter Twelve

One night, several weeks later, Tom invited me to supper in his billet, and I cursed myself as a fool for being at his beck and call. I saw him when *he* wanted it not when I wanted to, and yet I found myself enjoying the atmosphere and the company.

The food was plentiful; the Americans didn't know what rationing was all about. There was a dance that evening in the village hall, and after we'd eaten Tom invited me to go with him as his guest. 'My men will expect me to put in an appearance,' he explained as we walked the short distance to the village hall. 'And what lovelier lady could I have on my arm than my Miss Evans?'

I took in the 'my' with a sense of belonging. I felt suddenly happy.

It was a lovely evening, the last of the summer, with just a tinge of autumn about the air. Inside the hall it was hot, and the heavy scent of American cigarettes hung in the room like a haze.

Bright-eyed girls danced and laughed, and I caught sight of Mrs Ward's daughter with her soldier: a very hand-some man, his skin dark as night and shining almost blue in the dimmed lights. How Mrs Ward would disapprove!

Tom had followed my gaze. 'I do believe that young lady is asking for trouble. Airman Jenkins is married with three children.' Tom didn't seem to make anything troubling from the colour of his corporal's skin. But then he wouldn't; he had no prejudice. To him, the man was brave and clever and a good aircraft officer – and that was all Tom required of his men. But I knew Mrs Ward would treat the men as 'foreigners' out to exploit the untried young ladies of the village.

'He's married?' I felt a pang of anxiety. 'Do you think Rosie knows that?'

'I doubt it. Most men are tight-lipped about marriage when they have a pretty girl in their arms.'

I looked up at him as he took me in his arms and swept me on to the dance floor. 'And you… are you being tight-lipped, Tom?' I heard the anxiety in my voice, and Tom did too.

'I have no wife, no child, no girlfriend – not at home, anyway,' he said, his eyes twinkling. 'I've been too busy fighting a war for any of that. Though I have plenty of time for flirting now, if I can find anyone to flirt with.'

Was that what I was to Tom – a flirtation?

'Excuse me.' I left him on the floor and made my way out of the crowded hall and into the night air. What a fool I was thinking I was special to him. To Tom I was just a girl to eat with, dance with, fall into his arms and give him her all while he looked on her as just a flirtation. Well, I'd been warned now, and I knew my place.

I left the dance and made my way back home alone. I saw the flickering lights on the top landing, the lights the locals insisted were carried by the ghosts of the dead maids, but I knew they were caused by just the clouds and the moonlight playing tricks against the glass. Besides, I was too wrapped up in my anger and humiliation to think too much about ghosts.

I went to my studio and spent some time wrapping the painting ready for carrying to the gallery in London. I resolved just to carry on with my life and concentrate on my business, my paintings, my house, my ghost parties and to forget Tom Maybury and the few remaining Americans. Soon they would go home. They would leave my property, and I could have the huts taken down. I could extend the garden – perhaps have a rose arbour, some wooden benches, and a water fountain with a chained cup on it like in the parks. Somewhere my guests could sit and write and discuss the ghosts.

–

The next day I went to London, and I was warmly welcomed at the gallery. Now I had enough paintings to make a proper exhibition! Mr Readings was delighted and made a fuss of each painting, admiring what he called the 'misty excellence' of each one. 'Same talented hand, same brush strokes, but each painting standing alone. I do so like your work, dear Miss Evans.'

For the first time, he led me into his small sitting room at the back of the gallery and poured me a glass of sherry. 'We shall have an opening event! Champagne, some good cheese and biscuits, and publicity in the London art magazines. My dear girl, you are a precious find for me. We shall make each other very rich and famous.'

I drank his excellent sherry and took his words with a pinch of salt. Still, it felt good to have such enthusiasm shown over my work. I didn't think I was that talented, just inspired by my house to make some paintings Mr Readings thought 'different' enough to attract buyers.

We arranged the opening for the next month – the first of September – and I wondered if Tom and the few men he had left would be gone back to America by then. The thought make me unhappy, and I pushed it out of my mind.

I drove back to Aberglasney with a mixture of elation and disquiet, wondering if any of my paintings would sell. Would I let Mr Readings and the audience down? Would they be disappointed with my mythical type of pictures? On the other hand, it was an opportunity to advertise my 'ghost-haunting' nights at the mansion. I had two strings to my bow now, two means of making funds to restore the old house, so I might as well make full use of both of them.

As I drew my rattling old van up at the back of the house I saw a figure lurking in the shadows. I felt a stark fear for a moment, and then I realised it was only the slight figure of a girl coming towards me, a handkerchief held to her streaming eyes. 'Rosie what is it?'

'Can I talk to you, miss?'

I led her to the bench in the vegetable garden, where we would be hidden by trees from the kitchen window. 'What is it, Rosie? You're not...?' I gestured to her tummy, not knowing how to frame the words for the disaster I thought was about to happen.

Her drooping head and renewed sobs told me my guess was correct.

'Oh, Rosie!' I put my arm around her. How could she give herself to an American serviceman who would fly away out of her life? But then hadn't I almost given myself to Tom, so how could I judge her?

'I love him, miss. He promised to take me to America, give me a new life away from my mother, but now he's finished with me, he doesn't want me, he says he's leaving at the end of the month. How can I bear the shame of having a child with no father?'

'You'll have to tell your mother,' I said at once. I didn't know how to deal with this situation. I was only a young woman myself.

Rosie sobbed louder.

'Look,' I said. 'You and the baby can stay at the house. The talk will die down after a while, and we can all help you bring the little one up.'

'I can't *have* it.' She looked up at me in alarm. 'You'll have to find me a doctor, or a midwife. Somebody to get me out of this mess.'

I was startled. 'What do you mean to do? Kill your baby?'

'I know, I know, but what if its skin is dark like its father? I'd never live down the shame! No, I can't let it ruin my life.'

I felt like telling her she should have thought of that before, but that wouldn't have been very kind or helpful. 'Look, I'll talk to Tom. He's the boss, he'll know what can be done.'

For the first time, Rosie looked hopeful. 'Perhaps he'll insist that Carl takes me back to America with him and at least settles me there, even if he doesn't want to marry me.'

Some hope when he had a wife and children, I thought, but then it wasn't for me to break the bad news of her boyfriend's treachery to Rosie.

'Go to bed now, Rosie,' I said soothingly. 'It can all be sorted out in the morning, I'm sure.' I wasn't sure at all, but what else could I say? Selfishly, I was cheerful as I undressed, for I had an excuse to go and see Tom in the morning.

I was to be disappointed and so was Rosie – for when I tried, the next morning, the men had gone out on a training exercise and no one knew where. The only man left on duty was the cook, and he told me in no uncertain terms that officers did not consult him when they were on manoeuvres.

Rosie burst into tears when I told her, and again I had the job of comforting her.

–

I didn't have a chance to see Tom over the weekend because I had my ghost guests there again, and the house was full of excited, chattering 'hunters' with lighting equipment and cameras and all sort of items I couldn't even begin to understand.

I hoped something would happen to please my guests and take my mind off Rosie's troubles, and it did in a most spectacular way. As Mrs Ward and Rosie served the soup, the dining room door opened and a chill wind blew through the room. The sound of moaning and crying could be heard clearly from upstairs!

Dinner forgotten, everyone rushed up the elegant stair-case and along the landing to where the mysterious lights were flickering. Beatrice appeared briefly in her doorway, but retreated as soon as she saw the hoards of wild-eyed guests with cameras running towards her.

'Did you see that, the Victorian lady? Anyone catch a picture of her?' The old colonel was back, and he boasted this was the second time he'd seen the ghost. 'She's called Beatrice,' he explained all-knowingly.

I kept quiet as the guests moved more cautiously now along the landing. Lights still flickered. Even I could see them, and as there was no moon I was at a loss to explain them. I felt I had to say something dramatic, though, and give the guests something for their money. 'Here, on this landing, the five murdered maids are alleged to seek release from their chains of death.' I spoke in a sepulchral voice that suddenly silenced all the talking.

One lady, obviously of a nervous disposition, screamed and ran back down the stairs – but at the same time everything abruptly became silent and the eerie lights vanished.

'It's a hoax,' one of the men declared bravely. 'I shall search the rooms for trickery.'

'Please,' I said. 'Mr Bravage, all of you, search, and if you find anything rigged or to be a hoax I will refund your money.' I couldn't explain any more than they could what had taken place. I felt a little unnerved myself, but I led the way along the landing and into the rooms. When we walked back towards the stairs I hesitated outside Beatrice's room.

'Go on then!' Mr Bravage shouted. 'Let's see the lady ghost, find out if she's alive and kicking.'

Reluctantly, I opened Beatrice's door, worried about invading her privacy, but there was no one in the room – it was silent and empty. Relieved, I stepped back and let the other people in, led by Mr Bravage.

'I feel a distinct chill in here.' Mr Bravage spoke in hushed tones and looked around, evidently seeking an open window or two.

'I do feel a presence,' the colonel chimed in, his pipe suddenly smouldering into extinction as if it had been blown out by a ghostly breath. He took it out of his mouth and looked at it in disbelief. 'It's never done that before.' He sniffed. 'This room hasn't been occupied by anyone alive, not for a very long time. You can smell the scent of decay.'

That was going a bit far, but I closed my lips firmly. Dear Beatrice used an ancient violet perfume that *did* smell a bit musty. I wondered where she'd gone, but Beatrice knew every nook and cranny of the creaking old house. She was probably keeping out of the way until the nosy, camera-laden guests had gone.

We all returned to the dining room. The soup had gone cold, and Mrs Ward and Rosie, dressed in maid uniforms now – a new idea of mine – removed the plates. Mrs Ward had sniffed at the notion of a starched white apron instead of her wraparound floral pinny, but when I'd promised her a little bonus she had complied with my craven request for her to fit in with the mood of the night.

'Perhaps Your Ladyship should bring in a butler as well?' Her acid remark had left little circles running round in my head. I knew she had been joking, but would my budget stretch to a butler? It would be an added authentic touch!

The meal comprised of roast lamb, cooked and seasoned beautifully by Mrs Ward, with devilled slices of lamb's liver, mint, baby roast potatoes and several dishes of vegetables. Not from the garden, alas, but from a market gardener who'd sold me them fresh at a premium price. We had dishes of steaming suet pudding and custard after the main course.

My guests ate well – and they paid well for the privilege.

Tonight, the conversation was noisy and elated; the sounds and the noises and the ghostly scents of my dear, conspiring old house pleased the ghost hunters, as did the timely appearance of Beatrice – dressed, as always, as if she'd stepped out of a picture book of the past century.

'My dear Miss Evans.' The colonel swept off his glasses. 'I think your house is one that is truly possessed by spirits of the past. So many of these so called "haunted" houses are nothing but fakes, fooling gullible tourists into a cheap thrill, but this house, Aberglasney, is the real thing, and I will be a guest any time you have your weekend conferences.' He leaned over me, wiping the custard from his mouth with a pristine napkin. It was lucky Mrs Ward could still persuade the few Americans remaining in the huts to help her work the laundry.

'You know, Miss Evans, you should put out leaflets, advertise in the newspapers more. You would have waiting lists, you would need ghost weekends more frequently, and then you could repair more of the rooms. My dear young lady, you have a gold mine here. Not looking for a partner, are you, by any chance?'

I shook my head as if in regret. 'I like it as it is, Colonel. My regulars have become friends to me. What I hope to do is restore as many rooms as possible as bedrooms, and then the weekends might be able to accommodate a few more guests. What do you think?'

'Ah, I know I speak to my own disadvantage here, but I think you should charge more for the weekends. The hospitality is very good. I personally feel so much at home that I could get up in the night and make myself a drink.' He dabbed his moustache again. 'I like the stone floors of the kitchen, the old wooden cupboards, the china cups hanging on hooks, the kettle singing on the hob. It is a lovely house, my dear, and you are so fortunate to own it.'

'I know I am,' I agreed.

After the meal, I suggested a 'candlelit' search of the house. 'But be careful, don't disturb anything, and please don't be careless with the candles. We don't want the house to be on fire, do we?'

I left the guests to their search of the house and grounds and helped Mrs Ward and Rosie to wash up the dishes. Mrs Ward took an enamel jug, filled it with boiling water from the kettle, and I watched as she sluiced the cutlery and then put it in the jug of steaming water. All except the bone-handled cheese knives.

'Why do you leave the cheese knives out, Mrs Ward?' I was silly enough to ask and was subjected to a lecture about bone and ivory handles coming apart and falling off and of silver blades needing gentle washing and cleaning.

I could see Rosie hovering wanting to talk to me, but what could I say to her? I couldn't condone the operation she planned, and yet I could see her position was intolerable.

When Mrs Ward had left, shopping bag of leftover food on her arm, Rosie made a beeline for me. The guests were silently searching the upper floors, and now everything was cleared up, and the dining table laid for breakfast, there was nothing more for me to busy myself with. I sat down with Rosie, wondering what I could advise.

'Please, Miss Riana, you will have to help me.' She bit her full lip, and I could see she was at the end of her tether.

Suddenly, anger washed through me: anger at Tom for allowing his men such freedom, and anger at Pilot Jenkins for taking advantage of a young girl like Rosie. Granted, her reputation wasn't spotless, but at least the man could have been careful. 'I'll see Tom in the morning.' My voice carried conviction. 'It is up to the Americans to sort out all this, not me or you, Rosie.'

Her young face was awash with gratitude. 'Thank you, Miss Riana. Perhaps some hospital visit can be arranged and paid for, and then my troubles will be over.'

I didn't reply. I was thinking about a new unborn infant, a real child who had a right to life. But then who was I to make such decisions? Tomorrow it would all be taken out of my hands. I was determined on that.

My guests departed the next day, full of a good breakfast and tales of ghosts and noises and 'paranormal research', having booked again for another weekend in a month's time. I had planned on having them less frequently, but the events were so successful that I couldn't turn down the opportunity to make more of the weekends and to make money enough to restore my house.

Later I walked down to the barracks, my heart in my mouth, ready to confront Tom. His smile when he saw me made my heart beat more quickly, and my resolve to be firm wavered slightly.

'You look lovely and summery,' he said, his eyes warm and admiring. It was a warm day, without the autumnal chill that had seemed to pervade the house and gardens over the weekend. It almost seemed that the house, the weather, and everything else was colluding to make my 'ghost hunts' a success.

I plucked up my courage. 'Can we talk privately? There's a serious matter I have to discuss with you.'

'Please come into my office.'

Tom, I felt, already knew what the problem was. He poured me coffee from one of his electric contraptions brought from America, and we sat down at his desk, Tom facing me almost as if I was being interviewed. I felt suddenly as though he was an officer – a leader of men – not the friend I'd become fond of.

'It's about Pilot Officer Jenkins and Rosie Ward.' I spoke softly, willing Tom to help me.

He didn't.

'They seem to have a very big problem,' I said.

'And, as far as I'm concerned, a very private problem.' Tom spoke evenly.

'Rosie has told me she is expecting a child.' I knew I was being abrupt, but Tom's attitude was making me angry. 'I think you and your officers should be the ones to deal with it.'

'Surely it's more women's work?' He wasn't being actually hostile – more obstructive.

'I know he can't make an honest woman of Rosie.'

'If she was an honest woman she wouldn't be in this position in the first place,' Tom said, his tone one of reason.

'Oh, so your man couldn't have taken precautions?' Anger was making my voice rise. 'He's married with children, I believe – something he failed to tell Rosie – and he didn't even have the sense he was born with to take precautions!' It embarrassed me to be so frank, but I was so angry with Tom's cavalier attitude that I didn't care about the blush that made my cheeks hot.

'I tackled Jenkins about that, and his reply was: "You don't take precautions with a girl you first met in the Red Lion Public House."'

I was taken aback. I imagined Rosie had met Jenkins at the dance in my garden that night. Respectable young girls didn't go into public bars. I got to my feet and picked up my lace gloves and my bag, searching for something to say in mitigation of Rosie. 'Well,' I said hotly, unable to think of a defence, 'this is your problem not mine, sir. Please be sure to do something about it.'

'I'll call and discuss it with you tonight,' Tom said coldly.

I walked out into the sunshine feeling foolish and at a disadvantage and also feeling something else – a sense of having lost something precious to me.

Rosie was waiting for me. 'Did you see my Carl for me?' She was as flushed as any young girl in love, and I tried to make things easier for her.

'I saw Tom. He's going to speak to your Carl Jenkins, see what can be done.'

'Is Carl going to marry me then... or what?'

'Leave it all until Tom has had a word. Try not to worry. The men will soon have some answer for us, I'm sure.' I wasn't sure at all.

Rosie looked relieved. She evidently believed in my powers of persuasion more than I did. 'Thank you, Miss Riana. I've got to get out of this mess or my mother will kill me.' It was a phrase I was tired of hearing.

'Well, go and help your mother and act as though nothing's happened. I'll be seeing Tom later, and I'll find out what's going to happen. Try not to worry too much, Rosie, there's a good girl.'

There was no sign of Tom that night, even though I waited for him impatiently. I wanted to get something settled for Rosie's sake. I thought perhaps Jenkins could take Rosie to America, arrange a home for her there. Anything to get her away from the shame of bringing an illegitimate child into the world of a small Welsh village.

In the end, I cleared away the glasses of wine, Mrs Ward's elderberry wine, and switched off the gas light. The mantles popped as they died, and again.

I went to bed disappointed and quivered below the blankets, trying not to cry. I'd wanted to see Tom more than I realised. I wanted to put things right with him to get back on the old warm footing.

I didn't sleep very much. I kept hearing sounds... sobs, cries... Was it the wind that had whipped up dashing branches and stray bits of wet leaf against the windows, or were there really ghosts in my house, waiting outside my door ready to harm me? I turned my face into the pillow and closed my eyes. This was my house and I shouted, 'Shut up!' into the darkness, and suddenly, all was quiet.

Chapter Thirteen

The first of September soon arrived, and the art exhibition in the London gallery was a great success. I stood in the bright lights of the elegant room, a glass of champagne in my hand and a smile fixed to my face, and tried to look modest in the warmth of the praise that was heaped on my work. I knew I looked good, different, playing the part of an elegant artist. In one of the old wardrobes in my house I'd found a green silk pants suit, with panels over the trouser legs like an overskirt and a halter top that showed off my pale arms and shoulder length red-blonde hair to perfection.

With it I wore a colourful shawl in peacock greens and purples, so I looked like a picture of a wealthy woman from the nineteen twenties, not a product of the utility age of the war years.

'My dear, you are as ravishing as your paintings.' One of the art critics kissed my hand, and with his head bent he showed his glossy pink bald crown surrounded by grey hair. 'I'm Simon Bleesdale, dear lady.'

He expected me to know of him, and of course I did – he was one of the most influential art critics in London. 'How charming of you to say so.' I tried to sound enthusiastic, but I found his flattery a bit overwhelming.

'Not at all! You are very talented. The ghostliness of the lovely old mansion shines through the paintings. It was almost as if you were possessed when you worked on them.'

I realised, with a flush of pleasure, that he wasn't flattering me at all. His praise was genuine. 'Perhaps you would like to come to one of my ghost weekends?' I suggested. 'Good food, good company and ghosts, if we're lucky. As my guest, of course, Mr Bleesdale,' I added hastily.

'Call me Simon, please, don't stand on formality, and I would be delighted to come to your ghost weekend. The whole things appeals enormously. Now, dear lady, your public is waiting to meet you! Far be it from me to keep you from your admirers.'

I found myself smiling at, and shaking hands with, people I'd never met before – well-dressed ladies, and men with black ties. I received so many compliments I was quite dizzy. And yet my heart was heavy. I wanted Tom to be at my side, Tom to share with me the moment when I stood before my audience with a glass of sparkling champagne in my hand and gave a small speech of thanks to all who'd come to the exhibition.

Mr Readings spoke next, urging customers to buy my work before it became too much in demand and while prices were relatively low. 'Low' was not a word I would have used, each painting was marked at an alarming amount, and yet amazingly they were beginning to sell – and quickly. I saw Mr Readings taking orders and bundles of notes, making records of each sale meticulously in his little notebook.

At last the art lovers departed, and Mr Readings removed his glasses and stared at me as if he'd never seen me before. 'You are the new fashion, my dear, the new Pre-Raphaelite, but with a difference. Your figures are beautiful young things swathed in a deathly haze. Lovely white limbs like those of a ballet dancer, tiny feet not quite touching the ground.' He lifted his glass to me. 'I have found myself a genius. Even Mr Bleesdale bought several canvases, and he has commissioned more. What do you think of that, my dear Miss Evans?'

'I'm delighted and amazed,' I stuttered. And I truly *was* amazed. 'I didn't expect my work to be so popular.'

Of course, Mr Readings would take almost half the money in commission, he'd already made that quite clear, but I accepted that as fair. Mr Readings had launched me into the public, given me a showcase. He had taken a risk on me, and I didn't begrudge him a penny of what he'd truly earned. I'd still receive a princely sum for my work, and I was already planning what I'd do to Aberglasney with it.

'It's very late, dear. You'd better stay in town,' Mr Readings said. His concern, I suspected, was because of the money he could earn from my work, not for my personal safety. 'There is a nice little guest house just along the road, owned by a lady friend of mine. I shall put you up there for the night.'

'Very kind.' I truly was grateful. I didn't fancy the drive home through the dark lonely streets and lanes that led from London to Swansea.

The guest house was warm and comfortable, and Miss Treherne who owned it was obviously besotted by Mr Readings. I really looked at him for the first time. He was tall and quite handsome with grey wings of hair pointing the way to a silver beard. It was clear to me that he would also stay the night at Miss Treherne's little guest house.

I couldn't sleep at first – the house, I realised, was too quiet without the creaks and groans of old Aberglasney – but at last I drifted off: warm and comfortable and filled with cocoa and biscuits, not to mention the champagne.

Miss Treherne herself drove us back to the gallery where I'd left my old van. Her means of transport was an old-fashioned Ford car, but at least it meant I could see something of London itself. Some of the buildings were razed to the ground from the bombing, and yet the early morning cries of the street vendors were cheerful and clear, even in the fog from the smoking chimneys.

I drove back to Swansea at a leisurely pace, eager to get back to my home and yet enjoying the sun as I left the town and encountered the broad countryside. I tested the brakes of the van several times. I'd had enough strange experiences to be wary now, fearing someone was trying to hurt or even kill me. Why? It wasn't for my wealth, that was sure. Before the exhibition I'd had little money, and I was still nowhere near rich.

Was it an effort to stop me finding out the truth about Aberglasney and the deaths of the young maids? That seemed the most likely reason, but then that meant that someone with the guilt of it all, and the knowledge of what really happened, was still in the vicinity of the big old house, the mansion that had become my home...

At last, my thoughts turned to Tom, and I felt warm and comforted. Tom would always protect me; he cared about me, and even though we saw things differently at the moment he was a good friend. More than friends, on my part, which I wouldn't let my mind acknowledge. Our little disagreement would soon be over and done with. We were too close to allow other people's problems to spoil what we had built up.

I remembered how we sat in the shade of the cloisters, the old stone arching above us as solid as the day when the cloisters had been built. What hands had worked on those stones, on the gardens, making a paradise of the private world that surrounded Aberglasney?

And then I thought of Tom's warmth close to mine, his arm touching mine and his occasional kisses... they were friendly, but such kisses could quickly turn to passion. Or was I dreaming, wishing, wanting more than Tom had ever thought of offering?

I stopped to drink my bottled water and eat the small sandwiches Miss Treherne had prepared for me. This morning she'd had the glow of a woman who had slept in a lover's arms, and I envied her.

It was peaceful sitting near the grass verge, with the pale sun and the slight chill of the country breeze freshening my skin. I rested a little and then, with a sigh of resignation, I climbed in the van and drove the rest of the way home without stopping.

Tom was standing near the door of the house and my heart lurched as I expected a smile of welcome. Instead, Tom was frowning. 'I was worried about you, Riana. Where have you been all night?' He sounded like an angry father, or at least an older brother.

'I stayed in London, of course.' I was irked. I wasn't a child, I was an artist, the owner of property. What right did he have to question me?

'So you found a man to look after you then?'

'Mr Readings looked after me – the owner of the gallery – so I stayed in London. Have you any objections?' I forced myself to be calmer. 'All my paintings have sold, so at least the trip was worth it.'

'So you celebrated by staying with Mr Readings all night.'

Angry again, I faced him. 'Yes, I stayed all night, but not in the way you are implying.'

'And what do you think I am implying, Miss High-And-Mighty?'

'How dare you lecture me, Tom? You are not my keeper, and you are on my land, so please go back to your billet and stop interfering in my affairs.'

'Affairs being the operative word.'

His sarcasm hurt. 'Oh, just go away! Go on, clear off. You are not welcome at my house!'

I'd said too much. White faced, Tom marched away, his broad shoulders squared, outrage in every line of his tall body. I wanted to call him back, but the words stuck in my throat. How dare he assume that I would stay the night with a man I hardly knew? With any man, for that matter.

I entered the hallway of Aberglasney and was immediately in love with my house again, washed by the tranquillity of the pale thin sunlight falling through the stained tall windows. The house creaked and groaned though there was no one in sight. Even Beatrice seemed to be absent on one of her trips. I wondered where she'd gone, as I often did when she disappeared, but then she was part of the package that came with buying the house. I'd agreed to her staying over sometimes, though she seemed more often here with me than anywhere else, and right now I missed her.

I made some tea and sat in the spotless kitchen drinking it, feeling suddenly alone. Mrs Ward had been here cleaning while I was in London – that was evident in the sparkling cleanliness of the glass in the panelled corner cupboard and the well-swept wooden floor.

I wandered up to my studio taking my cup with me, warming my hands around the china more for comfort than because I was cold. On the landing, I thought I caught a glimpse of white cotton and the drift of floating hair, but when I blinked the corridor was empty. *I'm tired from the long drive*, I thought. *I'd better not begin a new painting today. Perhaps a rest will do me good?*

In my room, I finished the dregs of my tea and then lay back against the pillows. I must have slept because I thought a lover came to me… he was Tom but not Tom. A man a few years older than Tom. A man with laughter lines round his eyes.

When I woke, I wondered what it was all about, and then I stopped worrying about the dream and remembered that Tom and I had quarrelled.

Chapter Fourteen

I saw Carl Jenkins myself. I didn't want any more quarrels with Tom.

Carl looked shamefaced but mutinous. 'Sorry, Miss Evans, but I took what was freely offered. No man could resist such a lovely young girl. It's just asking too much of humankind.'

'You took precautions to protect her, did you? She was a virgin, wasn't she?' I stumbled over speaking such plain language, but Carl's head bent even lower.

'I didn't know she was a good girl, ma'am. I met her in a public house and—' he shrugged '—well, I just thought.' He stopped when he saw my expression.

'Was Rosie in the bar?'

'Why, no. She was in a tiny room at the back.'

'The snug?' I didn't wait for a reply. 'It's where the ladies go, officer. It is the custom for respectable women to sit together in a room away from the men and talk and relax. The snug is not a place into which a man usually strays.'

'I didn't know that,' Carl said in a low deep voice.

'So you ruined the girl's reputation, and what are you going to do about it?' He didn't reply. I persisted: 'Can you imagine the shame of bringing an illegitimate child into the village?'

He nodded silently.

'What are you going to do about it?' I demanded.

'What can I do, Miss Evans? I got a wife and children of my own back home. I got enough mouths to feed as it is.'

'Well, isn't that hard luck for you then?'

'What do you mean, ma'am?'

'I mean, this child is going to be your responsibility and so is Rosie. She's talking about having an abortion! It's against the law and dangerous as well. What if she died?'

Carl's head was almost touching his chest now. He was behaving like a chastised child.

'Sort something out.' I almost whispered the words, but they sounded like a clarion call in the pale misty morning air.

'Excuse me, Miss Evans.' Tom loomed out of the mist. 'Where do you think you get off chastising my men?'

'Someone has to if you won't.' I felt myself grow tense. I didn't want to quarrel any more with Tom, but he couldn't speak to me like that and get away with it. 'Jenkins has a responsibility to Rosie, and so have you. I can't let her risk an abortion, and I don't think you can either. Think of the bad publicity the Americans would get if it got into the papers.'

'Are you blackmailing me, Miss Evans?' His voice was icy. I thought of the times Tom and I had sat together close, warm in the summer twilight under the arch of the cloisters, and I felt like crying.

'I suppose I am.' My voice was equally cold. 'Your officer has ruined a girl's reputation. He's insulted her because he didn't know our habits. Here in the village respectable old women and young ladies can sit in what we

call the "snug" without being labelled "loose women"…
but that's what officer Jenkins did, isn't it?'

'That's a matter of opinion.'

'No, it is not!' I would have stamped my foot if I hadn't
been standing on grass. 'Rosie was *respectable*,' I said. 'Just
ask your officer; he took her innocence.'

Jenkins looked at his feet, and Tom had no choice but
to believe what I was saying was true.

There was silence, and then Carl Jenkins spoke in his
deep Southern drawl. 'I'll take care of it, sir,' he said, lifting
his head. 'I'll take Rosie back home with me, and we'll
sort something out for her.'

I sighed in relief. I couldn't wait to see Rosie and tell
her it would be all right. Tom, however, turned away and
walked off without a word to me. In my mind I made
excuses for him: he was embarrassed, upset, feeling guilty
at not believing me. And yet, as I turned to go home to
Aberglasney, I felt tears cooling as they ran down my hot
face.

Once I was home I managed to tell Rosie the good
news, and she closed her eyes in relief. 'I knew he wouldn't
let me down,' she breathed. 'He loves me, and I love him.
It's going to be all right.'

But the next day Carl Jenkins was killed trying a new
modification to one of the plane engines.

Chapter Fifteen

The next ghost hunt in September was another success. Even more people attended, and though the bedrooms were not quite finished I managed to fit fifty people into Aberglasney House.

Mrs Ward and Rosie did their usual cooking and waiting on tables, and even though Rosie could not hide her devastation at Carl's untimely death she rouged her cheeks and managed to look almost pretty.

One of the ghost hunters, a young man from Yorkshire, took a liking to Rosie's by now rather voluptuous figure and flirted outrageously with her all weekend. Even though Mrs Ward frowned, and tried to freeze young William with a look every time she saw him, he persisted in his attentions until at last, in spite of her mother's displeasure, Rosie agreed to sit with him in the dining room after supper and have a glass of sherry with him.

Later I talked to her. Her blue eyes were shadowed, her face pale beneath her rouge, and in spite of her burgeoning size her mother hadn't yet guessed her condition.

'You have to talk to your mother,' I said. 'Look, I'll help you. I'll have the baby here as much as I can.'

'But—' Rosie was almost in tears '—there *can't* be a baby. You can imagine how my mum would take it if I brought shame on her!'

'You can't still want to abort it.'

'Why not?' Rosie was uncomprehending.

'It's too late to get rid of it,' I said firmly. 'No doctor will do it now. You are much too far gone. Six or seven months, is it?'

Rosie shrugged helplessly. 'I don't really know.'

Mrs Ward came into the room her dark, bird like eyes bright with suspicion. She put her hand on her daughter's shoulders and shook her. 'You've fallen for a baby, haven't you? Tell me the truth, Rosie, before I smack it out of you.' Rosie started to cry, and her mother shook her roughly once more.

My heart was in my mouth. Mrs Ward was a formidable lady, but I had to speak out. It was clear Rosie couldn't say anything. 'Mrs Ward, please stop manhandling your daughter! You might harm her and the baby.'

Mrs Ward's mouth was a tight line, but she forced herself to speak. 'It would be the best thing. Who's the father, Rosie? Tell me.'

'He's dead, if you must know.' Rosie's voice was a wail of pain. 'I loved him, he was going to take me to America with him, but he's dead! Now are you satisfied?'

Mrs Ward froze. 'An American? Don't tell me your bastard child will be a foreigner!'

'Oh, Mum, can't you care about me for a change? Worry about *my* feelings, not your own?'

I was so sorry for Rosie, and when her mother didn't move I held Rosie in my arms myself.

She appealed to her mother. 'Will you help me, Mum?'

'How *can* I help you?' Mrs Ward was still stiff-backed, but I sensed her attitude had softened.

'I don't know!' Rosie burst into hysterical tears again, and at last Mrs Ward came to her and took her away from me, holding her tightly.

'I'll do my best, we'll go away somewhere, it will be all right,' Mrs Ward said, but her tone was rigidly cool, her brow furrowed with a frown. 'Though how I will be able to support us all without a job, I don't know.'

'You and Rosie can stay here with me,' I said, not being entirely unselfish because I knew I couldn't manage without the two of them to help me with the weekends. 'There are downstairs rooms at the back of the house, unused. We'll do those up between us.'

'But folk will still know. They'll talk about us,' Mrs Ward said quietly.

'Rosie will have to have the baby,' I said firmly. 'She's too far advanced in her pregnancy to abort the child now. I'll talk to Tom. He'll think of something, I'm sure.'

I hadn't spoken to Tom for some days, but I'd wanted an excuse to try to patch things up between us – and this might be it.

However, when I went to see him, Tom was cold and distant. 'If you've come to make a scene, remember I've just lost a good pilot and a good man.'

I wanted to retort that if Carl Jenkins was such a good man, why did he have an affair with a young innocent girl when he had a wife at home? However, I sat down in his office and just took a deep breath instead.

'I've had to write a letter home telling Carl's wife that her husband has been killed.' He spoke defensively, wearily.

'I only wanted to ask your advice,' I said.

His lines of strain softened. 'I'm sorry. I know you're trying to help the girl, and I've been hard on you as well as her. What can I do?'

I shrugged helplessly. 'I don't know.'

He poured us a drink from the bottle in his drawer and sat down again, reaching for my hand as I sat down next to him. It felt comfortable and comforting to have his fingers touching mine, however lightly.

'I wondered if the baby could go to America to be cared for… by his own sort,' I finished lamely, knowing I sounded patronising.

'Black-skinned folk, you mean.' Tom withdrew his hand.

'Yes.' I lifted my chin defensively. 'You can imagine what sort of life the child would have here among a white community, a very insular village community at that.'

Tom sighed. 'I do understand. Perhaps I can arrange something when the child is old enough to travel—' he looked up hopefully '—unless Rosie wants to go too?'

'I don't think she does. In any case, her mother wouldn't allow it.'

'Her mother can't run her life for ever.'

'I know, but Rosie is young, impressionable… Goodness knows what would happen to her if she went away with a baby and tried to manage without her mum.'

'How's the painting going?' He seemed to soften his voice just slightly.

I smiled up at him, longing for him to take me in his arms although he did nothing of the sort. 'Fine. My last exhibition was a great success.'

'I imagine so. After all, you stayed the night in London with your agent... or whatever he is.' There was now an edge to Tom's voice that I didn't like very much.

I didn't see why I should explain myself to him but I did anyway. 'That's right. Mr Readings had a lady friend who ran a guest house. I stayed there for the night because it was late and—'

'And your Mr Readings stayed there too, I presume.'

'He did, as a matter of fact.' I tried to gloss over the awkwardness between us. 'He was very pleased at the sales we achieved. Of course, I have to pay him for exhibiting and framing and all that sort of thing, so the profits are virtually halved.'

'Perhaps you have another arrangement – other than money, I mean.'

I took in his meaning, and the hurt made me stand up and step away from him. So that's what he thought of me and my work! That I sold my body in exchange for Mr Readings rustling up a few rich customers, who were then persuaded to buy my paintings. I felt like hitting Tom. He was maligning me and my work as an artist. 'Thanks a million,' I said sarcastically and walked away.

Fuming, I went into the house and walked upstairs to my studio. I heard footsteps running up the stairs behind me, and Rosie came into the room.

'What's happening miss?' She was breathless.

'Air Commander Maybury has agreed to send the baby to America to be brought up by a black family,' I said. 'Now please, Rosie, go away. I have to work if I'm to pay your wages.' I know I sounded sharp, but Tom's harsh and unjustified accusations had wounded me.

I mixed some paints and began to paint: angry colours, bright colours, red and yellow edged with white, the house on fire, flames leaping out of the old roof. And then I painted a faint figure on the roof and covered it with a few layers of a mixture of greyed down and white. She was almost invisible in a cloud of smoke. I don't know why I painted it. As far as I knew the house had never been on fire, but then no one said art should represent real events. And yet I shivered, hoping I wasn't tempting fate.

It was almost dark by the time I'd stopped work and, exhausted, I left the studio. When I went downstairs to the kitchen it was empty. Mrs Ward must have finished for the night, and she and Rosie had gone home. A tray of cold meat and pickle was left covered on a tray on the kitchen table, and an upturned cup was placed in the matching saucer, ready for me to make myself a cup of tea.

The house was silent, not even the creaking and groaning of the old boards disturbed the silence. I shivered, feeling very alone, but a cup of hot tea and some food soon put me in a better mood.

After, I wandered round the house looking for Beatrice. There was no sign of her; she was on one of her mysterious 'trips'. I never knew when she would be here or away, and I felt a momentary irritation. It wouldn't be much trouble for her to tell me her plans. It was rude to just vanish!

And then, as if my thoughts had touched her, she was there outside her door. It hadn't opened or closed, she was just there. I drew back, startled. Was she a ghost or a figment of my overworked, overwrought imagination?

'What's wrong, dear? You look as if you've seen a ghost.' She was so matter-of-fact that I laughed in relief.

I was tired, there were shadows on the landing and I was imagining things – foolish things like ghosts.

'You startled me, Beatrice,' I said. 'For a moment there, I thought I was seeing things.'

'Come and sit in my room, dear, you look worried. We can talk, if you like. I'm a very good listener.'

I thought of my nice cup of tea waiting for me in the kitchen. I'd made a fresh pot before I'd gone wandering. 'No thanks, Beatrice,' I said. 'I've got some paperwork to do.'

'Well, I'll say goodbye then, dear.' She spoke softly. 'I'm going away tonight to visit some of my people, and I'll see you in a few weeks' time.'

'Beatrice, I've got a ghost-haunting weekend in a few weeks. I want my guests to see you. They are convinced you are not of this world!'

'Are any of us, dear?' Beatrice said and went into her room, closing the door quietly behind her.

I quickly returned to the cheerfulness of the kitchen and sat near the warmth of the open fire. I had a gas stove in there but I loved the coal fire, and now I crouched near it with my cup of tea in my hands.

I must have dozed, because when I opened my eyes my cup was placed neatly on the floor between my feet and from outside I heard the sound of horse's hooves against the drive. I hurried to the front door and looked out in time to see an old-fashioned hansom carriage pulling away. Even as I watched, bewildered, the whole thing slowly vanished, and I was left gaping at the arch that led away from the house.

Was I going mad? Was I working too hard concentrating on ghostly images – imagining the house on fire, haunted? Next I would believe the five young maids were *really* haunting Aberglasney.

I hurried back to the kitchen and poured myself a sherry and sat shivering, afraid even to fetch more coal. I jumped when there was a gentle tapping on the back door. It came again more insistently, and then Tom's voice called out to me.

'Riana, are you in there? Will you let me talk to you? I want to apologise.'

Eagerly, I opened the back door. 'Come in, Tom. Want a cup of tea?' I was so pleased to see a real live human that I couldn't even keep my voice cool.

'You look so pale. What's wrong, Riana?' Tom sat at the table, his big bulk reassuringly solid.

'I'm being silly, Tom, but I thought I saw a hansom cab pulling away from the house.' The words were out before I could prevent them.

Tom smiled. 'I'm afraid that's my fault.'

'How do you mean?' I was unable to keep the tremble out of my voice.

Tom took my hand. 'I'm sorry, Riana. I was silly not to ask old Frank from the village to wait till morning to show it to you. I thought it would help the ghost weekend look more authentic to have an old carriage outside.' He looked rather sheepish. 'It's by way of an apology. I was wrong to accuse you of staying the night and… Well, you know. I apologise.'

I smiled forgivingly, although I was still hurt so I chose to ignore his apology. 'Thanks for the carriage – and how silly of me. I actually believed in ghosts for a while.' I spoke lightly. 'Anyway, come and see my latest painting.' I didn't know why I'd said it, I should have sent him packing after his accusations about my morals, but he followed me upstairs and my heart warmed that he was at least friendly to me again.

He stood before the canvas and regarded it, head on one side. I watched him, my heart in my throat. It was strange how much I wanted his approval.

'It's one of your best,' he said at last. 'It's powerful and colourful. The light of the flames is glowing off the canvas, and yet you've managed to put that ghostly image on the roof. It's really wonderful.'

I wanted to hug him. Even now, after my recent successes, I still felt anxious about my work, as if I was a fraud who would one day be caught out.

'Will you have a cup of tea with me, Tom?' I was almost humble, and when Tom put his arm around my shoulders and smiled down at me I wanted to throw myself at him and kiss him and beg him to make love to me. Of course, I did no such thing. I shrugged off his arm and went downstairs, worried that he would think me fast.

We had a cup of tea in companionable silence. I felt better than I'd done for days because Tom was here with me and we weren't quarrelling.

I poured both of us more tea, and Tom spoke at last. 'Tell me about the sale in London,' he said.

'Everything sold,' I said meekly. 'Thanks to Mr Readings.'

'And you stayed in a guest house overnight?'

'That's right. The guest house belongs to Mr Readings'... er... lady friend,' I added anxiously.

Tom smiled. 'I'm really sorry I implied anything else.'

'So am I.' I spoke a little tartly.

'*Really* sorry. Now, to change the subject, I've made arrangements for Rosie's little child to go to a good family in America.' He didn't look at me. 'It's the best I can do. Airman Jenkins might have been misguided, but he wasn't a bad man. Still, you can be assured the baby will be very well looked after by a good professional childless couple who want a baby very badly.'

'Thank goodness that's settled.' I heaved a sigh of relief. I would be able to tell Rosie in the morning that all was arranged.

'How many months before the child will be born?'

'About two, I think. She doesn't really know herself. She didn't realise there *was* a baby coming until she was well on.' I looked at Tom with half-closed eyes. 'That's how innocent she was.'

'OK, I get the message, Riana. I shouldn't have put the blame on Rosie, I realised that from the start, but I was defending one of my men. You can understand that, surely.'

'Yes, Tom, but you were very hard on Rosie and—' He held up his hand and I stopped speaking.

'Let's just leave it there before we start to argue about it again,' Tom said. 'What about another cup of tea? Or better still a glass of wine or something. You could put on your coat, and we could sit under the cloisters like we did in the summer.'

It was good to sit in the darkness with Tom, huddled against the warmth of his shoulder, knowing we were friends again. I risked a question. 'You didn't really think I'd spent the night with Mr Readings, did you?' My throat was dry, and if I expected Tom to make more and profuse apologies I was mistaken. He made a joke of it.

'Well, I've heard about you artist types! Your flamboyant careless lifestyles and all that.'

I smacked his cheek playfully, and Tom caught my hand and kissed it. It was an erotic gesture, his warm mouth in the palm of my hand, his tongue darting against my skin. I felt myself grow warm and I drew away, startled by my own feelings.

'I think I'm falling in love with you, Miss Evans,' Tom breathed against my cheek.

Enough was enough. I was moved and thrilled, and yet I had the uneasy feeling Tom was still joking with me. I stood up, putting the cold air between us. 'How do I know you haven't got a wife at home like poor Carl Jenkins?'

'How indeed?' Tom touched his forelock. 'But I've told you the truth; there is no wife. Goodnight, Miss Evans, dear Miss Evans, and sweet dreams.' And then he was striding away down my now neat garden towards the barracks.

Chapter Sixteen

The latest ghost weekend was well under way, and the house was fuller than it had ever been. It was October, and although it was only autumn it felt like deep winter had set in, and fires roared the rooms we used most. As for upstairs, I'd installed electric fires in the bedrooms, not wanting to take the chance of noxious fumes bringing death and destruction to my house. Luckily, the walls were thick stone and the heat seemed contained.

Wine was being drunk, and hearty, cheerful voices could be heard all over the house, but I was lonely. I'd heard that the few remaining Americans were finally packing up to leave Aberglasney, and Tom had not yet spoken to me about it.

As it neared midnight, I extinguished the lights. My guests held torches, as well as candles and box cameras and other equipment designed to detect the presence of spirits, and we all fell silent.

'The blue room is the area of the haunting,' I said in a hushed whisper that carried sibilantly around the silent guests. The colonel as always was at my side, and Mr Bleesdale had finally come along, accompanied by a peroxided young woman with large bosoms who led the crowd towards the stairs.

A serious young man with a notepad and pen had joined the group. His name was Colin Sharp, and he had his college scarf slung in a careless fashion around his neck. He never once smiled, though I suppose he thought his work serious enough. He was working for his doctorate in Pharmacology, which seemed to have nothing at all to do with ghost hunting.

There was a collective gasp as lights could be seen flickering across the landing: five distinct lights shrouded in a haze of mist. Mr Bleesdale faltered and stepped back down into the hall. His lady friend gave a little screech and clung to his arm.

Colin Sharp gave a disgusted mutter. 'Charlatans, frauds, it's a trick to separate you fools from your money. You silly deluded folk don't really believe in ghosts, do you?' He pushed his way up the stairs towards the lights, and when he reached the landing he seemed to be engulfed in the mist, the lights forming a circle around him. The mist grew denser and no one else ventured upstairs.

I was as puzzled as everyone else, and we stood and watched until the mist evaporated and the lights disappeared, and then I heard Mrs Ward shouting for help.

Someone turned the gas lights on, and the one electric light near the front door shed a warm beam into the hallway. The young college student was lying in a heap on the landing, and – with my heart in my mouth – I went up to him. He was pale but breathing, and he seemed to have just fainted, possibly overcome by the beer he'd drunk.

'Did anyone get a picture?' the colonel demanded, but it seemed no one had. With the help of the men I got

Colin back into the library, and someone gave him a sip of brandy.

He opened his eyes. 'What happened?' he said dimly. 'Why did I faint away like that? I'm a healthy young man!'

'It was the ghosts,' the young blonde lady chimed in, her face pale under her make-up. 'You should never have challenged them.'

'Don't be silly! What ghosts?' It seemed Colin's memory had been stripped clean of his experiences.

'Help!' Mrs Ward pushed her way towards me. 'It's my Rosie! She's in a bad way. Why are you all still fussing round this obviously drunk young man when my Rosie needs a doctor?'

I knew at once that the baby must be coming. Rosie must be even further along than we'd thought. 'Anyone here a doctor?' I asked, feeling very dramatic. To my surprise, Mr Bravage held up his hand.

'Will I do, dear lady? I'm retired now, but unless there's anyone else I'll offer my services.'

'Thank you so much! Will you follow Mrs Ward? She'll take you to Rosie.' I turned to the other guests. 'Tonight has certainly been very strange, and it's not for me to say what happened here, but I think you all need a drink to settle you down for the night. Please help yourself from the bar.'

The bar was small, newly installed with a few bottles of spirits and a crate of beer under the shelf. I hoped there would be enough to go round. The drink had gone well this evening and would probably be used in a 'medicinal' way after the events of the night.

I went to Rosie's little bedroom, and she was sitting up against the pillows – apparently as well as I was. 'What's all the fuss about?' I asked. 'You seem fine to me.'

'With respects, miss, you haven't had a baby,' Rosie said. 'It comes and goes, like, the pains. One minute everything don't hurt, and then the pitchforks of hell are digging into you.'

I looked at Mr Bravage, who appeared unfamiliar in his shirt sleeves.

He nodded, confirming what Rosie had just told me. 'Perhaps you'll stay and help, Miss Evans?' he said. 'My... er... niece is not very practical at this sort of thing. The sight of blood makes her faint away.'

'What a surprise!'

My sarcasm was not lost on Mr Bravage. He smiled wryly and said, 'In this life one takes what one can get, dear lady.'

Rosie seemed to crunch up and began to moan, grasping her stomach for dear life.

'Easy, child. Just try to go with the pain.' Mr Bravage gently settled Rosie back against the pillows. 'Conserve your strength, there's a good girl. It may be a few hours yet.'

Rosie looked horrified. 'Hours! But I can't stand all this torture for hours! What can you give me to ease the pain?'

'All I have with me is some indigestion tablets.' Mr Bravage stretched out his hands apologetically. 'I don't carry a bag with me, not any more.'

'I'll see what I can find,' I said, and with a sigh of relief left the room with Rosie's agonised moans following me.

Beatrice was away on one of her trips, but in her room there might be something we could give Rosie. I felt ill at ease as I mounted the stairs and even worse as I went into Beatrice's room. I hated prying, but I had to help Rosie.

There was a little medicine box beside the bed, and hopefully I opened it. Neatly arranged were some bottles all labelled in fine handwriting. I read them one by one, but there seemed nothing that would help Rosie through the pains of childbirth. In the bottom drawer of the little box, however, there was a bottle of laudanum. I put it in my pocket and hurried to the library to talk to my disoriented guest. He was a pharmacist; perhaps he could help.

'Colin, how are you feeling?' I asked.

He looked at me blearily. 'Never better,' he said. He was evidently more than a little drunk.

'Look—' I showed him the small bottle of laudanum '—is this all right to give to someone in childbirth?'

'Of course, Miss Evans. Laudanum is still being used and will be for some time to come. It is a derivative of opium, you know. Not so potent, but good for toothache or some such thing. Though, I must say, that looks like a very old bottle. Still, it should be all right, I think.'

Reassured, I hurried back to Rosie's room and gave the struggling, red-faced girl a spoonful of laudanum. It seemed to ease the pain, but it made Rosie rather lethargic and sleepy.

'The contractions are not so intense now,' Mr Bravage said. 'What was that medicine you gave her, Miss Evans?'

'Just a painkiller, some laudanum, Colin said it should be all right.'

'That's not good for this sort of situation. It has slowed down the labour, you see. The more severe the contractions, the sooner the baby is delivered safely into this world.'

'I'm so sorry.'

I think we all fell asleep for an hour or two because I heard Rosie groan and I woke up with a suddenness that brought me upright in my chair. Mr Bravage was slumped in his chair snoring, and only Mrs Ward was wide awake – her eyes beady like those of a bird as she stared disapprovingly at me.

'I don't know what you gave my girl, but she's no nearer to giving birth than she was a few hours ago.' I explained to her what Colin had told me, and she shook her head and put the small bottle into her pocket. 'Well, that was no use.'

The house was silent. *Everyone else must be asleep*, I thought. Not even the 'ghosts' stirred along the landing as I looked out. The wind had dropped, and a soft rain spattered the windows like gentle tears. I stood at the window and looked towards the barracks; lights were on, and I realised Tom must still be awake.

I went downstairs into the hall and reached for my coat and scarf; a walk in the fresh air would do me good. My head was aching, and I wondered if Rosie would ever have the baby.

In a way, I would be glad when it was all over and the child taken to America. But then Tom would be gone too and with him my hopes and dreams of a future together. Tom had never made any promises, Tom had said nothing at all to give me hope, and yet I knew I hadn't imagined the closeness between us as we'd sat so often under the cloisters in the gardens of Aberglasney.

Tom was in his room poring over a map as if he couldn't wait to get away. I felt hurt and betrayed, although I had no right to feel any of those things.

'Good evening... or is it good morning?' I spoke politely as if to a stranger.

Tom looked at his wrist, at the large watch he wore with the special dials. 'It's zero four hours,' he said. 'Four o'clock in the morning.'

'Rosie's still in labour, if you're interested,' I said briskly. 'When you leave, I hope you can take the child with you.'

'Just as well I'm not going just yet then, isn't it?' He smiled, and I was overwhelmed with a sense of relief – and, yes, gratitude.

'I suppose so.' I stumbled over the words. 'I suppose Rosie will have to get the baby used to boiled milk or whatever it is they give babies.'

'What's wrong, Riana? You seemed a little over-wrought,' Tom said.

Suddenly, I was insanely furious. 'Oh, nothing really!' I said in a loud voice. 'Tonight a man in my party nearly died when we were apparently visited by ghosts, Rosie is about to give birth to a illegitimate baby, and you are sitting calmly down in the barracks not concerning your little self with any part of it!'

'Come on, Riana, let me pour you some coffee. You should have sent for me. I'd have done all I could to help, you know that.'

I wanted to cry, and I wasn't sure why. I watched, stony faced, as he poured me coffee and then gulped the scalding liquid as if it would take the lump away from my throat.

'I'll come up to the house with you and see what's happening.' He took my arm, and I put down my coffee quickly, slopping a little on to the table. We walked up through the gardens in silence.

The lights were still on; my guests were still sitting up drinking with no thoughts of going to bed. I couldn't blame them, for the events of the night had been too exciting for them to give up and go to sleep. My ghost-haunting weekend would be more infamous than ever, I realised. I would have to get more help. Mrs Ward couldn't manage it all alone now that Rosie would be laid up for a while.

As we went into the bedroom, I heard the shrill sound of a baby's cry, and then I gasped in astonishment – the baby lying on the sheets was as white-skinned as I was!

Mr Bravage did some medical things to the baby, and then handed the little being to Rosie.

Tom went up to the bed and took Rosie's hand. 'I think it's time you told us the truth, Rosie.' He spoke firmly, but his voice was kind.

Rosie had tears in her eyes. 'The baby must be following me, sir. Fair, and all that.'

Tom examined the baby's knuckles and elbows and softly touched the fine golden hair. 'Rosie, are you sure the boy is Officer Jenkins' son?'

Rosie's voice was bright. She seemed revived, back to her old flirtatious self. This childbirth was a strange experience all right! 'No, sir, he must be yours.'

I felt the blood drain from my face.

Tom smiled and shook his head. 'Rosie, you and I both know that's not true, honey. Were you having a relationship with anyone else?'

'It's yours, sir. Remember that Army Air Force party in early spring? You were the only other one I danced with beside Carl.' Her laugh tinkled out, and it was as though Rosie had been to a party, not gone through hours of gruelling pain.

'Rosie, stop that at once,' Tom said sternly.

Rosie looked at me. 'Sorry, miss, I know he's your man and all that, but I couldn't help it. I was so flattered when Mr Tom danced with me and held me close an' all.'

'Rosie!' Tom sounded exasperated. 'You can't have a baby just with dancing, you know.'

Blind anger boiled in me. Tom had danced with Rosie, held her close... how could he? I didn't wait to hear any more. I ran across the landing and into my bedroom and locked the door behind me. I crept into bed and pulled the blankets up over my face and let the tears flow.

Chapter Seventeen

'When are you going to do another exhibition for me, dear Riana?' Mr Readings had become far friendlier since the last exhibition, when all but one of my paintings had sold. Now even that one had gone, and I was so pleased. It had been darker than usual, with blues and greens mixed and lots of velvety leaves with just a few purple irises to give a splash of colour.

Mr Readings seemed to read my mind. 'The last painting of foliage was very good, my dear, but when you put just a touch of ghostliness into the work it sells like hot cakes. Take this one now—' he pointed at my picture of the mansion on fire '—it could just be a blaze – very nice colour mix, well lit indeed against the dark skies – but that one solitary indistinct figure on the roof makes it so much more than just a house in flames... do you see what I mean?'

'I do see what you mean,' I said and meant it. I knew full well that my ghostly pictures had set a new trend of realism with just a touch of the unreal or 'other world' as Mr Readings liked to call it.

'You've hit on something there, Riana. Don't let it go, whatever you do. Somehow the inspiration you show when you paint the "other world" brings life to the work. The painting is so much finer for it. I can't explain it any better than that. It's as if someone else guides your hand.' He shrugged. 'But isn't that the way with most creative people? The spirit moves, and we react to it.'

He laughed at his own joke, but to me it wasn't a joke it was true. Just as Mr Readings said, it was as if someone guided my hand. Suddenly, I was afraid. What if the guiding hand went away? What if I couldn't really paint?

'Well, Riana, when can you have another exhibition ready?'

'I don't know, Mr Readings. When the spirit moves me, I suppose.' I couldn't help smiling, and he smiled back at me. He really was a very handsome man – humorous, too, now that I knew him better.

While in town I bought a new batch of paints, some canvases and a sketch pad. It all cost money, but these, I reminded myself, were the tools of my trade. I packed them away in my van, and then I went to find a nice cup of tea and somewhere to sit for a few minutes while I tried to make a list of things I wanted for the house.

The November sun, pale and wintry, was nevertheless warm through the bowed glass windows of the tea shop. The cloth on the table was pristine white, and my cup, saucer and teapot were painted with pretty delicate flowers.

I suddenly felt very alone.

Tom. I'd tried to put him out of my mind since the awful night when Rosie had accused him of fathering her baby. He'd protested his innocence, and the baby could just have inherited Rosie's fine white skin and blue eyes, but her words at the baby's birth had made me feel sick and hollow. I knew she was teasing, but a doubt niggled at my mind all the same.

The baby – Rosie had named him John – was still with us. He could hardly go to America to be brought up by a dark-skinned American family, not now. It didn't seem appropriate, in any case. Rosie had bonded with the boy and seemed to love him with such motherliness it would be a shame to part them. Still, Mrs Ward still asserted that John should be adopted.

My stomach seemed to cramp with pain whenever I imagined Tom dancing with Rosie. He hadn't denied that. She had probably been the worse for drink and lapping up the attention.

I finished my tea and asked for the bill, and then I stepped outside into the cold sunshine. My eyes were dazzled by the light, but I was aware of a tall figure blocking my way. 'Tom?'

It was as if he'd been conjured up by my thoughts. My arm was held tightly, and I was led back inside the tea shop. I sank down into the chair I'd just vacated, and Tom sat opposite me.

'Listen to me, Riana. I've never touched Rosie, I don't know why she thinks it a joke to accuse me. Unlike the summer American Army Air Force party, when I spent most of the evening dancing with you, honey, I was only at the spring party for about an hour.'

'You still danced with her,' I said hotly.

'I danced with many of the young ladies present, and then I left. Why should I lie?' Tom challenged.

'I don't know.' I shrugged in bewilderment. 'Just tell me the truth, Tom. What really happened?'

'I was on duty, so I only called in just to show my face. Then I patrolled the grounds until about ten fifteen, as usual.' He shrugged helplessly. 'That's all I can tell you, Riana. It was a long time ago.'

I knew there was no way I could be sure Tom was telling the truth. Carl Jenkins was dead; most of the other men had been sent back to America. 'But the baby is white, no arguing with that,' I said uneasily.

'I think I was the first one to point that out,' Tom said.

'Could the baby be a sort of throwback to another generation?' I think I was being hopeful.

Tom shook his head. 'I don't know. Carl Jenkins's family are all African American, but it's quite possible there was a white connection years ago. Anyway, the child could have Rosie's genes.'

'He could have white blood back along the line,' I said. Carl's name was Jenkins, a British name, after all. But that apart, I didn't like to think of Rosie being in trouble. I bit my lip and looked at Tom. 'What can we do to help her?'

Tom rubbed the gathering lines on his forehead. 'I don't rightly know.'

I rose from my chair. 'Anyway, I have to get back home to Aberglasney. I have a lot to do! There's another haunting party next week.'

Tom's mouth twitched into a familiar smile. 'Why not just ghost *hunting*?' he asked.

'I prefer ghost haunting. It's more descriptive, somehow. Anyway, it brings the guests in, doesn't it?'

'No need to be defensive. I was only asking.'

For a moment we seemed to back on familiar ground, playfully baiting each other, smiling and being happy. I sat down again and asked for another pot of tea. For an hour or two we laughed and joked as we used to, while Tom held my hand and I felt a warm glow of happiness as all our differences seemed swept away. Tom had that magical quality that made me believe everything he said while I was with him. And then, suddenly, he became thoughtful. It was growing dark outside by now, and the magic seemed to vanish. The silence lengthened. and there seemed nothing left to say. 'Well, I'd better get home,' I said eventually.

He made no move to stop me.

'See you, Tom.' I made for the door, and as the bell clanked behind me I half expected Tom to come rushing out after me.

He didn't.

I glanced back and saw that he was walking purposefully towards the centre of town. I wondered, worriedly, where he was going and what he was going to do so far from his barracks. Perhaps he had another lady friend somewhere in the village? Doubt blossomed, and then I told myself I was being silly, paranoid, totally unrealistic. If there had been any talk about Tom and a village girl I would have heard about it. Or would I?

I went to bed miserable and tearful that night and shut my ears to any sounds that the house was making around me.

Chapter Eighteen

The colonel, as usual, was the first guest to arrive. And, as usual, he'd brought a huge amount of equipment with him. As he alighted from his taxi he looked up at the windows and waved. I stepped outside to greet him and glanced upwards, but I couldn't see anything. 'Who were you waving at, Colonel?' I asked, and he winked at me and tugged his little moustache.

'Never you mind, young Riana, we all see something different in this house. *I* see the ghost of the old lady in Victorian dress.' He rested his cases on the ground, gesturing to the driver to help him inside with them.

'You mean Beatrice?' I said in relief. 'She's no—' I stopped speaking. I didn't have to let him know Beatrice was just a friend and not a ghost at all. She was old and a bit strange, but she was as solid as I was.

At dinner, later, when all my guests had arrived and were seated around the dining tables, Mrs Ward and Rosie served roast lamb and mint sauce. The whole thing seemed to have an air of familiarity about it, and strangely Rosie looked her usual comely self, exactly as she had been before she'd given birth to the baby.

The door blew open, and there was a sound of wailing and crying from upstairs. Everyone left the dinner and rushed out into the hall and up the stairs to see at close quarters the flickering lights. This had happened before; either I was losing my mind, or I was in some terrible nightmare.

Beatrice appeared briefly, but retreated as she saw the people rush towards her, cameras flashing.

The colonel spoke the exact same words he'd spoken before. 'Did you see the Victorian lady? Anyone catch a picture of her? She's called "Beatrice", you know.'

Lights still flickered on the landing, and I found *myself* repeating exactly the same words I knew I'd used before. 'Here on this landing, the five murdered maids are alleged to seek release from their chains of death.' My voice was sepulchral, and everyone fell silent. I *was* going mad.

One lady screamed, the lights vanished, and young William spoke up bravely. 'Search the rooms, everyone!'

'Mr Bravage, all of you, please do search, and if you find anything rigged or to be a hoax I will refund your money.' I felt I was reliving a terrible nightmare, but I had to speak in my defence. Nothing was rigged, I knew that.

I felt the same sense of fear and unease as I had the first time all this had happened. Or *was* this the first time it had happened, and I'd dreamed it before? I didn't know anything any more.

When we walked back towards the stairs, I hesitated outside Beatrice's room. I felt the same reluctance to invade her territory, but Mr Bravage shouted, 'Go on then! Let's see the lady ghost. Find out if she's alive and kicking!'

I opened Beatrice's door, but she wasn't there. The room was empty. Relieved, I stepped back and let the other guests in, led by Mr Bravage. I'd had enough. I clearly remembered the rest of it: how Mr Bravage had 'sensed a presence' and then the colonel had smelled decay in the room, a smell I'd put down to Beatrice's old lavender scent.

Later, as we sat down again to our meal, I still felt the same dreamlike quality pervading the room. People talked in loud excited voices. We seemed to move slowly through the same conversations. I drank a great deal of wine and went to bed and slept soundly, and in the morning – to my relief – my guests left, although not before telling me that Aberglasney was a real find and that I should charge more for the weekends. It was nothing I hadn't heard before.

Tired beyond belief, I returned to bed and slept like a baby. When I woke again it was sunrise, and when I eventually left my room everything was back to normal, the clock was the right time, the date was correct, and I sat and drank coffee in the silent peace of the dining room and wondered how I'd dreamed such an odd dream.

But Rosie's baby wasn't a dream; he was stark reality, and his paternity was still a matter of doubt. I tried to shake off the feeling of despair when I considered that Tom might be the father of Rosie's child.

As it happened, I didn't see anything of Tom for the next few days, and so I concentrated on my painting. I squeezed out the last of my oils, twisting the tubes round a thin stick to force the thickening paint on to my palette. I put a thin wash of ochre on the canvas and then lightly sketched in the stairs and figures of my guests looking upward to where the lights flashed along the landing.

A sense of excitement gripped me. This must have been what my 'dream' or 'vision' or whatever it had been was all about: inspiration for a new painting! Almost without realising it, I opened my new tubes of paint and worked in the wood of the staircase, adding highlights from the flickering lights above.

The colonel was there, and Mr Bravage, and the new young man who had joined us recently. I painted in the lady who had run screaming back down the stairs and then, with a sigh, put down my brushes. I needed a reviving coffee. I was in the frame of mind where I didn't want to leave my work, but my back ached from standing before the easel and my mouth was too dry.

Mrs Ward was in the kitchen. Her face was long and gloomy. 'I don't know what's going on with Rosie,' she said without stopping her task of drying up dishes. 'She won't talk to me, just hugs that little baby all day and sits and cries over it. I'm at the end of my tether, Miss Riana.' She carefully hung the tea towel over the rail of the cooker and rewrapped her apron with deft, impatient fingers.

'Would it help if Rosie stayed on with me for a while?' The words were out before I'd even considered the implications of what I was offering. A crying baby, a young mother claiming that Tom was the father of her child… could I handle the complications of it all?

'That would help, Miss Riana.' The words came out with a rush of relief. 'Perhaps Rosie will talk to you, you being young and all.'

I doubted it. Rosie was claiming that the man I was fond of had fathered her child. She knew it had hurt me, and I still wasn't sure she was telling the truth, but now I'd made the offer for her to stay I would have to abide by it.

When Rosie came, bag and baggage, to live in the house with me, I stared long and hard at the baby in her arms. He was fair-skinned, but other than that he bore no resemblance to Tom. His hair was turning dark and curly, and his little nose was becoming a proper shape and was a little broad in the nostrils. I suddenly wanted to paint him. Little John with the five maids attending him. I brought my pencils and did some quick sketches while the baby was asleep. He opened his eyes and it was as though he was looking right through me. His eyes were the darkest brown.

I put Rosie to stay in my room because it was the biggest bedroom in the house, and she could put the baby in the cot I'd found in the attic. She would be comfortable there. 'Don't worry if you hear strange noises in the night,' I said, forcing a smile. 'The old house creaks and groans, but it's nothing to worry about.'

'I don't believe in all that ghost nonsense anyway,' Rosie said. 'I've seen the people come and rush around looking for lights and things, and have any of them got any proof of anything? Not one picture, not one sighting, nothing.'

'Oh, that's all right then.' I spoke a little sharply.

Rosie didn't look at me. 'I know it's all put on for the guests, as you call them. All a trick to bring in the money. I don't blame you, mind. I'd probably do the same if I owned this horrible old house.'

'Well, if it's so horrible, why do you want to live here?' I felt my anger rising. Rosie could have plenty of doubts about ghosts, but she shouldn't malign my dear old Aberglasney.

'Anywhere is better than living with my mother, narrow minded prude,' Rosie said.

I left her and went back to the kitchen where Mrs Ward was baking pies for supper. She looked at me with narrowed eyes. 'Complaining already, is she?'

I shrugged. 'She's got the biggest and best bedroom in the house,' I said tartly. 'There's nothing else I can do to make her welcome.'

'Whatever you do it wouldn't be enough.' She glanced at me. 'I never allowed her to have callers when she lived with me, and if I were you I wouldn't allow any nonsense here.'

I looked at her in surprise. 'But I thought Rosie was in love with Carl Jenkins?'

'Oh, she was, for a time. That's her way, apparently. One today and another one tomorrow.'

'So do you think Tom is the father of her child, Mrs Ward?'

'Not a chance.' She snapped her lips tightly shut, and I knew I'd never get another word out of her on the subject.

That night I heard the usual noises on the landing: doors opening, lights flashing under the crack of the door of my unfamiliar bedroom. But, as usual, I ignored the noises and went to sleep.

The next day I worked on my painting while Rosie took the baby for a walk in the gardens. It was a sunny day in early spring and the light was good through my large studio windows.

I painted baby John and behind him ghostlike spirals of mist, depicting the five maids. There was almost no form to the figures, and yet the painting worked so well that I could see features and shapes in the mist bending over the child.

I sketched a lantern into the painting using my imag-ination, making a convincing orange-yellow glow shine through the lantern's tiny glass windows. I stood back, wondering how on earth I'd managed to create such a magical painting. I'd gone to art school, worked hard to get my degree, but I'd never been one of the outstanding pupils, the stars-to-be, who the teacher had favoured and respected and pandered to if they were late with their essays. It was Aberglasney that had worked the spell: the atmosphere, the ghostliness, the stone and fabric of the old house. I loved it and felt that it loved me in return.

'Stop being absurd!' I said out loud. And then I heard it: the giggling, the muffled voices. One was a man's voice, low and somehow coaxing. I froze. Was it true that Beatrice's husband had seduced the young maids and then done away with them?

I realised then that the sounds were coming from the garden. I peered out through my open studio window and below me I could see the baby in the pram, a tiny white-faced creature covered with blankets. And there was Rosie, her pink knees akimbo and the bare backside of an unknown man exposed for all the world to see.

Hastily, I withdrew into my studio and shut the window as if *I* were the guilty one, not Rosie. I held my hand to my mouth, realising at least that the man wasn't Tom. I knew by the heavy boots Rosie's lover had been wearing and by the rough cap on the mop of unruly hair. And then anger seized me. How dare she do it? Bring a man into my garden and let him… do things to her no decent man should be doing, and with the baby at her side! Wasn't she in enough trouble?

I washed my brushes, stood them in an old jam jar to dry and took off my canvas apron. I would have liked an artist's smock, but up until now I hadn't been able to afford one – and anyway, my apron had deep pockets that proved very useful. Restless now, I wanted to run down to Tom and apologise for doubting him. Of course he wasn't the father of Rosie's baby. Perhaps she didn't even know which man was. I stayed in the kitchen, however. I couldn't walk through the gardens in case I embarrassed both Rosie and myself, so I made a cup of tea, thankful that Mrs Ward would have gone home hours ago.

It was a long day, and I was glad to go to bed early and sit up reading *Rebecca* yet again until my eyes grew heavy and I turned off the gas light and went to sleep.

-

I woke to hear Rosie's baby crying from the next room, so I hastily made myself ready for the day and went to the kitchen to make some breakfast. From downstairs I couldn't hear if Rosie was up and about or not. I didn't know what I'd say to her when I saw her, because I wouldn't have her carrying on, risking yet another unwanted pregnancy, not while she lived under *my* roof.

It was with a feeling of excitement that, some time later, I left the house and walked through the gardens towards the barracks near the boundaries of my land. I had to see Tom and put things right with him, if I could.

He was working at his desk, and the sight of him, his hair fair and silky and his brow creased into furrows as he concentrated, made my heart melt. It hit me then, really hit me: I was in love with Tom, an American pilot who would soon be going home, leaving the country for ever.

'I'm sorry I doubted you,' I said quickly before I could lose my nerve.

He looked up and carefully wiped the ink from the nib of his pen. 'What?'

'I said I'm sorry. I realise I was silly and judgemental accusing you of being the father of Rosie's baby.'

'Well, it showed what you really thought of me. How little faith you have in my character.' His voice held no warmth.

I sat opposite him feeling as if I was applying for a job and feeling more than a little shocked at his coldly spoken words. 'I can't apologise enough,' I said. 'I really shouldn't have listened to her in the first place.'

'You should have had more trust in me.' He didn't give an inch. 'In any case, it hardly matters now. I leave for home at the end of the week. We've finished here, but thank you for your hospitality, Miss Evans.'

I was suddenly ice cold, and yet I felt in a chaos of panic at the same time. He couldn't go and leave me! Not now, when I'd just realised how much he meant to me! But I found myself getting to my feet and holding out my hand. 'Well, thank you for all your help, Tom – clearing the cloisters, the work you and the men did, all that. I'll miss you.' I stumbled over the last few words.

'Riana,' he began, but a loud knocking on the door startled us both.

I withdrew my hand… or was Tom the first to move? 'I'd better go and leave you to do your work,' I said.

I left by the back door and returned to the fresh air of the garden. My cheeks felt hot and I knew in my heart that Tom had been about to say something important, but I hurried through the gardens into the house.

Mrs Ward had arrived, with her shopping bag of polish and dusters, and was filling the cupboard under the sink with cleaning materials. 'Morning. You owe me three shillings and sixpence,' she said. 'Where's Rosie and the baby?'

'I don't know,' I said. 'They may not be awake yet. I've been down to see Tom, to say goodbye. The last of the Americans are leaving next week.'

'And good riddance to them,' Mrs Ward said softly. 'Master Tom was all right, kind enough and all that, but he's still a foreigner.' She glanced at me sheepishly. 'Sorry, miss.' Mrs Ward ran the tap and that was the end of the matter.

I didn't feel like working so I went in to the empty sitting room and tried to read the morning paper. There was an article entitled 'The Strange Happenings at Aberglasney', and I read a highly exaggerated account of the drama at the ghost weekend, the 'sighting' of a Victorian lady, and the strange lights on the staircase. Nothing new there, then. It was the same old local gossip, and surely by now some of the villagers must recognise Beatrice – who was eccentric, but certainly very much alive.

The story of the murder was dragged out again at the conclusion of the article and, bored with it all, I threw down the paper. I realised the publicity would do my ghost-haunting weekends a lot of good, but couldn't anyone think of something original to say? I felt a little niggle of resentment: why didn't my paintings get a mention, for instance? They were of the house and its supposed ghosts, and my work had sold well in a London gallery. What's more, the London newspapers had published small pieces about the new artist Mr

Readings had discovered, but I supposed that was more to do with the standing of Mr Readings and his gallery than with me.

I closed my eyes and tried to think of other ideas for my weekends. What more could I do but provide good food and accommodation, and the occasional flurry of lights and activity that the guests took to be ghostly visitations?

I think I was drifting into a comfortable haze – half asleep, half awake – when a blood-curdling scream brought me to my feet.

'Help! Get a doctor, an ambulance, Miss Riana. Something dreadful has happened to my Rosie!'

I ran up the stairs, my heart pounding hard in my chest. In my old bedroom, the curtains were still closed and there was a strange smell in the room. I couldn't identify it. Cigarette smoke, perhaps?

Mrs Ward was staring at the empty bed, transfixed with horror. 'She's gone, my Rosie is gone! And the baby too! They've been abducted, or the ghosts have got them, just like those poor maids.' She looked up at me, her face stained with tears. 'They must have meant to take you, Miss Riana. This was *your* room, and my girl was wearing your dressing gown, the one with all the colours and fancy patterns. I saw her wearing it when I brought her a cup of cocoa last night before I went home.'

I suddenly felt cold. Mrs Ward was right. Rosie must have been mistaken for me. 'But the baby, where is he?' The cot was empty.

'My dear, 'elp!' Mrs Ward was incoherent. 'The child has been stolen away! What in the name of heaven and all the angels has happened here in the night?'

I shivered. 'Someone wanted me out of the way.' I mumbled the words through dry lips.

Mrs Ward stared at me with cold accusing eyes. 'My Rosie will be another ghost for you to paint.' Her voice was cold, her hysterics pushed into the recesses of her reserve. 'We'd better get the police and report my daughter and my grandchild missing.' She left the room.

Once the police came, everything degenerated into a scene of noise and chaos. I was ordered out of the room and told not to pollute the crime scene any further.

At the door, a policeman clutched my arm. 'We might need to take your fingerprints, miss.'

'Look on the door handle.' My voice was crisp. 'You'll find my fingerprints on *everything*, officer. This is my house, and this used to be my room.'

'I see.' He eyed me up and down. 'You are Miss Evans then?'

'That's right.'

'You hold ghost weekends and you sell daubs?' The scornful way he said it implied I would sell my body if I had to.

'If it's any help, Rosie was last seen wearing my dressing gown. She could have been mistaken for me.'

'We'll do the detective work, Miss Evans, and draw our own conclusions. I would advise you to go and make a cup of tea or do something feminine and appropriate.'

'And I would advise *you* not to patronise me, sir.' I straightened, made myself as tall as possible and stared him down. 'Have you brought a senior officer with you?'

'Well, no, Miss Evans. This girl might have left here willingly.' He wasn't quite so sure of himself now.

'Wearing my dressing gown? I doubt that.' I lifted my chin. 'And when a senior officer *does* arrive I will talk to him not to you.'

'Very well, Miss Evans.' He still had an arrogant twist to his lips.

'And my paintings sell for more than you make in a year, so I will not have them called daubs. Aberglasney was on your doorstep, decaying under your stuck-up nose, and yet you didn't have the wit or the drive to restore the old place. Well, I have saved it from ruin, and so long as the way I do it is legal I hope you will respect that.' In that moment I didn't respect myself at all, however. Here I was, bragging about my achievements to a mere constable. What on earth had got into me?

I saw Beatrice on the landing and told her what had happened to Rosie.

She wasn't in the least surprised. 'At least they can't blame her disappearance on poor Eddie. It's this house, you see. It's always been this house.' And with those cryptic words she went into her room and closed her door with a snap of finality.

Mrs Ward was sitting in the kitchen. Her eyes were dry as she pushed a cup of tea towards me. 'Perhaps this is all for the best.' Her voice was low. 'Poor Rosie had no future here, not with the baby and no Americans willing to take the child away. She's run away. That's the answer, it must be! Nothing else makes sense.' Her eyes didn't meet mine. 'And me, well, if I keep my head down and my tongue still, I might survive all the nastiness.'

'Haven't you got a soul, Mrs Ward?' I asked in disbelief at her attitude to losing her daughter and her grandchild.

'Lordy, Miss Riana, I lost that many years ago when I was betrayed by a fine man.' She held her cup in both hands and I saw that she was crying, after all.

'You don't wear a wedding ring, Mrs Ward,' I said suddenly.

'I'm not married.' Her statement was bald, brittle and her eyes filled with tears. 'At least Rosie's been spared the shame, the menial work, the humbleness of being always lowly, a servant, unable even to attend the Lord's house because of the "good people" who don't deign to notice you.'

'You always speak correctly, Mrs Ward. You were well educated, I think.'

'Ah, I was. I was sent to private school by my guilty father. He was married – but not to my mother. History has a strange way of repeating itself, Miss Riana.'

As Mrs Ward put the kettle on again, almost unaware of what she was doing, I saw her in a new light and felt a new closeness to her.

Chapter Nineteen

The police interviewed everyone connected to the ghost weekends and then told me to cancel my booking for the next one, which had been due to take place at the end of November. I wrote letters to my guests and received replies from all of them, rebooking for the Big Christmas weekend. It seemed the disappearance of Rosie and her child had only served to whet the appetite of ghost hunters everywhere. There was even an article in the London papers about the tragedy at the 'house of Riana', now described as a 'famous artist', and one headline reported: 'Another ghost to haunt Aberglasney.'

I was still upset and worried. I missed Rosie, and I found it impossible to hire anyone from the village to come and work for me. Everyone was afraid and suspicious of me and the house, and no one favoured the coming and goings of my guests, even though they brought trade to the village.

Worst of all, Tom had kept out of my way. I knew he was destined to go back to America in a few days, and at the very least I wanted to say goodbye to him. The thought of him leaving filled me with dread; my heart ached at the thought of being without him. I was in love, but an unrequited love that left me hurt and shamed. But, in spite of my pride, I knew I would have to say goodbye to him.

It was a cold, damp day when I made my way down the garden, through the yew-tree tunnel and towards the gates where the barracks stood. To my surprise, some of the buildings had been razed to the ground already. Men were busy laying rolls of grass over the area, almost as though the huts had never been. One of the men looked up and nodded. He was wearing a cherry-red scarf that somehow brightened the day. I wondered who had sent them. Perhaps they were council workers, or maybe Tom had organised the restoring of the ground. Anyway, what did it matter so long as Tom hadn't gone already?

When I saw his familiar figure sitting at the desk, his hair curling into a quiff above his forehead, the strong broad set of his shoulders visible beneath his crisp shirt, I wanted to throw myself into his arms and hug him in relief that he was still there.

He got up when he saw me. 'Riana,' he said and my name fell softly into the cold air of the room. He seemed to straighten his back then, almost as if he was going to salute me. I could see at once he was keeping his distance. Gone was the Tom who had sat with me under the cloisters in the thin balmy air of a summer's night.

'I was very sorry to hear about Rosie,' he said in his best official voice, 'and the child. Does anyone know what's happened to them?'

'The police are investigating,' I replied, and the formality in my own voice placed a huge barrier between us.

There was a long silence, and I searched Tom's face for some sign of softening. I knew I'd been cold to him, stayed away from him without a word, and he was stiff with pride. Even so, if he came and kissed me and told me he loved me, I'd go to the ends of the world with him.

'I just came down to say goodbye,' I found myself saying 'I know you'll be going home soon.'

He looked round distractedly. 'This seems like my home now,' he said, and then he took a deep breath. 'But you are right. I leave tomorrow.'

'And you were going without talking to me?' I was aghast.

'What was there to say?' Tom didn't look at me.

I managed to speak after a while. 'Well, I want to say thanks for everything again. The gardening, the support, your faith in my painting. Everything.'

'My pleasure.' He half bowed.

There seemed nothing left for me to do but go. I went towards the door, just as it was pushed open and two burly policemen came into the office. Before my terrified eyes, they arrested Tom, put him in handcuffs and – without looking at me – took him outside. I followed, trying to protest, but the men took no notice of me. They pushed Tom into a car and slammed the door shut. The car was an unmarked one, and as it drove away I saw something bright sticking out of the boot: a red scarf by the look of it. Suspicions aroused, I memorised the registration number – or at least some of it – and ran back through the garden to the house and the phone.

The local police, I learned, had no knowledge of anyone picking up an American Wing Commander.

I sat abruptly on the chair near the phone table and tried to sort out my thoughts. Who could have taken Tom... and why?

—

I went back to Tom's office later that day, thinking perhaps I would find a clue to what was happening there. The office was no longer standing, however. It had been taken apart, prefabricated piece by prefabricated piece, like a jigsaw puzzle. Someone had been searching the place with complete thoroughness; not even a pin would have escaped notice.

I looked suspiciously at the workmen, but none of them was wearing a cherry-red scarf. 'What happened to the Wing Commander's possessions?' I asked.

The workman shrugged, uncaring. 'Boxed up and sent on to his home, I suppose,' he said.

I managed a smile. 'Has anyone got a forwarding address?'

'Don't know nothing about that, miss.' He turned away, finished with the conversation, and in despair I returned to the house.

'What's the police doing here, Miss Riana? Is it about Rosie?' Mrs Ward was pale with dark shadows under her eyes. She was evidently more worried about her daughter than she had let on.

I shook my head. 'We've had four visits from the police about Rosie and the baby,' I said quietly. 'They'll find her, don't worry, but this visit by unknown men is something to do with the Americans.' Though what, I didn't know, because I would have bet everything I had – even Aberglasney – that those men had not been real policemen.

'Well, it's those Americans who started the troubles here.' Mrs Ward spoke emphatically. 'We were all right before the war. *Then* the village was quiet and peaceable enough.'

'And what about the five young maids who were murdered?' I asked. 'That wasn't very peaceable, was it?'

'Well, I don't know much about all that.' Mrs Ward turned her face away from me, and I wondered how much she did know. She played her cards very close to her chest, I'd found.

Chapter Twenty

I met Miss Grist again when I went to Swansea the next day. I'd been to the police station to report Tom as missing, and although my comments had been written down by the officer on duty, I felt the sheet of paper would be put in the bin the minute I left. I wandered into the library, and Miss Grist followed me into the reference room. She was wearing a smart white blouse and a dark skirt that appeared almost a uniform. Even her shoes and stockings were black.

She was obviously intrigued by the latest stories about Aberglasney and wanted to know all the details of Rosie's disappearance. She was very friendly, talkative even, and coaxed me to go with her to the staffroom for a cup of coffee during her break and sat uncomfortably close to me.

'How was the room left? Any signs of an intruder?' Her eyes were bright with curiosity. 'Perhaps it was one of those American airmen who abducted her.'

I reined in my sudden burst of irritation. 'We don't know anything more than you do, Miss Grist,' I said. 'One thing I *am* sure about – it wasn't anything to do with the Americans.'

'But this girl had several "assignations" with these men. They say the baby was fathered by one of them.'

'Well, "they" might well be right, but her disappearance was during the night when the house was locked up, and there was no sign of a break-in.' I told myself it was only natural for people to be curious about events at Aberglasney; no doubt Miss Grist was only saying what everyone was thinking.

Her eyes narrowed. 'Are you saying it was the ghosts then, or have you yourself taken the girl somewhere?'

'Why on earth would I? If you have such evidence to back up such suspicions about me you'd better tell it to the police, or else stop being so nosy!' I felt like telling her she was reading too many of the books on the shelves of the library and allowing her imagination to run away with her.

'Did the police suspect you, Miss Evans?'

It was a good question. 'I don't think so. I didn't have a motive, you see. Rosie was my helper. I needed her to work for me.' I spoke wearily now. Miss Grist had the hide of an elephant and wasn't going to give in.

'But she accused the man you loved of being the father of her child. If that wasn't a motive, I don't know what was.'

I put down my cup with a bang against the saucer, and Miss Grist drew back, realising she'd gone too far. 'Isn't anything private any more? I'll leave you, Miss Grist, and I'll thank you to keep out of my business. I thought it was just idle curiosity on your part, but if even you think I'm capable of abducting a mother and baby, what chance have I with everyone else?'

'I do apologise.' Miss Grist looked distressed. 'I don't believe any of that myself. It's just what people will think and what they will say.'

'Precisely.' I left the library, my cheeks flaming as I walked down the steps and into the chill of the day. It was getting dark already, and there was a hint of snow in the air. I wanted to be home in my house with my dear Tom beside me, Rosie and Mrs Ward working in the kitchen, and guests about to arrive. I wanted everything to be as it was before Rosie had been silly enough to fall for a baby and ruin everything.

I suddenly realised Miss Grist was right. I did have a motive, and one of the strongest types: the vitriol of a woman scorned. How foolish though! Tom wasn't the father. He had always denied it, and I believed him. It was Tom who'd said the baby might not be Carl's son; why would he have pointed that out if he'd had something to hide? All the same, Miss Grist had raised the spectre of jealousy and mistrust in me once again.

I hurried towards the train station at the top of High Street. A drunken man staggered noisily in the echoing porcelain of the gentleman's toilet, rolling down the steps to disappear beneath road level. The train for Aberglasney was just steaming into the station, and I thanked my lucky stars I didn't have to wait on the bleak cold platform. I sunk into a seat in an empty carriage and thought of the things Miss Grist had said. Was I a suspect? Was I being watched? And what on earth had happened to Tom?

That night I left the light on in my room and took a hot toddy to bed with me. Tonight Aberglasney was quiet: no creaking floorboards, no groaning trees pressing like skeletal fingers against the old windows. And yet I was disturbed and afraid; for the first time I was uneasy in my own house.

The next day I went to the police station again, determined to talk to someone in authority about Tom's disappearance. I sat waiting in the hallway for what seemed hours, but I had decided that I was not going to go away, however long I had to sit there.

At last, a bored detective called me into his room. He switched on a tape recorder, and as I watched the wheels go round I was aware of a policeman standing behind me, guarding the door.

'I'm Inspector Morris. What can we do for you, Miss Evans?'

'I want to report a missing person. Again,' I said, and waited.

The inspector wrote something down, ignoring me completely.

'Do you want any details, or are you going to use mind-reading?'

My sarcasm was lost on him. 'Carry on,' he said.

'Tom Maybury, an American officer, was taken away by men dressed as policemen a few days ago, and there's been no sign of him since.'

There was silence. Morris rifled through some papers. 'There's no record of any such event,' he said.

'So I was told yesterday.' My voice was strong and Morris looked at me sharply.

'I'll write the details down, miss, but this American is nothing to do with us. Perhaps he's gone back to his own country.' His tone indicated that 'his own country' was the best place for him.

I forced a calmness into my voice I didn't feel and wondered how I could get through to this man. 'What if the Americans send someone over here and demand to know what the British police have done to find the officer? They will think we British are very unprofessional.'

The inspector looked a little uneasy. Finally, he wrote something on paper and then looked up at me. 'We'll investigate, of course, but I don't hold out much hope of finding the officer. Our resources here are very limited, you understand.'

'I understand, and thank you so much for your help. I will be sure to tell the American authorities about your understanding and command of the situation.'

This time the sarcasm hit home, and Inspector Morris grew red with embarrassment. 'We've done all we can to help these foreigners,' he snapped, 'and they've repaid us by drinking copious amounts of liquor, being free and easy with our women, and making trouble everywhere they go.'

'Hmm.' I walked to the door and then looked back. 'I think you might have to cut off that piece of tape, don't you?'

Inspector Morris stood up. 'See the lady out, Atkins,' he said abruptly, but he was already fiddling with the tape machine.

—

I stood outside the tiny police station and breathed in the cold, thin air. It cut like a knife, and I shivered involuntarily. I hurried into the tiny coffee shop and sat down, wrapping my scarf more tightly around my neck.

'Excuse me, may I sit with you? I think I've an apology to make.'

I looked up in surprise. 'Miss Grist! What are you doing down here? Aren't you supposed to be at work today?'

'I realise I spoke out of turn yesterday, and when I saw you at the police station I thought the worst. I thought you were being arrested!'

'Still the soul of tact then?' I said shortly, and Miss Grist pursed her thin lips.

'I'm *trying* to apologise,' she said. She looked pale and cold, and her eyes were an icy grey as they narrowed against the white of the falling snow. She had made an effort to see me, however, and so I relented.

'Let me buy us a hot pot of coffee,' I suggested.

She smiled at once, and it seemed we were on amicable terms again. I thought it would be helpful if I explained the situation. 'I went to the police to report a missing person,' I said. 'I won't go into it all, but let me assure you I'm not being accused of anything – certainly not Rosie's disappearance or the abduction of her child. She had a key to the house, naturally. I thought it remiss of the police not to ask me that right away.'

'So she might have left of her own accord. Again, I can only apologise.' Miss Grist was frosty again.

'My next ghost weekend will be just before Christmas. Perhaps you'd like to come, Miss Grist? As my guest, of course, though I wonder if you would be kind enough to help me serve the meals. I can't get any village girls up to the house – not since the awful night Rosie disappeared.'

'A superstitious lot, the villagers, and of course I would be delighted to help,' Miss Grist surprised me by saying. She appeared genuinely pleased. She took out a diary and meticulously penned in the date I gave her. 'If there's any secretarial work for me, I'm very good at typing. I could contact your list of guests.' She sounded eager.

'That would be a great help.' And it would; I hated handwriting all the letters and addressing all the envelopes to my growing list of guests.

'What about the cooking?' she asked. 'That's not one of my great skills, I'm afraid.'

'Mrs Ward does that. Rosie's mother.'

'Oh, is that what Gladys Williams is calling herself now?' There was a spiteful edge to Miss Grist's words. 'No better than she should be, is Gladys. Had an unseemly affair with a foreign gentleman, and poor little Rosie was the result.'

'You know Mrs Ward then, do you?' My tone was severe. I liked Mrs Ward, in spite of her spiky ways, and she was invaluable to me.

'Just gossip, you know,' Miss Grist said. 'Just gossip, that's all. I never met the woman, of course. She and I didn't move in the same circles, you know.'

I realised I didn't like Miss Grist very much. Why on earth had I invited her to my home? I quickly drank the hot, sweet, warming coffee and then picked up my bag and gloves and twisted my scarf around my neck. 'I'd better be getting back.' I tried to smile as Miss Grist rose too.

'I'll come back with you, if I may,' Miss Grist said. 'You can show me around the house, give me your list of guests, and I can get the letters done when I get back to Swansea.'

It made sense, and so Miss Grist walked beside me through the snowy streets and caught the train to Aberglasney. When my house came into view, my heart warmed with pleasure. As we passed the place where the barracks had been, I bit my lip in anxiety; would the police do anything at all to find Tom?

I suspected Inspector Morris would have to go through the motions after what I'd said about the Americans sending someone over to investigate, and I could only hope that Morris would at least do his best to track the men who had taken Tom.

I hesitated among the rubbish left when the workmen removed the huts. Those fake policemen had something to do with Tom's disappearance; who were they, and who had sent them?

A scrap of paper among the rubble caught my eye, and I picked it up. I realised Miss Grist was trying to look over my shoulder at it, and I pushed it quickly into my pocket, not really knowing why I wanted to hide it. All I knew was that I felt lost and empty without Tom and this might be a piece of him.

It was quiet in the house. I hadn't seen any sign of Beatrice for some time. I thought she'd gone away, having taken exception to my guests peering at her, poking into her privacy, but I wished – not for the first time – that she would let me know when she was going away and for how long.

'My, this house is so quiet,' Miss Grist said as she followed me into the hall. I realised we'd been walking through the garden in so great a silence that I'd almost forgotten she was there.

Mrs Ward took one look at Miss Grist and disappeared out of the back door without a word.

'It may be silent now, but it will be full of laughter and noise when my guests come again,' I said, realising I would be glad when the ghost-haunting weekends began again and filled the house with chatter and warmth and curiosity and all the paraphernalia that went with hunting ghosts.

'I've heard the ghosts are sighted along the upstairs corridor,' Miss Grist said. 'Flickering lights, and all that sort of thing.'

'That's what we've seen sometimes.' I sighed. 'I think the moon makes weird shapes through the trees and that's what causes the flickering lights.'

'Don't you believe in ghosts then, Miss Evans?'

I watched as Miss Grist took off her coat and hung it on the stand in the hall. My heart sank; she obviously intended her stay to be a long one.

She seemed to know the house well – something I hadn't expected – and she made her way to the kitchen and put the kettle on to boil. She gave a deprecating smile. 'I might as well get familiar with things while I'm here.' She almost hugged herself. 'I can hardly wait for the ghost weekend; heaven knows who I'll meet.'

'Mostly elderly colonels and sweet old ladies,' I said dryly. 'They are all intelligent people, mind you, and we do have one young man who might be good company for you.'

Miss Grist brightened up immediately. 'Really? What's his name?'

'I think his name is Colin. And then there's young William, of course. He always comes along to the weekends. He's quite the keen ghost hunter; even keener than the colonel, I sometimes think. Anyway, I'll fetch the list for you.'

She followed me into the study and looked around, as though appraising the house and its contents. I brought the guest list out from its drawer and gave it to her.

Miss Grist put it carefully away in her handbag, and after a moment she spoke again. 'I don't think I'll wait for that cup of tea,' she said. 'I'd better get back to the station, otherwise I'll miss my train.'

I breathed a sigh of relief and quickly opened the door for her, in case she changed her mind.

'See you soon then.' She gave a cheery wave, hurried off along the drive and disappeared through the archway leading to the side gate. She seemed to know her way around my house already. When had she been here, and why pretend she had never visited before? Eventually, I shrugged my questions away. So what if she had been to Aberglasney before? It was *my* house, and all she would be was an occasional guest.

The kettle had boiled so I made some tea and stoked up the fire so I could make some toast. I had some good Welsh salt butter, and my mouth watered at the thought of eating the hot toast with the butter almost liquidising into it. But then I thought of Tom, and abruptly my appetite faded. Where could he be, and what had happened to him? I almost wished it was the real police who had taken him. At least then I would know he was safe.

I remembered the scrap piece of paper I had picked up from the site of the barracks and took it out of my pocket and tried to read it. The writing was in pencil, the spelling all awry, with letters turned back to front as though written by someone illiterate or foreign.

I took my cup of tea and the note and sat near the fire, but it might as well have been written in Chinese for all the sense I could make of it. I needed a pen and ink and a fresh piece of paper – and perhaps a magnifying glass would help.

At last, seated with all my bits and pieces, I pored over the scrap of paper, slowly writing down what I thought each letter represented. The words made little sense, and at last I realised the note wasn't written in English at all.

I sat up straight as I heard the rattle of the front-door lock, and my heart leaped with a mingling of fear and excitement. Was it Tom returned to me, intruders bent on robbery... or worse?

It was Beatrice who stood in the doorway, her white hair covered in misty rain and her funny little bag, wrought with flowers, clutched in her hand. For a moment she did look like the ghost my guests believed she was, and then she spoke. 'Carry my bag to my room for me, dear.' Her voice sounded weak, as if she was very tired.

'Where on earth have you been this time?' I asked irritably. 'Why do you keep coming and going like some sort of ethereal spirit?'

'Just help me to my room, dear, I've only been visiting relatives. Do I have to report to you every time I wish to come and go, then?'

I remembered our bargain, when I'd assured Beatrice she could stay at Aberglasney any time she liked. I decided I was being unfair. 'No, of course not, Beatrice, I'm sorry. I'm a bit touchy today. Such a lot has been happening here. You get changed and rested, and I'll come up with a cup of tea and we'll talk. How's that?'

'Very good, dear. I'm very tired so I might just get into bed, if you don't mind, but we can still talk, if you like.'

'No, the morning will do, Beatrice. I'm being thoughtless.'

I helped her upstairs, and she disappeared into her room, shutting the door pointedly in my face. I shrugged. She was old, and she was entitled to be a bit eccentric.

—

It was the next day that I saw the advertisement in the *Daily Messenger*. 'Hunt the Ghost,' it read, 'in the beautiful surroundings of Oystermouth Castle in Swansea.' I gasped in disbelief. Someone else was doing a ghost weekend! The headline was followed by a mouth-watering description of the ruined castle near the sea, where the ghost of a minor royal was meant to haunt.

I sighed. I supposed I had to expect competition. My idea had been a good one, but I couldn't keep it to myself for ever. In any case, I had my guest base, my regulars. I would be all right. Still, I hurried to Beatrice's room to show her the newspaper, and she sat up in bed against her pillows, pale and ethereal in her little lace bed cap, and her hand shook as she read the piece.

She threw down the paper at last and shook her head. A stray grey curl drooped over her forehead. I suddenly realised how fond I was of the old lady. 'Makes no difference,' she said. 'Our ghosts are real. Your friends will soon realise and come back to us.'

'But I never expected to lose them in the first place, Beatrice,' I said. 'Do you think they'll desert us then?'

'Something new, my dear, is always an attraction at first, but they'll come back, you'll see.' She stared at me shrewdly. 'Now, what else is there?'

I told her about Rosie, about the terrible night she vanished. 'The police don't seem to be doing very much about it,' I said. 'Nor about the baby. The poor girl and her child seem to have vanished into thin air.'

'I expect the police will carry on the same way they did when Eddie died: show little concern and hope the matter is quickly forgotten.'

There was silence for a moment, and then I dipped into my pocket and brought out the transcription of the note I'd found in the rubble of the barracks. 'Tom's disappeared,' I said. 'I found a note but I can't make sense of it.'

'No wonder you can't read it,' she said. 'It's in very fine, very old Welsh. It's the name of a place in Carmarthen. "Cwm Elwyn." It's an old farmhouse under the mountains, near a winding stream. Of course, you'll go and look there for your Tom.'

'What area, Beatrice? There are many mountains here in Wales and lots of streams too.'

'I don't know!' Beatrice sounded exasperated. 'I'll translate the address for you into English, and then it's up to you.'

'But you think Tom might have been taken there?' I asked hopefully.

'It's a possibility, and only a possibility. This could be the address of someone's mother or grandmother, but I have a feeling Tom is there — somewhere under the shadow of the mountain.'

I was heartened by Beatrice's words. They gave me a sense of hope that I might see Tom again.

'Bring a pen,' Beatrice said, 'and I'll do my best to help.'

She waved me away with a lace-gloved hand, and I hurried downstairs to find a pen and some notepaper. I felt excitement flow through me, and I realised again how much I needed Tom around me, at my side encouraging me. If only he would say he loved me, I would be the happiest woman in the world.

I carefully wrote down the address Beatrice gave me, and when I hastened to the library in town that same day I found a map and plotted my journey with care. I reckoned it would take half a day to find my way to *Cwm Elwyn* in *Craig Melyn* and wondered if I would have enough petrol to take me there. My guest weekend was coming up and I would need to stock up on supplies, but that wouldn't take much precious petrol.

The next morning I set off early with my hamper of food and a Thermos of hot tea on the seat of the van beside me. I didn't know if Tom would be hungry and thirsty, and I shuddered at the thought he might not even be alive, but I began my journey with hope and enthusiasm and headed in the direction of the mountains of Brecon.

The journey was along country lanes, past endless fields, but at last the roadway led upward and I felt the air change from chilly to near freezing. Far below me I saw a long river snaking through the hills. On one side there was a castle, and in the middle of the water was a strip of land, rising like a sleeping animal from the river. A small building that might have been a church stood on it, and my heart stopped for a second as I read a crude notice with the words *Cwm Elwyn* painted on it in large letters that were blood red.

I stopped my old van on the bank of the river and, to steady myself, poured a small cup of hot tea. The journey had taken longer than I'd thought, and soon it would be dark once more. Nearby, boats were moored – a huddle of small rowing boats, and some bigger, sturdier boats for passengers tied to the jetty – but there were no people to sail them. The place seemed deserted.

I looked desperately at the small island. I had a gut instinct that Tom was there, and somehow I had to get to him. I strolled around the boats, and then, quite suddenly, a man appeared at my side.

'Can I help you, miss?' He had a strong accent, definitely Welsh but thick and almost intelligible. In this remote part of the country, Welsh was probably the first language.

'I just wanted to explore the island,' I said. 'Is that a little church out there?'

'It is, miss, but you have to be careful of the tides on this river. They can change with the winds and turn nasty.'

'Could you get me out there?' I searched in my rucksack for my purse.

He waved an extraordinarily large hand in dismissal. 'No need of that. I'll take you out there... if you really want to go.'

I smiled in what I thought was a winning way. 'Oh, I do. I love old, haunted places you see.'

He gave me an odd look and gestured me towards one of the boats. It was a small boat with an outboard engine that looked precarious, hanging as it was on the edge of the wooden planking.

At a fairly fast speed, we crossed the river, and I could see the boatman was right: the current swirled the water into circles around us. 'When is the tide due to rise?' I asked, and he looked surprised that I knew anything at all about tidal waters.

'Not for hours yet, miss.' The boat bumped against a mossy bank, and he helped me alight. 'What if I come back for you in—' he looked at his watch '—say an hour? Will that suit you?'

'Lovely.' I watched as he pulled away from the shore and had the distinct feeling I was being abandoned. I watched until he reached the other side of the shore, and then I turned to explore the island.

The church had steps leading down to a small door. The wooden posts at either side were green, and seaweed grew like strange medieval flowers in the surrounding land. That meant that when the tide came in it covered the church. Everything inside must be soaked and rotten. I realised that if I stayed here too long I would drown.

I pushed hard against the door and almost fell into the smelly, dark, seaweed-slippery porch of the building – if it could be called a building. There were holes in the roof, showing small beams of dull, fading light, and the windows were eroded and cracked by the rush of the water that must continually pound the glass.

'Tom?' My voice was subdued in the sodden surroundings of the church. I walked cautiously along the isle towards the pulpit, feeling the hairs on the back of my neck rising in fear. I don't know what I feared… Vampires, perhaps, or at least drowned sailors? But most of all my fear was for Tom. Was he still alive?

'Tom!' I called more loudly, and I heard a small sound above my head.

'Riana, over here.'

I could see Tom at the far end of the church; he was tied to one of the pillars! I hurried along the broken, rotting aisle and saw that he'd got his hands free, but was struggling to untie the rope around his feet.

'Riana, we have to get out of here – and quick. It's going to be high tide tonight, and then the entire island will be under water – at least that's what one of the men who brought me here today said.'

I ran to him and managed, with difficulty, to untie the knots around his feet. He stood up and towered over me, and I resisted the urge to fling myself into his arms. *Tom, please love me*, I thought – and could not tell if I had spoken those thoughts aloud.

Chapter Twenty-One

The moon was just a pale shadow in among the misty clouds as I looked up through the holes in the roof of the building at the grey, threatening skies above. I realised I was clinging to Tom, kissing his cheeks, his eyelids, his luscious mouth. At last, he held me away, and I came out of my dream, realising we were trapped in an old building with the water rising around us.

'We have to get out of here.' Tom's tone was urgent as he held me away from him.

'What's going on, Tom?' I asked. 'Why were you taken here and tied up like a cat about to be drowned?'

'No time for questions. We have to get away before the church is flooded.'

'It's going to be all right.' I smiled at him, which was something of an effort because I was shivering with cold and damp and relief. 'The man with the boat is coming back for me soon.'

'If you believe that, you'll believe anything.'

'You are being melodramatic,' I said. 'Of course he'll come back. Why shouldn't he?'

'They want me dead, that's why, and they don't care if you die too. You are a stranger who has poked her nose into things, and you'd be better out of the way.'

'Who are these people, and why do they want you dead?' I said, almost disbelieving.

'They think I know too much. As I said, there is no time for discussion, Riana. The tide is already creeping under the door. We've got to get away before it's too late.'

I hurried to the door and tried to push it open. It didn't budge. 'It's stuck!'

My words were unnecessary, however, as Tom barged against the slime covered door with all his strength and it failed to open.

'It's been nailed from the outside, probably with a strong beam across it. That must have been after you came in here. As I said, they don't care if you die too.' Tom looked up at the cracked windows. 'That's our best bet. Come on, Riana, we have no time to waste.'

'The river! How are we going to get across if it's in full tide?' I suddenly realised Tom was right; the situation was desperate. Someone wanted us out of the way!

Tom edged off one of his flying boots and began to strike at the glass with the heel. Water was already gushing up to my ankles; it wasn't a very high building, and the tide would soon reach us and be over our heads. The place was now almost pitch black, and it smelled of salt and seaweed and slime. I couldn't stop myself from shivering.

Tom was cursing under his breath in his honeyed American accent, and I resisted the desire to laugh hysterically. He kept hitting the glass, and at last it shattered outwards – like diamonds of light falling into the lapping sea.

Tom began to pull planks of wood from the benches in the gallery. 'Good thing they're rotting. These were once good, strong wooden seats. I'd never have moved them then.' He gasped as he manhandled one of the planks towards the window. 'Use this as a float,' he said, sliding the plank half out of the window.

I looked at the water outside. My feet and legs were already soaked, and the tide was beginning to lap at my waist. Soon it would be too late to get out at all. 'I'll wait for you. Come with me, Tom.'

'Go while you can.' Tom began to prise another plank from the benches, but the water was hampering him now. 'Go!' he said commandingly. He hesitated and then took my face in his hands and kissed me soundly.

'Go. Please, Riana, just go. Save me the pressure of worrying about you as well as myself. I think I must disappear for a while and let my enemies think I'm dead.'

'All right, Tom.' Before I could lose my nerve, I decided he was right I would have to go. I kissed him on his lips; his mouth was cold, but I felt the warmth of his emotions as he hoisted me up and then gently pushed me out through the jagged gap and into the cold sharp air.

I slid the plank into the water and lay on the full length of it. My sweater got stuck on a point of glass and I struggled with it for a moment, and then I gasped as I was in the sea, driven by the rushing tide.

I was lucky. The fierce wind pushed me towards the bank, but as I almost reached safety – after what felt like a lifetime of horror – a wave pushed me off the plank, and I was submerged in the freezing cold muddy water. Fronds of weeds reached curling fingers towards me, but then thankfully another wave drove me towards the bank and I felt the ground under my feet.

Gasping, I hauled myself up out of the freezing water and lay there – panting for breath, soaked and shivering, and almost crying with worry and fear. I scrambled to my knees and looked for Tom on his makeshift raft, but the water had risen even further and was rushing recklessly towards the sea, with no sign of Tom on the boiling surface.

I waited, shivering, for over an hour. Perhaps Tom had come ashore further up the river, I told myself eventually. Perhaps even now he was waiting for me by the car. Hope gave me strength, and with my feet squelching at every step, I made my way back to where I'd left the car. I stopped when I could just see the spiral of the tower of the church, for the rest was under the water.

I began to cry, silent tears that ran unheeded down my freezing cheeks. A piece of seaweed hung from my hair, and I pulled the slimy strand off with a grimace of disgust. I shouted for Tom, but my voice was carried away on the wind.

Chapter Twenty-Two

My van was where I had left it. Clearly, no one had
expected me to survive the floodwater at the church. I
climbed inside, wet and shivering and crying with shock.
At last, I managed to get home to Aberglasney – but
without Tom.

Mrs Ward didn't say a word. She made me some hot
sweet tea, and after my bath I changed into a fleecy nightgown and a warm woollen dressing gown and sat in my
room, cup in my hand.

Tom had vanished, Rosie and her baby had vanished,
and if that wasn't enough to worry about I hadn't sold a
painting for some time. I would have to borrow from the
bank to finance my next ghost-haunting weekend.

I started to plan the weekend to try to take my mind off
Tom. Perhaps he'd been washed downriver? He'd talked
about disappearing, and I felt sure in my heart he was
still alive. He'd wanted his enemies to think he was dead.
I must keep that in my mind, I told myself, and hope
and pray that his problems would be resolved soon, and
in the meantime I must immerse myself in my plans to
make enough money to keep Aberglasney afloat – and
that meant working on my ghost weekends.

I stayed in my bed for a few days, getting over a chill and
trying to come to terms with my despair about Tom. But

at last I knew I had to face life again – alone if necessary. So Mrs Ward and I went shopping together for food in the local market: meat, vegetables, fruit for puddings, cheese and biscuits, and bottles of wine that were cheap but looked good once their contents were poured into my decanters, which appeared like cut crystal in the gaslight. The villagers might scorn Mrs Ward for her past, and me for the present, but they took our money without a flinch.

–

Mrs Ward was busy setting the long table in the large hall for dinner on the first evening of our renewed ghost-haunting evenings. It was just before Christmas; the air outside was pure – crisp and cold – but inside the down-stairs fires roared and flamed with warmth and welcome.

The old colonel was first to arrive, and then Miss Grist turned up, briefly. 'I can't stay,' she said, staring round my empty hall with something like satisfaction. 'Something unexpected has come up.'

The lanterns were lit along the drive and under the archway to the road, and as the car drove Miss Grist away I recognised the driver: it was the young man Colin, who'd come to my last weekend. I felt piqued. Why hadn't he attended my get-together this time? What business could he possibly have with Miss Grist?

The colonel had the answer. 'I don't like to tell you, my dear,' he said and coughed a little, 'but another ghost hunt has been arranged, at a much reduced price to yours, and we were all circulated with letters of invitation. Someone has clearly got hold of your guest list, my dear.'

And I knew full well who that person was. 'Miss Grist,' I said bleakly. 'She's taken my list and used it for her own ends. Where is this ghost hunt taking place, colonel?'

'It's in an old castle. A huge place in a large park. The grounds are extensive, and the guests will not be fed or given any sort of hospitality, but the ghost of a royal duke is reputed to haunt the ruins at this time of year. Apparently, this ghost carries his head underneath his arm. Sounds a bit phoney to me.'

'Thank you for your loyalty, colonel.' I sat at the empty table and thought of all the food we had prepared. In bed that night I cried until I was weary, and I fell asleep knowing I was more in debt, I'd been deserted by people I thought were loyal guests, if not friends, and – worst of all – Tom still hadn't come back and I didn't know if he was alive or drowned beneath the waters of the huge river under the hills.

In the early thin light of the winter's morning, to my surprise cars began to arrive. My guests – full of apologies – begged to be given shelter and food, and Mr Bravage took me aside and told me what a miserable night they'd had at the castle. 'Frauds!' he said. 'The people were charlatans. They must have thought we were all idiots to believe such an obvious fake.'

'Why, didn't you see the ghost with no head then?' I was trying not to laugh; even saying the words sounded silly.

'Ghost, indeed. You could see at once it was no ghost. The man had his head hidden in a specially adapted coat, and as for the "head" it was that of a plaster mannequin, any fool could see that.' He shook his head. 'A man of my experience, being tricked like that... but then I was suspicious when I saw the "ghost". I've been a doctor too long to be fooled by a fake. I ran up the stairs, wrestled with the head, and when it came off I threw it down the stone steps and the wig fell off – and the nose too. Oh, and one ear!'

'A bit like Van Gogh then?'

'Eh?' Mr Bravage looked puzzled for a moment, and then he laughed. 'Oh, I see. The artist chappie who cut off his ear!'

'Did you see Miss Grist from the library there, Mr Bravage?'

'Who? Sorry, I don't know of the lady. Can't help you there, I'm afraid. Oh, she did sign the letter of invitation though. A Miss Grist, you say? Yes, I remember now, that was the lady. She sounded very forbidding too. Not the sort to have a jolly good weekend, with ghosts or no ghosts.'

In the kitchen, Mrs Ward already had the pots steaming on the stove. She looked brighter than she'd done since Rosie disappeared. 'I like it when the house is full,' she said, confirming my hope that she had nothing to do with the list and the other ghost night, and I returned her cheery smile, feeling better myself.

Tom would come back when he was ready, when he'd sorted whatever it was his problem was – I was sure of it. Rosie and the baby would be found safe and well, living with a good-natured man who would take care of her, and I would soon be able to paint again. Already, I had my guests back. Miss Grist's scheme to steal them away from me had failed, and her 'ghost' had been exposed as a fraud.

At least my ghosts were not trickery or deception on my part. Of course, there must be a natural explanation for the lights and the noises from upstairs – the moonlight, and the wind rattling the old house – but nothing *I'd* faked. *Except Beatrice*, a voice whispered in my head. But then I was just withholding the truth about Beatrice. She had once owned the house, and now still felt she had the run of the place. I knew she was tied to it by her dead husband, but it was strange that *he* never seemed to haunt the old house!

We had a jolly – if quiet – weekend, and though my guests drank a lot of mulled wine, and at midnight we ate the delicious mince pies Mrs Ward had made, no ghost or noises or lights bothered us – much to the disappointment of the ghost hunters.

It was almost dawn when the quiet was disturbed by a cry and a series of thumps, and I hurriedly pulled on my warm woollen dressing gown and hurried on to the landing, only to see that the colonel was crumpled at the bottom of the stairs! He was moaning and holding his side, but at least he was alive. I ran to him and knelt down. 'What's happened? Have you had a fall, Colonel Fred?'

'I've had a push, not a fall,' Colonel Fred said indignantly, 'and it was no ghost. It was a human hand I felt in the small of my back. Pushing with some strength, I may tell you!'

I felt along his body for breaks, and though he winced when I touched his side there didn't seem to be anything worse than bruising. 'I'm no nurse,' I said, 'but I did a first-aid course and I think you are going to be all right, but I can ring for an ambulance just in case.'

'No need, my dear Riana. I feel quite all right – just a bit shaken, that's all. I wish I could just find the fool who pushed me.'

Some of the guests helped me to lift Colonel Fred to his feet, and though he was pale and a little trembly he seemed pretty sound on his feet.

'I could do with a large brandy, my dear.' He hobbled into the sitting room and slumped into an old leather chair. I brought him a brandy, and he drank it with relish before holding out his glass for a refill.

'Here, colonel, have the bottle at your side.' I turned to the others. 'Go back to bed, if you wish. It's only just dawn.'

There was a chorus of protest, and I looked at Mrs Ward. 'In that case, we'll do breakfast now. Anyone wishing to stay for lunch, it's on me.'

Mrs Ward stepped forward. 'But if any of you good folk want to stay an extra night you'll have to pay up, because I'll need more groceries and such to feed you.'

Mrs Ward had said what I was too embarrassed to say, and I nodded my agreement.

Everyone wanted to stay, and Mrs Ward put a large bowl in the centre of the hall table. 'For the takings.'

Her explanation was unnecessary. The guests were already dipping into wallets and purses with an eagerness that delighted me.

Later, when my visitors had gone to bathe and dress and prepare for a good cooked breakfast, I sat with the colonel. He was still in his striped pyjamas and dressing gown, and his hand holding the glass to his lips still trembled, but the colour was coming back into his face.

'I'm going to arrange a bed for you in my back room,' I said. 'I don't want you climbing stairs today. Mrs Ward can bring down your things from your room.'

'That might be a good idea, Riana. I'm a bit sore, I must admit. Who,' he asked, 'would want to harm me?' He was puzzled, and so was I. 'I'm just an old retired soldier that's all,' he said, and I looked at him, really looked for the first time. His moustache and eyebrows were tinged with grey and so was his hair, but he wasn't really so old – perhaps sixty or so. If he wasn't so stooped, and if he were to wear glasses instead of an old-fashioned monocle, he would look much younger.

'You're not old.' I smiled at him.

He winked at me and then took out his pipe, which added to his elderly image. 'Compared to you, I'm geriatric, Riana. You are just a young bud of a girl, so take a tip from me: life isn't all about business and making a "go" of things – important as those things are at your age – it's also about the heart and about love. Which reminds me! Where is that charming American pilot these days? I rather thought he was keen on you.'

'Away on duty, I suppose.' I didn't know why I felt the need to lie to the colonel, but the story of Tom going into the river and wanting to disappear was something I had to respect, even though I didn't understand it.

'He hasn't met with some sort of accident, has he? You look anxious, my dear.'

I hesitated a moment. 'I'd rather not talk about Tom, if you don't mind.' I suppose my tone was cold, discouraging any further questions, because the colonel puffed on his pipe for a moment without answering.

'I wonder if we'll see any ghosts tonight, my dear.' He broke the silence, and I felt relieved. I hoped I hadn't offended him, but being a paying guest didn't allow someone the privilege of enquiring into my private life.

'Perhaps.' I didn't commit myself. Ghosts were touchy beings, if they existed at all.

Breakfast was a noisy, cheerful affair. It seemed that everyone had forgotten Colonel Fred's accident. But I hadn't. I looked around the assorted guests: Mr Bravage, young William, Colin, Mrs Timpson Smith with her neatly-cut hair and rather thin, rouged face. Plump Betty, her cheerful smile making her beautiful, and all the others who as yet were not personalities to me. None of them had any reason to hurt the colonel that I knew of. He must have slipped, missed his step. He liked his drink, and who was to say he hadn't had plenty of that when he went up the stairs?

–

That evening I had a call from Mr Readings. He wanted to come to Aberglasney to talk to me about another exhibition. I tried to put him off, explaining I had guests, but he was persistent. 'I haven't anything even started yet,' I said at last. 'I've been off my painting for a few weeks.'

'Even more reason for me to talk to you,' he said. 'Oh, and I'll be bringing my lady friend with me, so make it a nice double room, will you?'

I found Mrs Ward reading a postcard in the kitchen. She had a sour look on her face, and when I sat down beside her at the well-scrubbed table, she slid the card over to me. 'From our Rosie,' she said bluntly. 'She's safe and well and so is the baby, and she's living with some man in

Ireland.' The anger in her voice was tempered with pain, and I felt like putting my hand over hers to comfort her, but she wasn't the type for sentimental gestures.

'Well, that's a relief,' I said. 'At least she's all right – not murdered, as we all thought.'

'She's without shame, that girl.' Mrs Ward had tears in her voice, though her face was cold and stony. 'I brought her up to be a good girl, but she wouldn't learn from the mistakes I made, would she? She had to go and mess up her life – and the child's too.'

'Don't be too hard on Rosie. She's very young.' I tried to sound soothing.

Mrs Ward replied at once. 'She's no younger than you, Miss Riana, and look at you – making a business for yourself, as well as being a fine painter. I don't see *you* running off to bed any man who comes along and offers.'

I felt the colour bloom in my cheeks. 'No one's offered, Mrs Ward.' I made an effort to smile, but she wasn't amused.

'You are far too respectful of yourself to go to bed with a man without a ring on your finger.'

'Anyway—' I changed the subject '—we have two more guests coming, so will you make up a double room when you have time, Mrs Ward?'

'Aye, I'll do that after supper. We're having lamb stew and fresh cheese and for the main meal beef and vegetables. I thought we'd finish up with steamed pudding and custard.'

'I don't know how you do it.' I really admired her; no one could coax the local shops into generosity like Mrs Ward.

She lifted her chin in the air and went stiff with pride. 'The villagers know which side their bread is buttered,' she said. 'We are good customers, so it pays to keep the folks at Aberglasney well supplied.' She allowed herself a tiny smile. 'And, of course, the Americans created a lot of trade as well, and it has dawned on the shopkeepers that now the air force men have all gone back to America they need our custom.'

'Thank goodness for your contacts.' My words were heartfelt. In these days of austerity after the war I was lucky to get ordinary supplies, let alone extras.

Mr Readings and his lady arrived just as Mrs Ward was serving supper. With the good news about Rosie, I'd finally managed to hire the services of a village girl to help. She had the strange name of Treasure, and she really was one to me. According to Mrs Ward the girl was slow but was willing – and, as Mrs Ward put it, 'she'll train, given time'.

'My dear Riana.' Mr Readings kissed me on the cheek, and his lady friend did a little curtsey.

'I hope you'll call me Diane,' she said gently. She had a Welsh accent, and I was amazed by the coincidence when she told me she had been brought up close to Aberglasney, though this was the first time she'd been back in years. She was a sweet lady and very refined, but I knew she took Mr Readings to her bed whenever she had the chance.

As usual there was a great deal of chatter at the supper table, high voices and jolly laughter – that was, until the wonderful electric lights I'd installed in the ground-floor rooms went out. I could hear a small scream from plump Betty.

'Everyone stay calm,' I announced in my best author-itative voice. 'We have oil lamps and candles, so no one panic.'

Between us, Mrs Ward and I soon had the dining room lit again. Treasure, meanwhile, stood helpless with fright, her eyes wide. 'Is it the ghosts of the five maids playing tricks on us?' She was quaking with fear.

'I do hope so, dear girl,' Colonel Fred said heartily. 'That's what we are all here for, after all.'

'Don't be silly, girl,' Mrs Ward reprimanded. 'Ghosts, indeed. It's all a load of rubbish.'

'Keep your voice down, Mrs Ward,' I said. 'Don't let my guests hear you saying such things. We don't want to put them off, do we?'

'But you don't believe in such things, do you?' Mrs Ward eyed me with her usual common-sense expression.

I shrugged. 'Who knows? My guests believe it, and that's why they come to ghost-haunting weekends, so we don't bite the hand that feeds us, do we?'

Mrs Ward nodded sagely. 'Well, I will say I've never been in a house with such strange happenings before.' She spoke loudly so that the guests would hear. 'Shall I serve the pudding now, Miss Riana?'

The sombre mood was dispelled a little as large helpings of steamed syrup pudding were served with rich egg-filled custard. Wine glasses were filled, and soon the business of the failed lights was forgotten and the laughter and sound of voices raised in enjoyment could be heard once more.

Later, as Treasure carried heavy tray-loads of dishes through to the kitchen, the lights came back on and Mr Readings took me to one side.

'Don't worry about paintings until you are ready, my sweet little Riana.' He was a little carried away with the wine. 'Waiting only makes my customers more eager to own one of your precious works.'

Diane came anxiously to Mr Readings' side. 'I don't want to trouble you, dear, but I've a little headache coming on. Do you mind if I go to bed?'

'Of course not, my dear Diane.' Mr Readings turned back to me. 'I would very much like you to think of the next exhibition, however. Perhaps a little more "free" this time, with the ghosts – and the buildings or staircase or whatever – done in an impressionist style.'

Diane was pulling at Mr Readings' sleeve. 'I am a little nervous about going to bed alone. Will you come along with me?'

'Please do go to bed, Mr Readings,' I urged. 'It's been a long drive from London, and I promise to think over what you have said.'

To my relief, he kissed me goodnight on my cheek, and arm in arm the couple went upstairs. I wished all my guests were such early birds, but Colonel Fred was only just setting up his ghost-hunting equipment, while plump Betty was hovering nervously at the foot of the stairs, clinging to the arm of young William.

That night nothing happened, except that I started on a new painting – perhaps inspired by Mr Readings' words or by the need to make some money. The painting was adequate, but had no soul, and I left it half-finished and went off to bed. The guests were still making merry downstairs in the sitting room, but I was used to their noise by now and managed to ignore it.

I woke as dawn was creeping into the room and got up quickly and went to the gallery. At once I could see what was wrong with the painting. I squeezed out some fresh oils and – still in my nightgown – began to paint almost in a frenzy of enthusiasm; some might call it inspiration, but paint I did until my eyes began to close again in weariness.

I tiptoed back to my bedroom and fell asleep again, feeling relaxed and content with what I'd achieved.

Chapter Twenty-Three

I was wakened in the late morning by the appearance of a man at the side of my bed. I opened my mouth to scream and a hand was placed against my lips, a gentle hand. It was Tom.

I held out my arms to him, and he held me close. I could feel the hardness of his body against mine and had the almost uncontrollable desire to pull him under the sheets with me. He released me and sat on the bed, and I felt a sinking feeling of disappointment. I never knew if Tom wanted me in a special way, or just as a friend. 'Thank God you're safe,' I said. 'What's going on?'

'I can't tell you right now, hon. It's a military thing.'

'Rubbish!' There was anger in my voice. 'Why would the military need to try to steal my business from me? To threaten my life and yours? Tell me the truth. I'm not a child.'

'Our lives are linked,' Tom said. 'Whoever is after some information guesses that you know what I know.'

'And what do you know?'

'If I told you, you'd be in as much danger as I am.'

'I *am* in as much danger as you are,' I pointed out. 'From the time I arrived here, someone has tried to harm me. At first I thought the attacks had something to do with Aberglasney, but they have everything to do with you and your military secrets.'

'The two are inextricably linked. Don't you understand?'

'For heaven's sake, Tom, stop talking in riddles. Of course I don't understand.'

'Perhaps that's just as well. You can't tell what you don't know.'

'I wouldn't tell if I did know anything,' I protested.

'Ever had a root canal without anaesthetic?' Tom's voice was wry.

'You mean I could be tortured?' The thought made me wince. 'But the war is over, Tom, and so is all that kind of thing.'

'Maybe.'

I sat up, hugging the sheets and blankets around my shoulders. 'Anyway, why are you here? What's happened? By the way, you smell like you've been sleeping on a rubbish tip!'

'I'm not surprised I smell. I've been hidden on the island, remember?'

'I don't remember much of anything, except that I called and called for you and got no answer. You could have been drowned or captured or anything!'

'I did warn you it was best my enemies thought I was dead, didn't I, honey?'

Suddenly, I was furious with him. Angry that he didn't kiss me, that he didn't tell me he loved me, that he didn't even talk to me as if I was an intelligent adult. 'Stop treating me like a child!' I heard my voice quiver.

Tom took me in his arms, and his kiss was all I could have wished it to be. His mouth parted mine, and I felt my breath become ragged. I wanted him to caress me, make love to me, but he pulled away. 'I need a shower.'

'That's the truth,' I replied.

'You must have an exhibition in London soon,' he said into my ear. 'It's vital you have some work ready within the month. Understood?'

He left me, without another word, and I saw him lower himself from the window and my heart was in my mouth. I didn't know if I should love him or hate him. Did he love me, or was he using me for some scheme of his own? And yet I found myself in my studio, almost as soon as he had left, mixing my paints and obeying his command as if I was a slave girl and he my master.

My other painting was almost dry; soon I would glaze it and it would be finished. This time I did a painting of the stairs – in greys and blues, with just a narrow slant of yellow-orange light, falling from the landing down into the large ornate hall, to give the canvas some colour. A ghostly shadow sat on the stairs, one arm raised to the balustrade and a long thin sleeve revealing a slim delicate arm. The face was hidden by long sweeping hair, which was almost transparent against the darkness. It was good; even I knew it was good, perhaps the best thing I'd ever painted. I seemed to improve with every work I executed. Was I really such an accomplished artist, I wondered, or was something in the house urging me on?

My life was full of questions, the main one being did Tom love me. But I was also worried about my work – was it natural inspiration or some spiritual intervention? I didn't know the answers, and yet I finished the painting in two days: one for the initial composition, and the second day for making the small changes I thought necessary.

There weren't many: a little flare of light on the sweep of the hair; the pattern of colour in the carpet briefly revealed in a narrow patch of light; and one bare long finger highlighted as it touched the balustrade.

When I had completed the painting, exhausted, I went to the kitchen, where Mrs Ward had left me a cold pie and some beef sandwiches. I made a hot cup of tea, realising I'd eaten nothing all day. I was losing weight, and I was thin to start with. I could feel the clothes hanging off me, and so I decided to treat myself to a new frock when I went into Swansea. I rarely bought clothes so I had coupons to spare, and suddenly I was filled with the urge to dress up, have my hair done and put on some lipstick. What I must have looked like first thing yesterday morning I dreaded to think. And yet my heart lightened as I remembered the way Tom's mouth had parted my lips and how I'd wanted him to love me, to make love to me, however improper it might be, however wrong and forward, and me a single girl. Such behaviour could only have been excused in the war; then death had been an ever-present threat.

The next morning I was in my studio again when Mrs Ward came up to me with a tray of Camp coffee that smelled strong and delicious. 'Have you heard the gossip?' she asked, her eyes curious as she examined my face.

'No. I've been working hard for my next exhibition.' I made a gesture towards the painting.

She hardly glanced at it. 'More ghosts,' she said with raised eyebrows. 'Anyway, you know Tom, the American air force man?'

'Of course I know Tom.' I was impatient and a little worried. 'What gossip could there possibly be about him?'

'It seems he's run away to London and got involved with an heiress,' she said, watching my face carefully.

I managed to hide my shock. 'Good for him,' I said smoothly. 'I hope he'll be very happy.' I turned away and began to work like a fiend. I was outwardly composed, but inside I felt as if jagged glass was tearing up my heart.

—

In the next few weeks I found that work was my salvation from the bitterness, anger and jealousy that seemed to eat my soul. My paintings were executed with a frenzy of brush strokes and in strong colours, but always with a shadowy corner and an ethereal being, hardly there, behind a stone arch or similar. Outside the house and in, I painted scenes of the shadowed hallway, the landings, and even the blue room, and wished that Beatrice was there to talk to about my troubles.

Mrs Ward poked and pried, but I remained elusive and avoided her when I could; she seemed to feed off my misery. It seemed to me that she was blooming and I was fading away into nothingness like my ghosts.

—

The day of the exhibition dawned. In the early morning, a van arrived to take my canvases to London. Gone were the days when I was expected to transport them myself. Now I was treated like royalty, Mr Readings practically putting out the red carpet for me.

Red; that was the colour I would wear, I decided. Once the van had left, I took the train to London and sat in the first-class compartment like a lady born to riches and honours. No one would know I was grieving inside.

I'd heard nothing from Tom – not a word of explanation, not even a plain letter telling me of his whereabouts. I still felt his last kiss on my lips, and I pushed the thought away in case I began to cry.

At Swansea, Miss Grist got into the compartment and gave me a sunny smile as if nothing had ever been wrong between us. 'Lovely crisp day,' she said as she sat down, letting a flurry of cold air in from the corridor before she pushed the door shut and pulled her fur collar around her face. Her hat of soft felt with pretty bird feathers she pulled into place on her brow, and I realised she looked very smart; far from her usual frumpy self. 'I'm actually coming to see your exhibition,' she said, almost preening as she adjusted the hat. 'I thought it was time to see what all the fuss was about.'

'Might you steal my ideas for yourself?' I couldn't help the sarcasm. 'Just as you stole my list of guests. That didn't work, fortunately for me. It seems *your* ghost was a trick.'

'And yours isn't?' She took out a small mirror from her bag and reapplied her lipstick. It was a new lipstick – still very expensive and exclusive after the barrenness of the war years. I couldn't resist staring at it.

'Have you been left an inheritance, Miss Grist?'

'You could say that.' She didn't enlarge. 'Your ghosts?' Her eyebrows were arched. 'Do you really believe the old house is haunted then?'

'I couldn't say.' My tone was cold. 'All I know is there's no trickery involved. Strange things happen of their own accord at Aberglasney.'

'Oh, I know that, dear Miss Evans.' Her tone was almost offensive. 'I also know that your American disappeared and then got engaged to an heiress.' She smiled a thin smile. 'Of course, you didn't know *this*, do you? Tom Maybury is engaged to *me*, Miss Evans. I am the heiress in question.'

'You? Really?' I spoke as calmly as I could, though I was seething inside. I left her as soon as I got off the train, and I waved at Mr Readings as he came to greet me, walking along the platform at a smart pace. I could see his car outside the station; it was old, pre-war, but it gleamed with the loving care he'd lavished upon it.

'Riana, how lovely you look, but you are far too thin! We shall have to feed you up while you are in London.'

Suddenly, Miss Grist was at my side again. 'Well, I must say goodbye, dear Miss Evans,' she said, as though we'd been having an amicable conversation on the train. She smiled at Mr Readings, and from sheer politeness he bowed and took her hand.

'Charmed, dear lady. Charmed, I'm sure.'

As we stood there, a huge Rolls Royce drew up. Miss Grist waved her gloved hand and, with a sweet smile at the chauffeur, stepped inside the magnificent car.

'She must be a lady of good standing and landed gentry to boot. Where did you meet her, Riana?'

'She works part-time at the local library,' I said flatly.

His eyebrows shot up. 'She must be doing that as a hobby or something. By the look of her she's extremely wealthy and has very good taste. You should have invited her to the exhibition.'

'Don't worry, she informs me she's attending,' I said acidly. 'We must make sure she has the best champagne and we must sweet-talk her, though I warn you she's not the sort to buy my work.'

'Humph!' Mr Readings chose to ignore my ire. 'Talking about the exhibition, your work is as colourful and as excellent and individual as always – with just a touch of melancholy, if I might say so.'

'I'm glad you're pleased. I've worked really hard on the exhibition.' I hadn't actually. The work had come easily to me, the brush strokes quick and sure. When I stood at my easel in the studio and painted the house I loved it was as though it was wrapped around me, urging me on, inspiring me in a way I'd never felt before. 'And of course you are entitled to say so! You are exhibiting the paintings for me, after all.'

'And selling them, my dear Riana, and selling them. We shall have a triumphant day tomorrow, you'll see; the opening will be a great event.'

I wondered why I wasn't feeling excited. I used to love the exhibitions; being the centre of attraction still felt like a new experience for me. Of course, I was still trying to swallow the shock of being taunted by Miss Grist. Was Tom *really* interested in her because she had come into money? And why had Tom asked me to put on this exhibition in the first place?

I could feel my hands shaking. My nerves were strung taut; I felt I would snap into little pieces at any moment. Tom engaged to be married was pain enough, but Tom married to a grasping, duplicitous woman like Miss Grist was impossible to believe!

And then I calmed down. It wasn't true, of course it wasn't true, none of it was true. Tom was lying low as he'd planned, so he couldn't be planning to marry anyone. The way he'd kissed me and held me, the kindness he'd shown me, the love – yes, *love*... He was *my* man. Wasn't he?

I realised then Mr Readings was talking to me.

'You feeling all right, Riana?'

'I'm just tired. That's all, I suppose. Working day and night on the paintings and then the journey up to London... It's all been a bit wearing, to tell the truth.' My physical tiredness was nothing compared to my emotional exhaustion, but I had to make some excuse to Mr Readings. 'I'll be all right after a rest on a cosy bed, so please don't worry.'

'You'll be all right for the exhibition I'm sure, my dear Riana. Put on your best glad rags and rouge your pretty cheeks and you'll be just fine.'

–

That evening at the exhibition I did feel fine. My weariness vanished as I coaxed myself into believing that Miss Grist was somehow behind the story about Tom and her sudden wealth. What was she up to now? She'd cheated me once over my list of guests, so why should she be telling me the truth now about her engagement? Come to think about it, I hadn't seen a diamond ring on her finger – just some huge stones that could have been bought from any traveller's basket of cheap trinkets.

The exhibition was a great success, and in the end I began to enjoy myself – although mainly because Miss Grist didn't show up. I was fawned over and praised and received so many compliments and smiles that it was a wonder my head wasn't turned. But I knew something the eager buyers didn't: it was the influence of Aberglasney that helped me create such emotive paintings, with the feel of age and ghostliness and mystery. But still. Seeing the pictures framed and hanging on the wall of the well-lit opulent gallery I was impressed myself – and surprised at what I had achieved.

I sipped at the gin and tonic Mr Readings handed me and suppressed a grimace at the taste. Alcohol was a luxury I appreciated, but I would have preferred a nice hot cup of tea. As it was I slipped my rather utilitarian shoes off when no one was looking and stood in my stockinged feet, feeling the softness of the carpet under my toes with a sigh of pleasure.

'You look very lovely tonight, Riana.' Mr Readings suddenly stood beside me. 'I didn't realise how tiny you are, and all that luxuriant red hair! You should have your portrait painted, young lady. Why not do a self-portrait?'

'I couldn't,' I said quickly. 'I can paint other people, but not myself. I'm afraid I'd find too many faults.' *Or see through my own image*, I thought, *and see the flawed unsure being I really was.*

'All right, I'll get young Justin to paint you. A new talent, Riana. Not as original as you or as talented, but worth watching all the same. Come, I'll introduce you.'

Still shoeless, I trailed along reluctantly behind Mr Readings. I didn't want my portrait painted, and I was tired. All I wanted was to go to the privacy of my room in the guest house and go to sleep and dream of Tom.

Justin was pleasant and very handsome, in a film star sort of way. His hair was brilliantined to his head, and his features were in perfect proportion. He was dressed in a fine suit and a black bow tie, very proper for the occasion, but for me Tom's rugged good looks were far more attractive than this picture of male perfection standing before me. I held out my hand and murmured a greeting.

'Charmed to meet you, Miss Evans.' Justin bent towards me and kissed both my cheeks in what I thought was a very French way and somewhat affected for an English man. 'I do love your work,' he enthused, and although I knew as an artist himself he probably meant what he said, I made the appropriate modest replies, and after a few minutes of stilted conversation I tried to move away.

Mr Readings wasn't having it. 'Justin, I would like to make a suggestion. How would you like to paint Riana's portrait?'

Justin stood back a little and regarded me from head to toe in an embarrassingly detached way. 'Yes, I can see a field. Poppies, perhaps, to compliment that lovely red hair.' He rubbed his fingers through my hair until it was wild and curling on my shoulders. 'And a peasant dress,' he said.

'I'll leave the details with you, Justin.' Mr Readings spoke as if I wasn't there.

'Where on earth am I going to get a peasant dress?' I asked, a little piqued.

'Oh, a detail, my dear Riana. Ask that woman, that Mrs Ward, she seems able to pick up just about anything.' Mr Reading smiled. 'I would like to make it a commission. One painting to hang in my gallery permanently.'

'All right,' I said dubiously. 'I'll try, but I'm not promising anything.' Inwardly I groaned. It seemed I would have my portrait painted whether I liked it or not.

The door flew open just then. Some men came into the gallery, and one of them flashed a badge at Mr Readings.

'We have to ask you to come with us, miss,' he said to me. He spoke with such authority that I stepped back, stunned.

'Hang on. I want you to prove you are really policemen before I go anywhere,' I said, remembering the 'policemen' who had taken Tom away.

Mr Readings telephoned the station on my behalf, and then nodded at me. 'They confirmed that these are real policemen.'

'What have I done?' I asked as my arm was caught and I was hustled to the door.

Mr Readings tried to intervene but he was pushed away. 'I shall get you the best lawyer in town, Riana,' Mr Readings said. 'Don't worry! I'll have you free by the morning, and all this nonsense can be explained.'

The pavement was hard and cold beneath my feet; I hadn't had time to find my shoes. I was taken to a big black car and helped – or rather pushed – inside, and five minutes after we'd driven away from the bright lights of the gallery I sat stunned and silent in the back of the car, knowing in my heart that these were not real policemen and wondering if Tom had betrayed me.

Chapter Twenty-Four

I was taken to a small house, and although it was dark and I couldn't see much, I could smell the sea, feel the breeze and so I knew I was probably near the coast.

'Just keep quiet.' One of the so-called policemen grinned down at me, and I felt stupid in my evening dress and bare feet, and shivery in the coldness of the bare, utilitarian house.

'What's the charge?' I asked in reply. There was no response, but eventually one of the men asked if I wanted a cup of tea. I nodded helplessly. At least some hot tea would warm me and perhaps comfort me a little.

I was led into a small cell with a single bed and a rickety table as the only furniture. There was a high window – too high to see out of – but at least the sea wasn't coming in, so these men, whoever they were, did not intend to drown me.

The man came back a few minutes later with tea that had been kept in a flask. It tasted metallic, but it was hot and refreshing, and I sat on the bed and drank it gratefully.

He left me then, and I heard the key turning in the lock and guessed there was nothing I could do right now; it was dark and cold and I had no shoes. Better try to sleep and then find a way to escape tomorrow.

I finished my tea and clambered under the bedclothes. They felt a little damp – or maybe it was just the cold – but slowly I began to feel warm and drowsy, and as my eyelids began to droop I realised the lethargy I was feeling was due to some sleeping draught or drug dropped into my tea. I didn't care though. All I wanted to do was let blessed darkness claim me.

I woke to a sharp, chilly but sunny morning, and I had no hangover from the drugged tea. Instead I felt refreshed and calm and ready for some breakfast. Eventually, the policeman who had given me the tea, now in civvies, brought me some: a tray with tea and toast and scrambled eggs that looked as though they were meant to be poached eggs and had gone wrong. All the same, I ate the breakfast with enthusiasm, feeling inexplicably better than I'd done for some time.

It was, I supposed, the sense of having no responsibility for myself or my actions, and of having some time to be alone when I could refresh my mind and face my feelings. I had no sense of danger. If the men had meant to hurt me they would have done so by now... or so I hoped and reasoned. Was it some ransom plan? I decided it must be – otherwise what would anyone want with me?

Later in the morning, however, things took a sinister turn. My hands were tied behind my back and I was blindfolded; that meant I knew the person who wanted to question me. 'Why are you keeping me here?' I was led to a chair and sat down gingerly, afraid of falling. 'If it's money, I haven't got any.'

'It's for your own safety, ma'am, and *I'll* ask the questions.' The voice was American, deep Southern American with warm, deep overtones. Like Tom's, but not like Tom's. And I wondered again if Tom had set me up.

I waited silently, trying to absorb the sounds and smells around me. I could smell salt and fish and the wash of the waves, and I thought again that we were very near the sea. In the background I could hear feminine tones; obviously, there was a woman in the next room. Her voice was subdued, but again faintly familiar.

'I want information about Tom Maybury. Where is he?'

That surprised me. 'Last I heard he'd got engaged and was being lavished with gifts from his new, rich lady love.' I could hear a touch of bitterness and not a little anger in my voice.

'We all know that's a cover, so what's the truth?'

'I wish I knew,' I said on a sigh. 'How dare you!' My voice was clear and firm. 'I don't know anything about Tom Maybury, and I don't wish to. He was stationed at Aberglasney during the war and we became friends for a while, but then he went away. I have no idea where, and why should I?'

'We don't believe all that rubbish! We know he fell in love with you and the big house you live in.'

'You know more than I do then,' I said doggedly. 'I only wish that was true – the bit about him loving me I mean.' I was babbling now. 'He's engaged to some other woman, remember? Anyway, what's he done?'

I felt the brush of a skirt as someone knelt beside me. So there *was* a woman present!

'We might as well leave you here to die.' The words were whispered more to disguise the voice than anything else, I suspected. The whispering continued eerily in my ear: 'You will be trapped here to starve to death…'

—

After the whispering woman had finished talking, my captors had gagged me – and left me. For a while I made a keening noise, hoping to call Tom to me, until I realised it was impossible to talk coherently, so even if Tom *did* come to save me there was no way I could warn him of the danger. I tried to struggle, but the cords had become twisted and I was only making things worse, so I kept still and rested my head against the thick stone wall. Above me I could hear the beating of rain on the roof, and I had a sense of being here before – and, of course, I had been… in a way… with Tom. We'd been shut into that derelict church building to drown. But this time I was alone. No one would ever know where I was, and even if by some miracle Tom found out where I'd been taken, he would be caught and captured – perhaps even killed. I struggled again, but it was useless, and so I rested my head once more and tried to think.

I was beginning to despair – for I could hardly breathe with the tightness of the tape over my mouth – when my captors came back for me. I watched in amazement and relief as one of the men silently untied me, and then I was out of the building, gasping in the fresh salty air. I was thrust into a van and lay on the metal floor in the pitch dark, bouncing around for what seemed hours. Anything was better than starving to death alone, I told myself as my elbows hurt more and more and my head felt as if it had been constantly hit with a rock. I must have blacked out, because when I was let out of the van I fell to the ground on my own arched driveway, too numb to stand.

A light fell on me, and Mrs Ward came rushing out of the house. She wrapped a blanket around me and helped me indoors and through to the kitchen, where the welcome sound of the kettle boiling filled my heart with cheer.

'Some men came here, miss,' Mrs Ward said huskily. 'Searched the whole house, they did. Didn't ask permission – just went through, room by room.'

'What were they looking for?' My hands closed around the cup Mrs Ward put in front of me.

'Don't know, Miss Riana, and when I asked they pushed me into the kitchen and shut me in. I kept my mouth shut after that, didn't like the look of those villains at all. Rough men, they were, with glinting evil eyes.'

'Could you give the police a description of them, Mrs Ward?' I asked.

She shook her head, and her mouth twisted in a grimace of regret. 'They had scarves covering their faces, but they had foreign voices and glittering eyes – oh, and dark thick hair, I can tell the police that much.'

'Were they tall men? Fat? Thin? What colour clothes did they wear? What sort of voices did they have... were they Americans?'

'American- or Canadian-like, I'd say. Gruff and rough they were. Both big men – broad with big, calloused hands. You know, working men's hands.'

'That's very observant of you, Mrs Ward. Have you called the police?'

'Can't,' she said baldly. 'They cut the wires... and,' she added, 'I was too frightened.'

'All right.' I looked round, but everything in the kitchen was as neat and tidy as it had always been.

'They didn't mess things up, I'll say that for them. I did hear a bit of noise from the blue room, mind, as if they were moving furniture, that sort of thing.'

'Good thing Beatrice isn't there, though goodness knows where she is now.'

Mrs Ward shook her head. 'Who can say? Heaven or hell, one of the two.'

'What a funny thing to say, Mrs Ward.'

She frowned back, but before she could make any comment there was the sound of hammering on the front door. 'Oh my Lord, they've come back.' Mrs Ward looked as if she might dive under the table.

I stood up shakily.

'Police!' The voice rang out, and I tensed and put my hand to my lips, beckoning Mrs Ward to be quiet. I wasn't going to be caught like that again.

I crept across the dark hall and peered through the little window. There was a real police car outside and a plain-clothes officer and a uniformed constable standing on the drive.

'I want to see some identification please,' I shouted and obligingly the constable held up a card near the window. I knew anything could be a forgery, but I decided I might as well trust them. Reluctantly, I opened the door, expecting any minute to be thrown back against the wall. But the men walked calmly into the house and stood politely as I examined the card more thoroughly.

'We're from Carmarthen Police Station, miss,' the constable explained. 'We had a call stating there was some sort of disturbance at Aberglasney House.'

'Well—' I was a bit on edge '—come in, but the "disturbance" is well and truly over. You're too late to apprehend the perpetrators.' I was speaking like a policeman's notebook, but I was still in shock – my clothes still wet from the rain and my skirt sticking to my legs. 'In any case, who reported the matter?'

'Didn't leave a name, miss. They usually don't. But it was a woman; someone with a sore throat, by the sound of it,' he added helpfully.

'We'll search the house, miss.' The detective spoke at last. 'And I suggest you change your clothes before you catch your death.'

I could see he was longing to ask what had happened to me, but didn't quite dare to in case I reported something unpleasant that he didn't wish to deal with right now. He glanced at his watch, confirming my suspicions that he was reluctant to do this job. Had he heard about the ghosts? I wondered.

'Please carry out your search,' I said. 'The criminals have been through the whole house, though they didn't do any damage. Please look carefully for clues. A few more people searching my house won't do any harm.'

'I hear you have parties here, miss?' The constable's face was eager – almost as though he'd heard there were orgies taking place under the elegant roof of my house.

'Not parties,' I said, 'but ghost-haunting evenings, when witches fly and men turn to wolves in the full moon.' I was teasing him, but his eyes widened. 'I have visitors come to see if they can take a picture of the ghosts, the five maids who died here some years ago,' I explained. 'I'm sure you've heard the stories, officer?'

After a swift look at his superior officer, he didn't comment, but his eyes were large.

At last the men began their search of the rooms; of course, they didn't find anything, but in the meantime I was able to change into dry clothing.

We met again, after a remarkably short time, in the hall. 'Nothing out of the ordinary, miss.' The constable was usually the one to speak, as though his superior thought the whole thing beneath him. The constable's next words confirmed the doubts of both men. 'Sure this isn't all a publicity trick, miss, just to get your name in the papers and these parties some free advertising?'

'I'm sure,' I said. 'I was dragged away from a big opening night and I—' I stopped talking, realising it sounded exactly like a publicity stunt. 'Mr Reading phoned the police station, and someone there confirmed the men who took me away were real police officers.'

'Easy enough to fake,' one of the men said dryly. 'Well, as you don't seem to be in imminent danger, we'll have to leave, but be sure to lock up tonight just in case.'

'Aren't you going to guard the house or anything?'

The well-dressed plain-clothes officer took charge at last. 'This is really not our case, Miss Evans. You were taken from a *London* gallery. We've only come out as a courtesy to our London colleagues, you know.'

'So if I'm murdered in my bed, or abducted again from Aberglasney, it won't be your case then?'

'Goodnight, miss. Call us if you see anything suspicious.' They left abruptly and drove away in a cloud of black smoke.

I closed the door and bolted it and hurried into the kitchen.

'They were about as useful as a cow with a musket!' Mrs Ward said in resignation. 'Sit down, love, and I'll make you a bite to eat.'

'Just some toast and more hot tea, Mrs Ward, please.' I sank down into a chair and put my head in my hands. 'Thank goodness you were here! At least I wasn't alone when those officers came; they thought I made it all up as it was.'

'Aye,' Mrs Ward said dryly.

'What on earth is going on here? What does someone think I know about Tom? I only knew him for a few months. I know we were "fond" of each other... Well, I thought he was "fond" of me, anyway, and now he's vanished and it seems he's suspected of all sorts: espionage, perhaps, I just don't know.'

'Forget it now, Riana. Keep all the windows closed and your door locked and I'll double check everything is secured down here.'

I ate the hot buttered toast with relish and then took Mrs Ward's advice and slowly made my way upstairs to my bedroom. I wished Beatrice was here; she and Mrs Ward were the only friends I had now. Could I even trust Mr Readings and his lady friend? I just didn't know any more.

I climbed into my cosy bed, heavy with the blankets, and rubbed my sore head against the softness of the pillows, grateful to be warm and comfortable. My summer days with Tom seemed far away now; the hours we shared in the sun and in the shade of the cloisters when it was too hot seemed a distant dream. And at last I slept.

Chapter Twenty-Five

A sort of normality had returned to my life when we had the next ghost-haunting weekend. Beatrice had returned home with her little bag of belongings and, as usual, gave me no inkling of where she had been — but it was clear she loved the house to be full of people, of laughter, and of the cheeriness that came from wine-drinking and the scent of food cooking.

I always took her a small meal on a tray because she refused to join the crowd for dinner. 'Look, dear,' she told me this time, 'the good people who come to these things think I'm a ghost, so don't let's spoil the illusion.' She gave me a sweet smile. 'It's the way I dress. I know I'm eccentric, dear, but that way I'm comfortable.'

I left her then and joined the guests, thinking she had a point. I didn't mind her presence and her constant comings and goings. When she was at Aberglasney, the house, absurd as it might seem, was happy and restful.

My guests were in high spirits, full of the news of my abduction. The actress in me came to the fore, and I told the story of being chained in a strange building, with thugs telling me I would starve and die there, in a dramatic manner that had them all riveted.

Mr Bleesdale was the first to speak. 'Poor Riana, what on earth did those people want from you?'

'They think I know something I shouldn't about the Americans,' I explained. 'Because Tom and I were friends, I was mistaken for some sort of spy. Of course, I don't know much about any of the Americans, except what everyone knows – that they were billeted here during the war.'

'Oh, there was some talk a while back about a new aeroplane engine the Americans were testing. Perhaps it was something to do with the plans,' the colonel said importantly. 'Remember that poor pilot who was killed in a flying accident – Jenkins, was it? Well, he was involved in all this testing business, I heard. That's why his death was kept rather quiet.'

All this was new to me – and a light went off in my head. Tom had never said a word about testing a new type of engine – though why should he have? But perhaps that was why I had been abducted: so my house could be searched for some sort of designs. It didn't explain why Tom had asked me to hold the exhibition in the first place though... But I remembered once more that Mrs Ward had told me that the men who'd searched the house had had American accents. Perhaps Tom had learned that the house was to be searched and had wished me out of the way for my own safety. It was just bad luck that I had been targeted by the very men who were after Tom himself!

Another thought struck me, and after dinner was over and the ghost haunting was given up for a good night's sleep I went to see Beatrice. She was sitting on the bed reading, as if she'd been waiting for me. 'You want to know what Edwin did for a living,' she said at once.

'Have you been listening on the stairs?' I asked with wry amusement.

Her smile was sweet. 'No, dear, I'm clairvoyant. Didn't you know?' She nodded. 'He was an engineer and an inventor. He designed a new engine of some sort for an aeroplane, and the Americans – who always had too much money – took it up. The money never came, of course, once my dear husband was accused of murder, though I don't believe he had given the final designs to the Americans before he died.'

I went to sit on the bed, but Beatrice waved me to a chair. 'My old bones are too brittle, dear. Please don't put your weight on the bed.'

'Where are his plans now?'

'If you knew that, dear, you'd be in more trouble than you are now. If you'd known you'd have told those horrible men and they'd have taken the plans from you and Edwin's innocence would never be proven *and* you'd never have got the money from the Americans.'

'But that's your money, Beatrice! If you'd that you wouldn't have needed to sell the house. Anyway, how do you always seem to know everything that goes on?'

'You'll find out all about me, Edwin and the house one day, Riana, I'm counting on it, and then the money will be yours. You own Aberglasney now, and I want you to bring it back to its former glory.'

'I'm doing my best.' I was a little piqued.

'I know that, dear, and I do my best to help by showing myself on the ghost nights, just now and then, to encourage the story that the house is haunted.'

'Don't you think it is then?'

'Of course I do. Don't be silly, dear. Clearly, the house is haunted. It wouldn't be honest to say so otherwise, would it?' Did she wink or was I imagining it?

'Go to bed, Riana,' she said brusquely. 'You seem very tired all of a sudden.'

'I am,' I said. 'It seems to have been a long day.'

If the ghosts came out that night, I never heard them. I slept deeply and dreamlessly and woke in the morning, ready to tackle breakfast with my guests.

'You missed a spectacle, dear Riana.' The colonel greeted me with old-fashioned courtesy, rising from his chair and bowing slightly before tucking into his bacon and eggs once more.

'What do you mean?' I poured some coffee from the pot on the sideboard. Mornings, we'd agreed, were 'help yourself' times, when Mrs Ward brought in platters of food and pots of coffee and left the people who deigned to rise early to fill their own plates. I usually was up from bed in time to help her, but this morning I'd slept late.

'The ladies appeared, dear. The five maids.' The colonel's eyes were quite serious, and I realised he wasn't joking. 'They came along the corridor, drifting like clouds of mist, and then they just disappeared when the young lad William came along to go to his bed.'

'Did he see them too?' I asked innocently, suppressing an inane desire to laugh. Not surprisingly, Colonel Fred shook his head.

'Unfortunately not. He was too busy trying to load his camera with film. He did see the wreath of mist disappearing into the blue room though.'

'You were very lucky then, colonel. Not many are privileged to see the maids.' I guessed he'd had too many brandies after dinner and the 'mist' had probably been the smoke from his pipe.

'They do say there's going to be a disaster when the maids appear.' Mrs Ward had come into the dining room with fresh coffee and was standing there, her eyes large. *Good old Mrs Ward*, I thought. *Anything to drum up business for the weekends.* I smiled approvingly at her.

'It's true, Riana,' she said in all seriousness. 'They only appear when something bad is going to happen.'

'I've had my guests taken away from me, and I've been kidnapped – I didn't see the maids any time then,' I protested, forgetting the presence of guests. I could have added that my beloved Tom had become engaged to a dreadful, scheming woman too, but that would be giving too much away about my own feelings.

I sat down abruptly and drank my coffee, trying to see beyond Mrs Ward's serious expression.

'You'll see, Riana,' she said soberly.

I ate some toast, nearly choking with every mouthful. Not even the marmalade helped. I drank more coffee, just to keep the guests company.

–

The 'something dreadful' happened very soon; dear Mr Readings was found dead in his gallery.

I travelled up to London for his funeral and stood at the graveside with Diane, who was dry eyed and despairing as she stood and watched his remains being put into the cold earth.

I touched her arm. 'How are you?' A stupid question; I knew it as soon as the words left my mouth.

She stared down at her sensible shoes. 'I'm desolate, dear.' She even used Mr Readings' phrases. 'We were married quietly last week. I've only been his wife for a few days.' Tears blurred her eyes. 'For so long I've wanted him to make an honest woman of me, and now he has died and left me a widow. How can I bear it?'

'I'm sorry, Diane. Are you all right for money? I know Mr Readings will have left you well provided for, but if you need help right now please just tell me.'

'I have my guest house, Riana. It doesn't bring in a fortune, but I'll be far from destitute, and as you say my dear man will have left me well provided for. But what about you? What about your work? Who will market your paintings for you now?'

'I don't know. Don't you worry about that, Diane. I'll manage.'

After the service – during which I shed some tears for the honest, encouraging Mr Readings – we went back to Diane's guest house for a small glass of sherry and some very dry cake her cook had made. The loss of Mr Readings' influence and money was already making a difference. The black market served those who had money to spend very well indeed. Now that Midas touch was lacking, and it showed.

That night I slept at the guest house and drank some more sherry with Diane as she reminisced about the good times she and Mr Readings had shared. It helped her to talk, I could see, and in spite of my tiredness I was happy to listen.

The next morning I travelled home from London, cursing the train that stopped at every small station on the way back to Wales.

As I stepped out of the train, a tall, big shouldered figure came out of the shadows of the station platform. As he came nearer I realised it was Tom. I gasped as he came forward and took my overnight bag and kissed me on the cheek as if I was his maiden aunt.

I pulled away sharply. 'None of that! You are spoken for now, or have you forgotten?'

Tom tapped his nose. 'Don't believe all you hear and only half of what you see,' he said cryptically.

I shook my head and let him lead me to his car, a beaten-up old Ford that I'd never seen before. 'What's happened to all this money you're supposed to have had? Has your new girlfriend spent it? I understood she's some kind of heiress. Or have you come into some sort of plans? Drawings of engines, that sort of thing?'

He just chuckled, but didn't answer.

'What's going on, Tom?' I demanded. 'I think you owe me some sort of explanation.'

He didn't reply, but drove in silence all the way to Aberglasney. I felt a bit intimidated by his closed-in look and didn't ask any more questions.

Once outside my home he stopped the car, took me in his arms and kissed me deeply and thoroughly. I should have slapped his face, but instead I melted into his arms, breathing in the scent of him, the feel of his arms around me, his mouth against mine possessing me. We belonged together. It was unspoken, but known to both of us. What was he doing planning to marry another woman?

'Whatever happens, remember I love you,' he said, and then he opened the door, practically pushed me out of the car, and ground into gears and shot away in a cloud of dust.

Mrs Ward was waiting for me in the doorway. 'Was that Tom?' She was craning her neck to watch the disappearing car.

I didn't answer, wanting to clutch his words and his kiss close to me – something of mine, something precious that I didn't want to share.

'Kettle on, Mrs Ward?' I shrugged off my coat in the hall and let it dangle over the hallstand like a lifeless body. I shivered.

'You're cold, Riana,' Mrs Ward said. 'Come into the kitchen. It's warm there, and I'll make you a nice cup of tea and a sandwich. I have some cold beef and pickle in the larder, will that do?'

I nodded, not wanting to eat anything, but feeling a sandwich might give me some warmth and energy.

'Was the funeral very dreadful?' Mrs Ward asked. 'They usually are.'

'Very dreadful,' I replied. 'In more ways than one. I've lost a dear friend and a patron of the gallery where most of my work was sold.'

'Well, Riana, we'll just have to have more weekends,' Mrs Ward said practically.

'The profit from the weekends will help keep the place going,' I agreed, 'but I needed the money from my work to pay for the improvements to the house.'

'We'll manage.' Mrs Ward looked at me thoughtfully. 'What about taking me in as a lodger?'

'What?' It was something I'd never thought about.

'I only rent Mill Cottage,' she said, 'and you could take rent out of my wages. That would help a bit, wouldn't it?'

'That's very kind of you, Mrs Ward,' I said thoughtfully. Did I really want a live-in lodger? But then my house was open to whoever chose to come to the weekends, and Mrs Ward was with me most of the time anyway – sometimes until late at night.

'I do hate the walk home when it's dark,' she said. It was as if she read my thoughts. 'I wouldn't need much room, mind, just a small place to sleep. After all, I spend most of my time in the kitchen here as it is.'

'Yes, that sounds like a good idea,' I said at last, 'but I don't like the idea of taking money from you for rent.'

'Bless you, I'll be having bed and board, and all I need is a few shilling for a pack of Woodbines every week. In any case,' she said, smiling, 'my lease comes up for renewal soon, and my grumpy old landlord is bound to put the rent up if I sign again.'

'I see. Well, all in all, it sounds as if it will work.' I thought of Mrs Ward being in the house all the time; it would have its detractions, but it would have benefits too – like company when I listened to the radio or had a cup of tea. It wasn't as if I had a husband or a boyfriend or anything close to it; not with Tom playing silly games with me.

I held out my hand and took Mrs Ward's red scrubbed fingers, and yet a strange doubt lingered. Was I doing the right thing?

Chapter Twenty-Six

Mrs Ward was right about making more money from the house, and fortunately the next ghost-haunting weekend, which would take place in February, was oversubscribed. I had to make a waiting list of people and arrange another weekend quickly.

All the old crowd had priority for this weekend: Colonel Fred, young William, plump Betty, and all the other 'oldies' like Doctor Bravage and Mr Bleesdale. I was able only to allow a few new guests in for the weekend.

Colonel Fred's accident at the Christmas ghost-haunting weekend had hit the newspapers some time ago and caused quite a stir: it seems the public believed he had been attacked by vengeful ghosts; a story he had no doubt fostered. Also, the 'sightings' of the five dead serving maids from the last weekend had made a big story in the newspapers, and now were linked with poor Mr Readings' death. One headline had read: 'CURSED BY THE GHOSTS OF ABERGLASNEY.'

I feared even more for my paintings. No one would want them if they believed the whole enterprise – even buying paintings of mine – was 'cursed'.

The maids, as if on cue, appeared again that night, to the delight and terror of my guests. I even saw shadowy ghostly figures flitting along the landing myself, but I put it down to the flickering lights and the large amounts of sherry I'd consumed. The shadowy figures drifted across the landing wearing sweet cotton nightgowns, but faded to nothing as they reached the stairs. I blinked and put the 'vision' down to imagination. I didn't want to believe that anything bad would happen after seeing the maids, as it had the last time they had been seen.

Young William took photographs on his Brownie camera, clicking away as if he was going to make a fortune for his pictures from the newspapers – and maybe he would.

Beatrice also put in an appearance: peering out of her room with a frown, as if her sleep had been disturbed, and wearing a 'Queen Victoria' kind of sleep bonnet, and then disappearing abruptly with no sound of footsteps, almost as if she was floating on air. I don't know how she managed it, but she was very convincing.

I went into the kitchen and drank some thick coffee, trying to still my reeling brain. Mrs Ward was sitting with her feet up in the rocking chair and didn't sit to attention as she usually did when I came into the room. But now she was a lodger, and lived in, she had every right to make herself comfortable. 'The visitors seeing things again, are they?' she said dryly.

'So am I!' I sank into the old armchair in the corner of the kitchen. 'I don't know what I saw, but it certainly looked like ghosts trailing across the landing and turning into thin air.'

'Trick of the light, I expect.' Mrs Ward took my now empty cup. 'I'll make some more coffee. You've had rather too much alcohol,' she said sagely.

I sighed heavily. 'I expect you're right – or else it was mass hysteria gripping us all.'

'Whatever, it will be good for business.' Mrs Ward was, as ever, practical. She handed me the fresh coffee and sat down again, this time resting her slippers on the thick rug that covered the slate floor. A good fire burned in the grate, and even as I looked at the flames Mrs Ward added more coal. I was only glad she had no more dire warnings about bad things happening when the maids appeared.

The heat made me sleepy, and I let the haziness overtake me. I wanted to paint the maids while they were fresh in my mind or my imagination – whatever it was – but I was far too tired.

Later, I felt arms lift me, and I was being carried upstairs to my bedroom. I could smell Tom. Not the reeking smell of the water and the island, but a fresh-washed tobacco smell, and I put my arms around his neck and clung to him. If it was a dream, I meant to enjoy it.

He kissed me and held me tenderly, and I wanted more from him than kisses and hugs.

'I am not the engaged man everyone thinks I am. You must trust me on that, Riana,' he whispered, his breath sweet against my face.

I felt so young, so in love, and reason flew out through the window. I pressed against him and felt the hardness of his masculine body against my softness. I yielded to him willingly, and that night was the most thrilling, fulfilling night of my life. I felt happy, loved and desirable. That night I had become a woman – and in the morning I was lying in an empty bed.

Chapter Twenty-Seven

I painted furiously the next day. A glow of shame was filling me, but my head was clear as an icicle. I knew Tom had made love to me, but did he love me or was he taking advantage of my feelings for him? I was in a pain of rejection, of being a fool... and yet there was a certain kind of joy too. I had felt the thrill of possession, of arousing passion, in Tom and in myself. I had wanted him as much as he wanted me, and that night, that experience, would be mine for ever.

Later I had a phone call from the gallery. Diane had taken control of the business! Dear Mr Readings had left it all to her: the gallery, the paintings, the goodwill... Everything.

'May I come down to see you, dear Riana?' Diane's voice was still cool with grief, but she told me she wanted to display some of my work at her grand reopening exhibition. 'We'll make it together, Riana,' she said, and I'm sure I heard a catch in her voice. 'My dear man would have wanted us to go on, don't you think?'

'I really do, Diane. Please come and stay as soon as possible. I'll meet you at the station, and Mrs Ward and I will make you very welcome and comfortable, I promise.' I hesitated, running the phone cord through my fingers.

'Just so long as ghosts don't disturb you,' I added, only half joking.

'There's only one ghost that would be important to me, Riana, and that's of my dear Mr Readings himself. If I could see him again just once to tell him how much I care, I could be happy.'

'Come *soon*, Diane.' I didn't know what else to say.

'What about tomorrow?'

'Tomorrow will be wonderful!' I was enthusiastic. I could do with some company, and Diane would be an excellent confidante. I felt I could tell her about Tom and my love for him, and I would see if she could understand the strange way he was behaving. She was an older woman and must be wiser than I was in affairs of the heart.

That night I stayed up late painting, inspired by Diane's news about the gallery. Once again I had a home for my work, a showcase where art lovers could see what I'd done and hopefully appreciate the paintings and buy them.

Diane would explain how long I had to paint the pictures when she arrived; so far I'd only painted the one picture, and even that wasn't finished. At last the lack of light defeated me though, and I cleaned up my pallet and wiped the rims of the tubes of colour and put them aside for the morning.

I stood back and looked at the painting I'd created of the young serving maids, hair flowing over white-gowned slender shoulders, tapering away to a ghostly mist of grey and blue thinned down with white spirit. I sighed; it had worked. The light shone from the candelabra on the landing, the door to the blue room was open, and there was a glimpse of a bed with a distant figure sitting on the quilted cover.

Again I'd painted Beatrice into the picture, all dressed up in her Victorian nightwear – out of time and sequence with the maids, who had died in the nineteen twenties and would have thought themselves modern young women. I'd seen pictures of well-off, elegant women wearing bobbed hair and fox furs, but young women servants wouldn't have been allowed such luxuries, even if they could afford them.

I went to my bedroom and looked at my reflection in the long mirror. My frock had a narrow skirt and a sweetheart neckline. There was nothing elegant about me. My hair was rolled back, and I could have easily passed for a wartime housewife. I untied my hair and it fell wild and loose, hanging down to my waist in vibrant red curls. Now I looked more like an artist. I flung a red scarf around my waist and tied it in a knot, and against the dull grey of my frock it looked good, almost gypsy-like, as if I was going to dance the rest of the night away around a blazing open-air fire with gold earrings sparkling in the dim light.

I sighed and almost hugged myself. What would Tom think if he could see me now, looking wanton and free, with bare feet and ready to dance? But he had seen me more wanton than this, he had taken me in the very bed I was standing near, and I felt my cheeks grow hot at the memory. I felt thrilled too. He had made me his woman, and whatever happened now he would always be the love of my life, the only love I would ever want.

Diane's visit came and went; we hardly had time to talk about my life. Diane was busy planning the way she would run the gallery, the exhibitions she would hold. 'Of course, Riana, you will be my first and principle artist always,' she promised.

Inspired by her words, for the next few weeks I worked unceasingly on my paintings, barely eating or sleeping, but creating pictures that – in spite of my frenzy – turned out well. They were colourful and atmospheric. It was almost as if I'd entered a new phase in my life… and in a way I had.

I saw nothing of Tom in those weeks, but I always felt warm when I thought of him taking me in his arms and making love to me. I was his woman now, whatever he chose to do, and when I saw him again I would tell him so in no uncertain terms.

Love surged through me at the thought of him in his flying jacket and boots. Even soaked and dripping with seaweed, his hair plastered over his face. He was always handsome, and that lovable smile that seemed especially for me was always there, crinkling up his eyes and showing the tantalising curve of his mouth. How I loved Tom and wanted to make love with him again!

Mrs Ward remonstrated with me one day on a rare visit to the kitchen. 'You should eat more, Riana. I don't know how you keep going. You peck at your food like a bird.'

'Once the exhibition is done I'll relax,' I said. 'I've painted enough pictures now, and I have just one to finish. I'll eat my fill then, don't worry.'

'You have remembered we've got a ghost weekend next week, haven't you?'

I hadn't, but I put on a brave face. 'Don't worry. I'll be ready to ease up by then.'

'What about this exhibition of yours? Won't you be going up to London for the opening about then?'

I made a quick mental calculation. 'No, it's the week after; I've got everything organised.' I breathed a sigh of relief; it was pure luck that the two events were a week apart.

–

The ghost-haunting nights were becoming very well attended now, and a bigger crowd than usual had booked for the next event, giving Mrs Ward and Treasure and me more beds to make up. I had to double up rooms now, as well as the dormitories, with two beds in each. Soon I would be able to furnish other bedrooms – and maybe some more of the unused downstairs rooms – to accommodate more people. Now that I had an outlet for my paintings again, anything was possible. But even with the extra rooms, there still wasn't enough space to fit all the people who wanted to attend the next event – so, thinking of the profit, I decided to arrange an extra ghost-haunting weekend for the week after the exhibition.

I had worked day and night and completed six paintings. The grand reopening exhibition at the gallery would contain a small but select variety of paintings, and if all of mine sold then I'd have some income to spend on the house.

The ghost weekends were bringing in a healthy regular profit, and even though sometimes no supernatural events took place – no sightings, no noises in the night – the reputation Aberglasney had gained for being haunted was well established by now. However, even though no one expected ghosts to appear to order when there were guests staying, so far the 'ghosts' had been extremely cooperative. Even I was beginning to believe there were certain presences in the house that couldn't be explained.

Beatrice believed in the uneasy spirits of the dead serving maids and always did her bit as a 'Victorian ghost' to make some excitement happen on quiet nights. I lived in fear she would be caught – grabbed by the colonel or one of the younger guests, who could move more quickly – but she never was.

Tonight was a cold winter night, with frost designing patterns on the glass in the windows. I knew that next time I painted a picture I would have windows filled with traceries of frost in the background. I did a little pencil sketch that attempted to catch the mood, but frost on glass was going to be difficult to recreate in paint, a challenge. My heart lifted. It was just as Tom was a challenge; all I didn't know about him was a challenge I would love to solve.

This weekend 'young William' had brought a new young lady to hunt ghosts with him, much to the disappointment of some of the other ladies who'd hoped to bag him for themselves – especially 'plump Betty', who fancied herself irresistible to men.

Miss Connie Spears, as we were introduced to young William's girlfriend, was tiny and dark-haired and very slender. She looked as if a puff of wind, let alone a gaggle of ghosts, would blow her over, but she had an incredibly strong voice which she demonstrated after dinner by singing a medley of songs to us.

I wondered how the 'ghosts' were appreciating it and smiled as I thought of Beatrice covering her ears in the bedroom. I'd asked her to join us, but she'd said, 'No—' very firmly '—I couldn't spoil the image the guests have of me as a ghost,' which made sense, I supposed.

I felt guilty though at leaving her out, and asked Mrs Ward to take some supper on a tray to the blue room.

She shook her head so much that her greying curls came loose from the pins and fell against her face, making her seem much younger. 'You won't catch me going in there,' she announced, folding her arms firmly across her breasts.

'I thought you didn't believe in ghosts!' I was amused, but she obviously wasn't.

'I don't care about ghosts, but have you seen the state of the ceiling in there?'

'What on earth do you mean?'

'Well, you can see the daylight through the hole in the tiles. It must be terrible there when it's cold and raining. You couldn't expect anyone to live there, not even a ghost.'

'But you've seen Beatrice go to and fro on the stair, surely? She seems to like it in there. She's cosy and warm, and she always has the little electric fire to heat the room. I saw to that myself.'

'More fool you. Of course I've seen *Beatrice*, but she's nutty as a fruit cake, though I'll admit she makes herself useful in those strange clothes of hers, but if you think there are ghosts in the attic then that painting stuff is softening your brain!'

'Don't worry then. I'll take the tray up myself.' I was irritated, but it didn't do to upset such a valuable asset as Mrs Ward.

I caught Beatrice doing some needlework; her fingers were deft, slender and skilled as she stitched away at the embroidery. I glanced up at the ceiling, and I couldn't see any holes there at all. Mrs Ward must have had too many glasses of wine – or else she was making excuses not to climb the stairs. Perhaps she was tired or getting arthritic; it was a good thing I'd brought Treasure in when I did.

'Party going with a swing, if I'm hearing correctly,' Beatrice said dryly. 'Nice enough voice, but we could do with lowering the volume a bit. Who on earth is singing?'

'Young William's new lady friend. You wouldn't think it, but she's tiny and dainty and frail! I don't know where that big voice has room to hide. Anyway, she's adding to the spirit of the weekend. She's at least thirty – much older than William – but he clearly adores her.'

Beatrice raised her eyebrows. 'Likes older women then? Perhaps even I have a chance!' She giggled, and I giggled with her, but I was wise enough not to get too close to her. Beatrice didn't like anyone close to her.

The singing began again, some jazzy tunes from the wartime, and I could hear that Miss Spears was not going to let up.

'Do me a favour, Beatrice,' I suggested. 'Do your bit along the corridor, cause a diversion from Miss Spears' good intentions.'

Beatrice nodded and put down her sewing, waving her hand impatiently at me. 'Depart then, go.'

I thought of kissing her cheek, and then thought better of it and ran down the stairs. I burst into the dining room, just in time to see Colonel Fred cover his ears. 'Ghosts,' I announced dramatically, 'on the landing. Come quickly, all of you.'

The guests flooded into the hall, and Beatrice was doing her bit – her head raised, her hand pointing at the window. She looked so convincing that I almost believed she *was* a ghost.

Miss Spears, predictably, fainted away, her fall cushioned by the carpet. William knelt at her side to hold a bottle of smelling salts under her nose. Apparently, she was given to fainting spells. Meanwhile the 'ghost' discreetly vanished.

'Look at the window!' the colonel suddenly shouted.

We all stared upward and there, silhouetted in the window, was a face, a ghostly white face. The face of a bearded man! It seemed to hover there for a moment and then disappeared. Even I was shaken, as William's girlfriend fell into a decline again.

'It's the first time we've seen the ghost of a man.' Plump Betty pulled at her corsets, a beam of sheer excitement on her face. 'Ooh, Mr Bravage, might I stand next to you? I am just a little frightened.' She did indeed seem to be trembling.

'Brandies all round,' Colonel Fred declared. 'I've brought a whole case full with me,' he added as an afterthought.

Rather subdued now, we sat in the large drawing room, quietly discussing the new phenomena. Until now the story of ghosts, of young maids, of the appearances of Beatrice, and of the noises in the night had all seemed a game. I'd been able to explain everything away to myself... but not this. The disembodied face of the old man, hovering in an upper window, was really spooky and frightening.

I wandered into the kitchen looking for some aspirin and heard a slight sound behind me. Frightened I'd see a disembodied face staring at me, I was relieved to see a flesh-and-blood man standing there. 'Tom! You're here again.' I hurried towards him. 'What are you doing trying to frighten me like that? What tricks are you playing on us and why? Do you want to ruin my weekends?'

'I don't know what you're talking about, honey.' He sounded genuinely puzzled. 'I've only just driven up in my old army car, so what am I supposed to have done?'

'I don't know what's happening here!' I ran back into the drawing room, where everyone was talking together. Colonel Fred raised his voice as he held forth, and then young William rushed outside to examine the old building for signs of trickery, such as ladders. When he returned to the drawing room, his cheeks red with cold and a sprinkling of snow on his hair, he sank into a chair gasping with fright and lack of breath.

'No sign of intruders. This is no trick, Riana. What we all saw was the ghost of a man, a desperate spirit trying to tell us something!'

'Could it be Edwin Mansel-Atherton, the man accused of the murder of the young maids?' Colonel Fred had, evidently, been reading up on the history of Aberglasney. I shivered, suddenly cold.

I went back to the kitchen where Tom was sitting, leaving my guests to discuss the arrival of a new ghost between themselves.

'What are you doing here?' My tone was sharp. 'The lights of your car must have thrown up images on the window.'

'Don't be silly, Riana. My lights are still hooded. It's an old official car, remember? The lights were kept dim for the blackout, so I don't see how I could have thrown up lights on any window.'

I was embarrassed about accusing him of something he clearly hadn't done... and more so about our last meeting when I had fallen into Tom's arms so readily, like a desperate wanton. And yet, even as I tried to be indignant and angry, I wanted to press myself against him and feel his mouth on mine. 'Well, you surprised me, that's all.'

He smiled his crooked charming smile. 'You're getting in the habit of saying that every time we meet,' he commented.

'And we meet so often, don't we, Tom?' I knew I was being sarcastic. 'Not bad for an engaged man with responsibilities, I suppose. Taking your new lady love back to America soon, are you?'

'You are being foolish again,' Tom said. 'Miss Grist is really Mrs Grist. She has a husband who is alive and well and living in the highlands of Scotland. Our "engagement" is a ruse. I can't explain things now.'

'You never can explain! Tom, you say you love me, you *make* love to me, and then you vanish again. Talk to me, please! Just tell me the truth about what's going on.'

He took a deep breath, about to speak, but we were rudely interrupted by a thundering at the door. Tom caught me swiftly in his arms and kissed me. 'Remember, whatever happens, I love you.'

He'd gone then, disappeared like a shadow, leaving me with more questions than answers. All right, he'd gone through a sham engagement with Miss Grist, but why?

When I returned to the drawing room, my guests were standing against the wall, hands in the air, and two men were pointing savage-looking firearms at them!

'What's going on here?' I demanded.

A gun swivelled in my direction and I flinched, taking a step backwards. The men were dressed as soldiers, armed and threatening, but after my previous encounters with bogus police I looked at them doubtfully.

'On the floor!' one of them snapped.

I straightened my back. 'No!' I stated firmly. 'I want to see some identification – if you are genuine soldiers you should have some.'

The man pointing a gun at me appeared agitated and waved his gun about wildly.

I pushed his arm aside and pulled off his mask, and he stared at me in disbelief. 'What are you looking for? Tell me and I might be able to help,' I said calmly.

My guests began to sit down, still wary, their hands clearly visible on the table.

'We have been informed there's an American deserter at large.' One of the soldiers came forward taking charge. 'Has anyone been here in the last half hour?'

'Only the ghost of an old man,' Colonel Fred declared in a roar. 'Proof of identity, if you please, sir.' He bravely approached the man we recognised as leader, and a card was duly produced. The colonel took it, grunting like an old boar. I chuckled, amused by my own unspoken pun, and I was given a frozen look by the man whose mask I'd ripped off.

'Careful, lady,' he said, and then the penny dropped. These men were Americans sure enough, and I could see the flash of dog tags on one soldier's shirt. Tom was an airman… though not a soldier, like these men. Something must have shown in my face, because I was pushed into a chair. 'Tell us what you know, ma'am, otherwise things might get a bit nasty here.'

'I don't know anything! I don't even know which man you are talking about, and why should I? I'm getting sick of being attacked in my own house!'

My face was slapped hard, and then all hell broke out as Beatrice came out on to the landing, joined by the misty figures of 'the girls', as I had come to call them.

'The ghosts!' young William shouted, while his girl-friend hid under the table as shots rang out, aimed towards the landing. They made no noticeable difference to the mist, however.

To my relief, now there was no sign of Beatrice. She must have taken cover – as had all the guests, with the exception of William, who was now on the landing trying to grasp hold of the mist with very little success. I saw his hand run clean through one of the shadowy figures, and I saw a glimpse of ghostly hair swinging over a cotton nightgown, and then the images faded and all was silent.

'What the hell was that!' One of the soldiers, white faced and cringing against the wall, was wide-eyed and terrified, his words coming out on a sibilant whisper.

'It's the ghosts of Aberglasney,' I said boldly. 'That's why we're here! This is a ghost-haunting weekend, and you've messed it all up on a wild goose chase. Why would we want spies here? Don't you think we've got enough excitement as it is?'

'I'm out of here!' The soldier without a mask edged towards the door, and I could hear him lighting up a cigarette outside, and then he began to run, his feet pounding against the drive.

The leader looked doubtful. 'We should search the place,' he said. 'We need to find out if that cursed airman has been here or not.'

'To hell with all that!' The other soldiers filed out of the house at quick-march.

The leader looked at me apologetically. 'Sorry for the trouble, ma'am.' His gaze was directed at the landing, his eyes wide with disbelief, and he continued talking – almost as if reciting a well-known speech. 'I didn't mean to be so rough, but this man is dangerous. If you see him, keep away from him. He's quite liable to kill you; he's killed before.'

'*Sorry!* What sort of man are you?' The colonel came forward. 'May the ghosts of Aberglasney haunt you for all the days of your life – sir,' he added as an afterthought.

As if on cue, Mrs Ward appeared with a tray of hot drinks, apparently without knowing what had happened. 'Sorry I've been absent for a while, Riana. I fell asleep in my room with the radio on, heard a bit of noise – some banging – and guessed the ghosts had put in an appearance, so I got up.'

'We've been shot at and frightened to death and you didn't know?' I asked in disbelief.

'What! What happened? I'd taken a drink, Riana. It fair knocked me out it did. I'm sorry, but when I woke up I washed my face and came straight down to help.'

'Who gave you a drink?' I asked suspiciously.

The colonel came to rest his hand on Mrs Ward's arm. 'It was my fault,' he said. 'I'm afraid I gave Mrs Ward a cocktail made up of some almost empty bottles – gin, vodka, brandy. I do hope you didn't suffer any ill effects, Mrs Ward.'

She beamed. 'No, I just had a wonderful few hours' rest that's all,' she said happily.

I relaxed. *I must be getting paranoid*, I thought.

The colonel was beaming happily down at Mrs Ward, and my eyes must have opened wide; surely not a romance in the air? Not between pragmatic Mrs Ward and the bluff old colonel?

Mrs Ward's eyes fluttered downward in what looked suspiciously like a coquettish manner. 'I'd better get these hot drinks served,' she said. Was that a wink?

'Let me help you dear lady.' The colonel and Mrs Ward went around the room handing out tea and coffee, and I sank into a chair, exhausted.

I heard the cars start up outside the door and guessed the soldiers had left. I had no idea what they'd really wanted, but I was angry with them – and with Tom. So far I'd behaved like a weak fool, letting him treat me so casually. He'd only given me the smallest of hints as to his life and his 'activities', and yet my whole life was being disrupted by him. Next time he chose to come calling I'd send him away with a flea in his ear!

Eventually, we all went to our rooms, and from next door I could hear William and his lady friend arguing. I gathered that while William was fascinated by the hall and its unusual residents, Miss Spears was appalled and afraid and wanted to go home to her cottage in the Brecon hills. Frankly, I didn't blame her. It seemed ludicrous to pay to spend a weekend being shot at and frightened half to death!

–

In the morning, the guests were up bright and early: going on walks in the fresh air, sitting in the library reading, and young William himself was on the landing, looking for bits of string or mirrors or goodness knows what. In spite of being a serious ghost-hunter, he was still trying to discover if there had been some sort of trickery.

I could scarcely believe what had happened myself. It wasn't so much the appearance of ghosts, or the intrusion of the soldiers and the way the men had treated me, that had upset me. It was Tom.

On the other hand, I was tired of being treated roughly, as if I were some sort of traitor. Tonight I would make sure the doors and windows were securely locked. Later, I would get a dog – a big dog that would bark and growl and maybe bite any intruders.

At breakfast the colonel was missing, and worried I went to his room. I knocked and opened the door, and there he was, handling a fierce-looking handgun. He turned and saw me. 'Let anyone insult you again, my dear, and I'll use this on him.' His voice was booming fierce, his handling of the gun was clumsy, and I guessed his title of 'colonel' was 'honorary'.

'I'm going to get a dog,' I said. 'Maybe a *big* dog. At least then we will be warned if anyone tries to break in on us.' *Even Tom*, I thought to myself.

'Very well, Riana, but I think you should report all this to the police.'

'No, no. I don't want to alarm the local people. We might be shut down or something. Our ghost weekends might even be banned!'

The colonel nodded thoughtfully. 'I think you could be right, least said soonest mended, but at least have someone on guard outside. Back and front doors and windows, and someone at the gate perhaps.'

I doubted I could afford all that, but I nodded placatingly. 'We'll have to do something,' I agreed.

I spent the day painting and fuming about Tom and the trouble he'd brought me, while the some of the guests lazed about or read up on the ghosts of Aberglasney and young William took his no-longer lady friend into Swansea to catch a train home. I worked a hasty loose painting of the events of the night before, omitting the shooting incident. That would be hard to explain. Instead, I did the landing scene and below in the hall the mixed reactions of the guests. I spitefully painted in Miss 'Young William' bottom up, crouching under the table, and 'Plump Betty' clutching the arm of Mr Bravage. It worked well, it was good... but I didn't like it, so I painted out William's girlfriend and put in a bit of moonlight on the parquet floor instead. It kept the colours muted and blurred and worked much better.

In the afternoon, Diane arrived on a short visit from London and asked to look at my work. She admired my painting, but with a head on one side she regarded it speculatively. 'Not with the "heart" you usually put into your work. Well executed, but something is lacking.' She stood back a bit. 'I know!' She snapped her fingers. 'The face in the window!'

'How do you know about that?'

'I've been talking to some of the others,' she said. 'Betty was full of it. She said it frightened her much more than the ghosts of the young maids. It was an oldish man with a weary face, and "despair was written all over his ghostly features". Her words, not mine.'

Enthused, I quickly painted in the face as I remembered it – pale, hollow-eyed, a grieving expression about the hooded eyes – and I painted in just the hint of tears. I stood back and breathed a sigh of relief; now the painting had meaning, life or death according to how the observer looked at it.

'Good!' Diane said. 'That will sell, as sure as eggs are eggs. I love it.'

'Thanks to your input,' I said, 'it's worked. You have a good eye, Diane, and perhaps even more intuition than dear Mr Readings had.'

'Ah, dear Mr Readings. I miss him like anything, Riana, and I told you, the lovely man left me everything he owned – the house, the business and, most important to me of all, the wedding ring he bought for me.'

I glanced at her hand where the gold band shone in the bright light through my studio windows. Impulsively, I hugged her. 'You were always his wife in every way,' I assured her. 'He loved you very much.'

'I was a mistress for years. I don't suppose I will be accepted in polite society.'

'There's no "polite society" left after the devastation of the war,' I protested.

She looked at me with eyebrows raised. 'You are mistaken, Riana. Snobbery will always exist, whatever the state of the world.'

'Let's go to the kitchen and have Mrs Ward make us a nice mug of hot chocolate, shall we?'

'Hot chocolate! That sounds wonderful. Where do you manage to find such luxuries, Riana?'

'It's Mrs Ward's doing. She conjures up various goodies! I think she's got a list of the local people's misdoings and blackmails them for luxuries.'

We had to make our own hot chocolate, for I saw Mrs Ward out in the vegetable garden, with the colonel helping her to pick spring vegetables for tonight's dinner.

I smiled. 'Those two unlikely people are getting on very well, aren't they?' I said.

Diane stood at my side and watched as Mrs Ward's head fell close to the colonel's, clearly examining the produce from the garden. 'They certainly are,' she agreed, somewhat enviously.

—

It was quiet that night, in stark contrast to the events of the night before. For all that, we sat up in the drawing room, bathed now with firelight, and talked quietly about the ghosts and the strange men who had intruded on us.

'It must be something to do with the American airmen who were stationed here,' William observed, newly knowledgeable after his research trip. 'They intruded into the big houses and took all advantage of all the ladies, offering stockings and food as an inducement to wrong-doing and loose living.'

'That's extremely prudish of you,' Betty said, perhaps feeling she should justify her own kind of approach to men. 'Don't forget that Americans were killed in the war as well as British.'

'I agree,' the colonel said at once. 'There was that young pilot who died when the house was first open to us. Carl Jenkins – was that his name, Riana?'

'That's right.' I thought of Rosie and the furore about her condition and how I'd blamed Tom for it all and felt ashamed. Poor Tom! He did so much for me, and yet I continued to blame him for everything bad that happened. But I couldn't deny, even to myself, that he was tied up in all the mystery. I just hoped it was military secrets and nothing too sinister... like arms-smuggling or, even worse, murder and some sort of revenge.

'May I pour some drinks, Riana?' the colonel asked meekly.

'Of course, it's all part of the weekend,' I said quickly. 'Drinks all round, everybody?' That was the latest innovation of mine – to provide a bar and a variety of drinks. I could afford these little additions now.

I helped myself to a small sherry. I felt very tired after my day's painting. It was something I loved doing, but I still wore myself out every time I created a picture. I supposed that I put too much of myself in it. I tensed up at the thought of the haunted face in the window, but when I drank some of the golden sherry it warmed my throat and my stomach and relaxed me a little.

Eventually, the guests departed for bed. It seemed once one made a move, everyone followed, much to my relief.

I visited Beatrice briefly on my own way to bed and asked her, in a whisper, about the events of the night before.

'The man in the window... that was my Edwin,' she whispered back. 'He wants you to get on with it and prove he's not a murderer, and then we can all rest in peace.'

I nodded. I had been so bound up in my own problems that I'd forgotten my wish to clear Beatrice's husband.

'Why don't you start by searching the house for suspicious signs,' she said. 'I'm not going to be here tomorrow, so make a start in the blue room. That's where the gals died, you know.'

'All right, Beatrice,' I agreed wearily. 'The guests return home tomorrow so the place will be mine again, and I promise I won't work at all. I'll just make a search of the house and see if I can find anything.' I paused. 'But surely you would have found something by now, Beatrice, if there *was* anything to find?'

'I haven't the ability, dear, nor the strength. You are young and alive, and you can do anything you choose. You'll fight for me. You are the owner of the house now. It's your place to sort everything out, and then we can all rest.'

'Goodnight, Beatrice.' I stumbled out and into my room, and without even undressing I kicked off my shoes, climbed on the bed and immediately fell asleep.

–

There was the usual bustle of departure in the morning. Even Diane went off home early. Although, of course, William's girlfriend had already left. I felt he would do much better without her presence. As if reading my thoughts, he came up to me. 'A wonderful weekend, Miss Evans. I shall certainly come again, although probably alone. My girlfriend didn't really fit in. She is too sensitive for her own good, you know.'

'I know,' I agreed, finding it difficult to keep my thoughts to myself about his girlfriend's sensitivity. 'Ghosts and armed men aren't everyone's cup of tea,' I said tactfully. 'But I do admire the way you investigated the landing area of the house to find out if there was any trickery involved.'

He blushed.

'It's all right,' I said. 'I doubted the evidence of my own eyes. I don't know, even now, if I was seeing things.'

'If you were, we all were,' William said. 'And we certainly didn't imagine the disembodied face in the window, did we?'

'No.' I made a mental note to start searching the house once the last guest departed.

When it was quiet, I watched Mrs Ward prolonging her farewells to the colonel and smiled to myself as I put the kettle on. The war hadn't managed to kill off all the romance in the world then!

I made a hot pot of coffee, and when Mrs Ward came into the kitchen, her pale cheeks flushed, I poured us a cup. 'You like the colonel, do you?'

The question was superfluous, and Mrs Ward turned away to pour milk in her cup. She shrugged eventually, and I realised it would be wise to drop the subject.

'I'm going to search the house today,' I said firmly. 'I want to look for clues as to what's hidden here.'

'What on earth do you mean?' Mrs Ward gave me her full attention.

'For one thing, why do people keep running in here with guns and things? What are they looking for?'

'It's just because of those Americans, I think,' Mrs Ward said. 'In any case, don't you think we'd have found whatever it is they're looking for, with all the renovation work that's been going on here?'

'You have a point,' I agreed. 'But what on earth do all these armed men think we've got here?'

'Well—' Mrs Ward's voice was dry '—you've certainly been the target for their violence. If the ghost silliness hadn't happened, they might have begun to torture you for information! I still reckon that Tom bloke has got something to do with it – and him so nice to us, too.'

'I don't think Tom could be involved,' I protested. 'I'm sure he wouldn't want anyone bullied and humiliated, and he was abducted himself at one stage, remember?'

'A cover,' Mrs Ward declared, her lips pursed with disapproval. 'Those Americans caused us enough trouble during the war, and why hasn't that Tom gone back to America with the rest of them, that's what I want to know.'

Again, Mrs Ward had a point. I sighed; there was no use arguing about it. I was too weary and too puzzled and too afraid of what I might find out about Tom to continue with the conversation. Instead, I started a systematic search of the house, starting with the servant's rooms at the top of the house. I found nothing untoward in the recently refurbished and brightly-curtained rooms, however.

I knew Beatrice would be away, so I went to the first floor, entered Beatrice's room, and immediately wondered if there was a window open. Everything felt cold and damp and decayed, and yet when Beatrice chose to be in residence the room felt warm and normal.

I felt dreadful as I searched in drawers and cupboards and even tested the floorboards for anything coming loose – but there was nothing. I left Beatrice's room, having made a thorough search, but feeling uneasy that I'd intruded on her privacy. The blue room, which up until now had been unoccupied, was where the whole thing had begun, the scene of the deaths. The paint was still on the wall, the windows unchanged. So far as I could tell, the room was the same as when the maids had died. Why they hadn't been housed in the servant's quarters at the top of the house, I didn't know. Perhaps the rooms were left to flake away as they weren't needed. But lead from the paint in the blue room had killed the girls, the stories claimed, and indeed it did smell strange in there. I shrugged and went outside and shut the door. There was nothing to find, and I hardly thought it worth searching the other rooms. But I'd promised Beatrice that I would look for evidence of her husband's innocence, and look I would. Perhaps in searching Aberglasney I would find some answers to my own problems.

Chapter Twenty-Eight

To my great happiness and relief my paintings continued to sell well, in spite of the gallery having changed hands. The art-loving crowd knew Diane well and trusted her honesty and judgement. One or two of the more senior critics watched on the fringes for a while, expecting – or perhaps hoping – Diane would make mistakes and have to put the valuable gallery up for sale, but that didn't happen.

At the official reopening exhibition, my six new works, including the painting depicting the haunted face in the window, were put on display, with lights fixed above each picture to reflect the colours and the nuances of light, and to highlight the progression of shadow and brightness across the canvas.

There were paintings by some old masters too, including one owned by Diane that I'd seen hanging in her sitting room in the guest house. It must have been a real wrench to part with it, but I knew that Diane needed to make a living as much as I did. Mr Readings would have left her well-provided for, I knew that, but perhaps there was some hold up with releasing all his private fortune to her? Diane had not confided in me, but that she had to sell one of her precious paintings told me enough to know she was short of immediate funds. This thought inspired me to vow to work harder once I returned home.

The exhibition was well attended, both by the curious and by those who genuinely wanted to buy. Silk gowns and fur capes shone under the glittering chandeliers and diamonds sparkled on white fingers: the art-loving crowd from London were out to show how prosperous they were. Nowadays, they arrived in cars, but in the olden days carriages with finely decorated horses would have been waiting outside in the stables, and suddenly I was inspired to paint something from the past.

Diane seemed to dance around the room. There was a smile on her face and a glass of champagne in her hand, though I noticed she didn't drink much of it. And underlying her smile was an air of sadness, because she'd lost the man she loved.

I, on the other hand, was determined to forget Tom. Why should I continue to waste my love and my passion on him when he had disappeared from my life yet again? And yet I ached for him. Not just for his touch, but for the familiarity and friendship we used to share, sitting under the cloisters in the garden Tom and his men had worked to bring into some kind of order.

'Excuse me, Miss Evans. I'm Justin. I'm supposed to paint your portrait, remember?'

I looked up to see a handsome man about my own age staring into my eyes.

'Your work is so atmospheric,' he said. 'Even more so than when I saw it at an earlier exhibition. I have bought one of your new paintings, and may I say that although the face in the picture is ghostly and haunted, the image reminds me of my late father?'

'Your father!' I was fearful and suddenly wary. 'Who was your father?'

'Edwin Mansel-Atherton,' he said. 'Unfortunately, my father is dead, so he's the *late* Edwin Mansel-Atherton. Did Mr Readings mention it when we last met?'

I saw him suddenly as a threat to my future in Aberglasney. After all, might he not be the rightful heir? I liked him very much, but I didn't want him taking my home from me. 'So you've bought my painting?' I said with false brightness.

Just then Diane came and took my arm. 'Some people want to meet the talented lady artist,' she said, hurrying me away. 'You must mingle, dear. You can't stand talking to the most eligible man in London all night, even though he *is* gorgeous!' There was a proprietary air about the way she spoke of Justin, and I imagined she'd met him many times before.

My head was ringing with confusion and questions: most importantly, was Justin the legal heir to my house? I stopped Diane as she made a beeline for the other art lovers. 'Wait! I'll meet your other clients later. What do you know about Justin Mansel-Atherton?'

Diane appeared puzzled. 'He was a friend of dear Mr Readings. Why? Are you interested in him?'

'In a way,' I said softly, 'but not romantically. I'll tell you all about it after the exhibition.' I'd arranged to stay the night in London with Diane. I could trust Diane and confide in her. She'd find out all she could about Justin – and use her discretion into the bargain. Once I got home I would also question Beatrice about the man, although I would have to be tactful and careful.

Most of the paintings sold that night, leaving only three – one of them mine. I knew I could look forward to some money to spend on the house. Providing, I thought, the house was really mine.

I knew I'd bought it legally, but if Beatrice had no right to sell it then I'd be in trouble. I knew some of these old mansions used to be entailed to the eldest son; I could only hope that wasn't the case with dear old Aberglasney.

Diane was sympathetic and comforting. 'If you've a legal document signed by the owner you must be all right, dear,' she said firmly.

'Yes, but was Beatrice the legal owner? What if Edwin left the house to his eldest son?'

'Don't panic.' Diane poured me a glass of the left-over champagne. 'Justin might be illegitimate. Have you thought of that?'

'I've thought of nothing else.' I sank into a chair with my glass.

Diane sat opposite me. 'I wish dear Mr Readings was here. He'd know who to contact and what the legal position was,' she said. She gave a wan smile. 'And the dear man would have celebrated such a good sale too.'

And *I* wished that Tom was here and was truly mine, instead of blowing hot and cold and vanishing at every turn, and that Justin would disappear from the face of the earth. Unfortunately, wishes didn't always come true.

'Don't worry about it, dear.' Diane's voice intruded on my thoughts. 'At least you've sold your paintings, and you always have that – your talent to paint evocative scenes of Aberglasney.'

'The house is my inspiration,' I said, and I knew I sounded despondent, but I was tired and it was time I went to bed. I kissed Diane's cheek and went to my room, and there I climbed into bed, turned my face into the pillow, and cried bitter, self-pitying tears.

In the morning, everything seemed clearer and much more hopeful. I had a legal document that confirmed I was the owner of Aberglasney. It had been signed and sealed by Beatrice, by me, and by the solicitor. Of course I was the legal owner, and no one could take the house from me.

Chapter Twenty-Nine

Some days later, when I'd returned home, Justin came to visit. The house seemed to crackle with hostility, and Beatrice, who I'd longed to question about Justin, was away on one of her frequent jaunts. I still couldn't help but wonder where she disappeared to, but whenever I asked her she was vague and unwilling to talk about her life, and I couldn't say I blamed her for that. Still, I dearly wanted to know about Justin and his history.

'Come into the sitting room.' I forced a pleasant smile as Justin handed Mrs Ward his cap. Today he looked like a country squire; I wouldn't have been surprised to see him carrying a gun beneath his arm.

'A tray of coffee, madam?' Mrs Ward was staring suspiciously at Justin, and I wondered if she'd seen him before or if she knew anything about him. I was surprised at her formality; she usually addressed me by my Christian name.

'That would be lovely, Mrs Ward.' I gestured to the sofa. 'Please take a seat Mr… er… Justin.'

He was staring round at the high ceilings and the beautifully moulded cornice, and I felt an instant antagonism to him. 'You like my house?' I emphasised the 'my', and he smiled as he took a seat.

'I rather think the old place is mine.' His words fell into the room like cold chips of ice. Mrs Ward almost dropped the tray of coffee she was carrying into the room. She frowned, and I shook my head, hoping she wouldn't say anything. She took the hint and retreated, glaring at the visitor.

'I don't understand you,' I said vaguely, unwilling to argue such an important point without professional advice.

'It's quite simple. I am the only son of Edwin Mansel-Atherton, therefore I am his heir.'

'Then why have you taken so long to come to see me or the house – or, for that matter, a solicitor? Is there a will to that effect – that you are heir, I mean?'

'As it happens, I haven't searched for one, and what's more I live in a very fine house in London. What would I do with this place? It takes so much money, and to what effect?' He took a seat as if he owned the place. 'A little bit of tidying and building isn't going to change the bad ambience of the place, is it?' He paused to drink some coffee, and with a grimace of distaste he put down his cup. 'Chicory coffee from a bottle, I take it?'

'The war hasn't long ended, and we are still on rations,' I pointed out, beginning to dislike Justin very much.

'I could let you rent the old place, of course.' He sounded smug.

I stood up, forcing my hands together to stop them shaking. I felt a cold fury turn to a fire in my belly. 'How dare you come here and patronise and whine and then offer me the tenancy of my own house?' My tone was raised.

Justin came towards me and I flinched, expecting a torrent of abuse. I'd got used to being roughly spoken to since I'd bought the house. Instead, Justin took me in

234

his arms and kissed me, deeply and passionately, before I instinctively pushed him away.

'We'll talk again when you are a bit calmer,' he said. He left me, and I heard the door slam after him as I almost fell into a chair.

I painted for the rest of the day, but my heart wasn't in it. I went to bed early, wanting the night to pass.

–

In the morning, an early sun was shining and I felt refreshed. Feverishly, I searched for the document Beatrice had given me when I'd bought the house, and I sighed with relief when I found it filed away in my desk drawer. I read through it avidly, line by line, trying to learn if there was any loophole in the agreement. After reading and rereading, I could find nothing to disprove the legality of the document. Tomorrow I'd go into Swansea and see the solicitor who had witnessed my signature, I decided, just to be certain. I was still shaking, however, when I put the agreement away carefully and locked the drawer, hiding the key beneath the clock on the mantelpiece.

A knocking on the door made me freeze. I knew it was Justin before Mrs Ward announced him.

'Do come in.' My tone was frosty as I led the way into the sitting room. 'Please tell me what I can do for you. I'm very busy today.' I sat well away from him, with a low ornate table as a barrier between us. Mrs Ward brought us coffee, and I held my cup like a guard against his undoubted charm and good looks.

'There's no doubt the house is mine,' he said without preamble, 'but I have a solution, seeing as you don't want to rent the old place from me.'

'The house is mine,' I said firmly, 'and I have no intention of arguing about it.'

'What I was thinking,' he said, continuing as if I hadn't spoken, 'is that it would solve everything if we got married. Then there would be no dispute, and the house would belong to both of us.'

I was breathless with the cheek of it. 'What makes you think I would want to marry you?' My tone was angry, and I felt the heat come into my cheeks at his arrogance.

'Well, you would be Mrs Mansel-Atherton for a start. You would have rights to the house, indisputable rights, and no one could take it from you.'

'And you. What would *you* hope to get from such a marriage? My money? A very easy living?' I asked, my voice heavy with sarcasm. 'I've checked, and you have very little money except what you win at cards. You rent a good address in London and put yourself about as a man of means.'

'I have charm and respectability, and *I've* done some checking too. You are — what shall we say? — a fallen woman, aren't you? Rumour has it that you've had at least one man in your bed, not to put too fine a point on it, and some say these weekends you run are an excuse for all sorts of goings on. Didn't one of the girls here have an illegitimate child, for instance?'

I was so angry I could have picked up one of the heavier flower vases and hit him over the head with it. What really upset me was that there was some truth amid all the slander he was spitting out. I put down my cup and got to my feet. 'If you don't leave *my* property at once, I will send Mrs Ward for the police.'

He got up, but laughed irritatingly. 'Poor old Sergeant Price on his bike will take an age to get here, Miss Evans. This is not London, you know, with efficient police cars able to cover the miles quickly – horns blazing out, and blue lights flashing. Face it! You might just lose everything if I take the legal way out of this dilemma.'

I took a deep breath. 'Why don't you come along to the next ghost-haunting weekend and see for yourself what really happens?' I spoke sweetly, and he looked at me suspiciously.

'And be murdered in my bed? I think not.'

'Don't be hysterical and absurd. Alert the police, your friends, the London public to your visit, if you like. Bring cameras, newspaper men, anyone of your dubious circle of acquaintances you like, so that your whereabouts will be well accounted for.' I was issuing a challenge, and he would look weak and silly if he wasn't man enough to take it.

At last, he nodded. 'Very well, I will accept your invitation. And don't worry, I will bring some friends with me.'

'There will be the usual charge, of course.' I wrote the date down for him on a card, and then met his dark eyes. 'Now, if you wouldn't mind leaving, I have a great deal of work to do.'

When he'd gone, I helped myself to some hot coffee and sat thinking about all he'd said. 'How on earth did Justin know about me and Tom? He could easily have learned about Rosie from village gossip, but I had told no one about my one night of passion with Tom except Diane, who I now counted as a close personal friend.

Perhaps Mrs Ward knew? But then she was the soul of discretion!

I sat in a chair with my head in my hands and tried to stop the hot tears from brimming in my eyes. If ever I needed Tom's arms around me, his deep reassuring voice, it was now – but as usual he was not with me when I needed him most.

Later I went into town to see Beatrice's solicitor, Mr Jeremy, and to my relief he told me there were no legitimate heirs and that Aberglasney was indisputably and legally mine.

I stared around his dusty office and asked idly if he knew of the murder case where five young serving maids had died.

'Of course I've heard of it, but it's all stuff and nonsense!' he said, waving a pale, effete hand. 'Five young girls don't die of lead poisoning on the same night. Lead poisons the blood slowly, you know.'

'And Mr Mansel-Atherton. Do you think he killed the maids?'

He looked at me over his glasses. 'This is not a legal opinion. I do know old Edwin was a bit of a boy, if you take my meaning, but murder? I think not, Miss Evans.'

'And what about this man who claims he is the heir to Aberglasney?' My mouth was dry as I asked the question.

Mr Jeremy was reluctant to reply. 'I don't wish to defame anyone's character, but the young man could be a by-blow. I mentioned Edwin was a "bit of a lad", didn't I?'

I visited the library next, determined to read through the articles about the murder case again. This time I asked the new young librarian – who had obviously replaced

Miss (or was that Mrs?) Grist – for the Bristol and London newspapers, as well as the Cardiff and Swansea editions, to see if there were any other comments about the murder. I took the bundle of newspapers to a table and sat down to read.

In the London issues there was a great deal of coverage of the deaths of the young girls – great columns of print, and a picture of Edwin in his younger days standing outside Aberglasney. The house looked big and grand and as old as the surrounding landscape – almost as though it had grown out of the hills – but the picture of Edwin showed the face of a slim, rather fragile young man wearing spectacles, a beard and a worried frown. There was nothing I didn't already know, however, which was disappointing.

I picked up the *Bristol News* and the same story was repeated – without any pictures of Edwin, but with the gruesome picture of a hangman's noose instead. I was almost ready to hand the newspaper back to the librarian when I noticed Edwin's name in another column: a small piece about some machine he was building. I felt a dart of excitement. The engine, it seemed, was fuelled by some-thing new, something yet untried… but no name was given to the fuel. I supposed that was for security reasons. The plans for the engine had been missing since Edwin's death, and it was assumed they were either destroyed or burned.

So the intrusion and searching of my house, my kidnapping, and perhaps, I thought painfully, Tom's interest in me and in Aberglasney, was all because of these missing designs, which could be used to build a new and better aeroplane engine for any future war! The designs must be truly revolutionary, I thought, for the American military to still be so desperate for them, so many years after Edwin's death.

I copied the small column down word for word in careful writing, using the pencil the librarian had pointedly put down before me. I looked up to her when I had finished. 'Miss Grist doesn't work here any more then?' I felt as if I was scratching a sore spot. I would have liked to have known why and how Tom had become mixed up with Miss Grist.

The young woman looked blank. 'We never had a Miss Grist working here, madam.'

'But you did,' I said flatly.

'I'll check, madam, but I'm sure we did not.'

She came back some time later, looking smug. 'The only Miss Grist who came here from time to time was an investigating officer from the police force! She definitely was not a librarian.'

'Thank you.' I tried to digest the information, but nothing fitted. Miss Grist was spiteful, a piece of fluff who had little brain in her head... Or had that all been a cover? Was she a very good police investigator indeed?

Eventually I turned my attention back to the papers and read again about Edwin's engine designs. I felt in my bones I was definitely on to something. If only I could find Tom I could ask him outright, I thought. If only I could find Tom I would be the happiest woman in the whole of the country... but I suppressed that lift of my heart.

As I travelled home on the train, I wondered where Justin fitted into all this. Perhaps he, too, was seeking the elusive plans. I supposed they would bring a fortune if sold into the right hands.

To my delight, Beatrice was back. She was stood on the landing as I entered the hallway. She waved to me briefly with her lace-gloved hand and disappeared into her room.

I hurried up the stairs without even taking off my coat and hat, and if Beatrice was surprised to see me so flustered she didn't show it. It was freezing in the room, and I switched on the electric heater I'd installed for her. She raised her eyebrows but said nothing. I crouched in the old basket chair and stared at her. 'I've met Justin,' I said, not willing to be patient. 'Does he have a legal claim to this house?'

'Certainly not!' Beatrice was stiff with hostility. 'He was just a moment of weakness on Edwin's part, the child of a London society lady I believe. Edwin was a very attractive man, you know. The women chased him, even when he was a mature gentleman, and whenever he was on a lecturing tour, I was sitting at home. Alone.'

She twisted her hands together. She still wore her gloves, and I noticed there was a hole in one of the fingers. I would buy her a new pair as soon as I went to Swansea again, I thought absently.

'This Justin might have called himself Mansel-Atherton but he's no son of mine. The boy is illegitimate.'

'Did Edwin leave a will?' I was almost afraid to ask. Beatrice was old and rather vague at times, and she might well have a grudge against Edwin's son.

'He didn't have time,' she said. 'He was whisked off to prison so suddenly, you see, but they had to let him out until they did further investigations. But then he forestalled them and took his own life. As I told you.'

'But most people make a will early on in their lives. I would have thought Mr Mansel-Atherton would be that sort of man.'

'Oh, Edwin was always drawing things,' Beatrice said. 'Always making plans that didn't work. But he lectured well, you know, was invited all over the world, and he was a brilliant engineer.'

I felt my pulse quicken. 'Where did he keep his drawings?'

Beatrice smiled. 'No one knows, dear. He was working on his drawings the night the maids died, and after that everything went crazy here.' She looked at me sadly and then pulled herself upright. 'When he... he died, I couldn't afford to employ any more maids – and in any case no one would work here.'

'Where do you go when you leave? Here, I mean.' I was suddenly curious about Beatrice's absences, curious about everything. I had a suspicion that Beatrice was guilty of something, though I didn't know what.

'Why, I go to stay with my friends and family, of course.' She seemed surprised that I'd asked, and suddenly I felt foolish and intrusive.

'I would love to see Edwin's work.' I felt the colour rise to my cheeks, sensing my lie would be obvious, but Beatrice shook her head.

'Yes, have a look around the place any time for his drawings, dear. It's your house, you know! But do search when I'm out visiting. I don't think I could stand the noise and dust if I was here.'

'You could always go to the sitting room or into the garden.' I'd seen her in the garden several times when the weather was good, but she pursed her lips before replying.

'I would prefer you to wait until I was away,' she said firmly. 'I might come across Mrs Ward. I wouldn't like that and neither would she.'

I frowned. I hadn't been aware that Beatrice and Mrs Ward didn't like each other. Mrs Ward hadn't spoken of any falling out. I began to feel uncomfortable sitting in Beatrice's room with my outdoor shoes on, and I got up. 'I'll leave you to get some sleep,' I said. 'I'm sorry to intrude on your privacy, very sorry.'

I hurried downstairs and went into the kitchen. As usual, Mrs Ward was sitting there before the fire, her feet up on a stool.

'Oh, Riana, just come in from Swansea, have you? I'll make you some milky cocoa. It will settle you down for the night.'

I was going to say I'd been talking to Beatrice, but I took the cocoa and came straight to the point. 'Did you know anything about any drawings Edwin Mansel-Atherton made? Plans of engines, that sort of thing?'

Mrs Ward suddenly looked furtive, but then her face cleared. 'Oh, I know what you mean. The drawings that disappeared when he died?'

'That's it.' I looked at her, wondering if I'd imagined the strange look that had come over her face. 'Know anything about them?'

'A lot of rubbish was talked when Mr Edwin died.' She shook her head. 'Who's to say what the truth was? Not me, that's for sure.'

I sighed, suddenly tired and feeling that everyone was an enemy. All the people I thought were friends were keeping the truth from me. I put down my cup. 'It's been a very long day.'

'Oh, I forgot to tell you. Mr Tom called here to see you.' She went to the drawer and took out a note. 'He left this for you.'

I took the note. It was not even in an envelope, and I wondered if Mrs Ward had read it. I went to my room, sat on the bed and devoured the words, feeling a thrill that this was Tom's writing and he'd actually been here in my house.

> *Sorry to have missed you. Will call again to*
> *explain everything.*
> *Love,*
> *Tom*

It could have been written to anyone; my name was not even on it. I felt like rushing downstairs to ask Mrs Ward: had Tom delivered it in person? Was it really intended for me? And if so, what did it mean? What was he going to explain – his strange behaviour? And what he was *really* after at Aberglasney?

I kicked off my shoes. I was weary of it all: the mystery of the house and the deaths of the five girls, and of the strangers bursting in any time they chose. I was even tired of my ghost-haunting weekends and the people I'd come to know as friends. Colonel Fred, young William – did all of them spend their time in my house looking for hidden treasure in the form of futuristic designs, rather than looking for ghosts? And the ghosts... Were they real, or had it been mass hysteria when we'd all seen the mist and ghostly beings on the landing? I fell back against the pillows and began to cry.

In the morning, I began to paint again – anything to take my mind off the fact that Tom might call. After a restless morning, I had a solitary lunch: some salad and cold potatoes, and a glass of milk. I stood on the doorstep for a while looking along the drive, but there was no sign of anyone arriving. Tom wouldn't come, I knew it in my bones, and at last I went back to the studio and became involved once more in my painting.

I painted the grounds from memory – the cloisters, the now neat gardens, the wooden bench where Tom and I had shared our time and enjoyed each other's company – and the tears welled blurring my eyes. The effect of tears in my eyes altered the painting, and I began to paint in heavy rain sleeting down over the gardens, darkening the stonework on the arches of the cloisters, and making the plants look dark green.

On an impulse, I painted in Beatrice – just a small figure in the distance, bending over the plants, oblivious of the rain. Instinctively, I knew Beatrice didn't worry about the weather. Sometimes she went out in the rain and snow, and very often she would sit in her room, never using the electric fire unless I switched it on for her. I felt a flood of warmth for Beatrice. She was other-worldly in many ways, but so practical, so understanding when occasionally I spoke to her about my fears and about Tom and his strange ways. And the way she put in an appearance when I held my weekends, being a 'ghost' for a few fleeting seconds and then discreetly disappearing! I guessed she must have a hiding place somewhere, because guests often looked into the blue room and she was never there.

I stood back from the painting, and I could see it was all but finished. I would wait for the oils to dry, and then I would put on the finishing touches. As I left, I made sure

I locked the studio. I always locked the door now – ever since my paintings had begun to sell well.

Later the sun came out from behind the clouds and the sweet smell of spring flowers filled the garden. The grass needed cutting, the sap was rising in the plants and trees, and after the rain everything looked fresh and green. Suddenly, I ached for Tom – to be in his arms, to feel his body fill mine, to have his mouth claim my lips, and to know that for a short time he was completely mine. *One night of love.* I smiled wryly. Surely that was a cue for a song? I felt wet on my cheeks again, and in a sudden frenzy of anger I wiped them away, unaware I was dabbing ultramarine paint on my cheeks. But then I noticed, in the distance, my guests arriving and I tried to pull myself together. I had completely forgotten that I'd arranged an extra weekend of ghost haunting! Fortunately, Mrs Ward hadn't. As I rushed into the house and into the kitchen, she was busy cooking, I could smell broth made with lamb and saw a fresh piece of cheese cut into chunks in a bowl.

'Oh, thank you for getting on with things, Mrs Ward,' I said. 'What would I do without you? I can see that Treasure is working like a whirlwind too; that girl is invaluable.' I touched Mrs Ward's shoulder. 'What would I do without you?' I said again.

'What indeed? You've been away with the fairies all day, working in your studio. Still, that's how you earn your living – mine too, if the truth be known. We work well as a team, Riana.' She gave me one of her rare smiles, and I knew by the light in her eyes that she was looking forward to seeing Colonel Fred again. 'The *cawl* is ready for the starters, made with lovely fresh veg from the garden and pieces of the lamb to make it tasty,' Mrs Ward said. 'Real

Welsh soup is my *cawl*, and fresh cheese cut ready for the dressing. I've got a *joint* of lamb for the main course, and I've picked fresh mint from the garden. As for pudding, I managed to make apple pie and custard, though the custard is a bit on the thin side, mind.'

She looked up at me then and laughed. 'Which tribe have you joined, Riana?'

'What?'

'You're painted up like an Indian brave.'

I hurried to the mirror in the hall and burst out laughing. But then I noticed Mrs Ward's face, reflected behind me, and there was a strange, almost hostile, look in her eyes. 'Do I look that bad?' I asked, and she smiled and the image altered. She was once again the Mrs Ward I knew – never one to give of herself, but loyal and hard working and reliable. 'Anything wrong Mrs Ward?' I turned to her, and she looked down at her shoes. All I could see was the crown of her grey hair, smoothed down tidily as always.

'It's Rosie,' she said. 'She's coming back home.'

'Oh.' I hesitated. 'Aren't you pleased?'

'She says she wants to be free again and young and lovely. She's fed up with being a slave for a man and his impossible family. Her words, not mine.'

I didn't really know what to say. 'She can come here, of course.' I swallowed hard. I could imagine Rosie disrupting the place, flirting and arousing the ire of all the respectable village wives.

'Oh, I don't think that would be wise, Riana,' Mrs Ward surprised me by saying. 'I think she'll stay in London – for a while, anyway.'

'In London? Oh, good.' I felt relieved. I didn't know if I could cope with Rosie's overenthusiastic presence in the house. 'What will she do there?'

'Doubtless she'll meet some gullible man. In the meantime, she'll wait on tables, be a cook, something of that sort.'

I didn't want to enquire further, and fortunately just then there was a knock on the door and the tooting of a horn outside in the yard. 'Looks like more guests are arriving,' I said, sighing heavily. 'We'll talk later if you want, Mrs Ward. And don't worry about Rosie, she'll be all right.'

'I'm not worried about Rosie,' Mrs Ward said bluntly. 'I'm worried about that baby of hers.'

–

It was good to have the old colonel, Betty, and all my guests arrive and fill the house. Soon the dining room blazed with candles and lamplight and happy diners were drinking wine from sparkling glasses and eating the good food Mrs Ward and Treasure had prepared.

Now the whole house was wired for electricity. It was long overdue, but I knew my guests preferred the old-fashioned lighting that heightened the atmosphere of the old mansion. It was also conducive to ghosts, so it seemed, with the apparent 'happenings' on the landings.

I never saw ghosts when I was alone; I never felt threatened by anything other-worldly in my house. It was the humans I feared and mistrusted.

'How is your romance progressing?' Plump Betty pressed against William with her large bosoms.

'Not very well, as it happens.' William was unusually terse.

Betty wouldn't allow matters to rest there. 'I'm so sorry to hear that, but you are among friends here. You can talk freely to us.'

Colonel Fred leaned forward. 'While that is true, Betty, some things are best left alone, don't you know?' He held the brandy bottle towards William. The colonel had no truck with wine – 'newfangled nonsense' he called it. He loved his brandy and insisted on bringing his own brand, which he always took to his room. He saw me glance at him and the bottle and smiled. 'You see, dear Riana, I have my own spirits to keep me warm of a night. Try some, William. It will help you to relax and sleep.'

William accepted, more for the sake of peace than because he wanted to drink the brandy, but he continued to share the brandy for the rest of the evening. Later, I winked at the colonel, as I could see William was getting merrier and relaxing very well against Betty's plump shoulder. Betty herself was flushed with success. She'd always had a fancy for William.

There were no ghost sightings that night so instead the gathering became a party, with someone putting the gramophone on and playing dance music. I helped the colonel roll back the carpet to reveal the wooden floor, and he took a new guest, a Mrs Lampeter, in his arms and performed a creditable slow foxtrot. Betty inveigled William to dance, and he was propelled round the room with Betty's full bosom projecting into his skinny chest.

I heard the front door open, and my heart beat faster as I hoped Tom had come to see me at last, but it was Justin. He entered the room, immaculately dressed in a dinner suit and a gleaming white shirt with a black bow tie. He held out his hand, and reluctantly I accepted it. 'What brought you here?' I asked none too graciously as we danced.

He smiled down at me and bent to kiss my cheek. 'A very beautiful lady,' he said. I gave him a wry look, and he shook his head, laughing at me. 'No, dear Riana, not you, lovely though you are. Diane wanted me to ask you to give her more paintings. It seems she has a commission for you, so I thought I'd drive down straight away.'

I frowned. Diane knew that Justin wanted my house. Why would she speak to him about coming to see me? 'I think you must be mistaken,' I said icily. 'Diane would contact me herself if she wanted me. I doubt if she'd ask you, of all people, to bring me a message.'

'Ah, but I have won her over.' Justin sounded smug. 'She believes I am the true heir to Aberglasney, and she thinks we should try to get along. It would be in your best interests, seeing as we will be married as soon as you come to your senses.'

'Don't be so silly!' I pushed him away from me. 'I don't even know you why you imagine I should take your word for anything, and why on earth would I want to marry you?'

'Expediency, my dear Riana. We could live here together, and we would be very happy, I'm sure.'

'I take it you have no money and you would let me pay to do up the house and live on my earnings in the meantime. Now, if you are really the legal heir then go fight your case in the courts. Until then, leave me alone.'

I left my guests to party, and on the stairs I encountered Betty leading William to his downfall. She had a wide smile on her face as William fondled her plump rear. There was no sign of ghostly images as I made my way to my bedroom. I lay fully clothed on the quilt and closed my eyes. I could scarcely hear the music from the drawing room, but I wished all my guests a happy night and smiled as I thought of William, who was about to learn what passion was all about. And then I fell asleep.

Chapter Thirty

Once my guests had departed on the Monday morning I dressed and took the train to Swansea and then on to London. I had to see Diane to find out what she was thinking of, encouraging Justin to come to Aberglasney!

Diane was not tucked away in her little sitting room, mourning her dear Mr Readings, but instead she was out visiting his grave, so the maid told me. I thought how fortunate Diane was to still have maids and a cook. I had only Mrs Ward and Treasure, and I was lucky to have them. So I waited, enjoying a cup of real ground coffee instead of the usual Camp coffee I had at home. No doubt Mr Readings had purchased a stock of it before he died, and Diane had found it and was enjoying her usual luxuries.

At last she returned, and in attendance, much to my surprise, was Rosie. Mrs Ward's daughter had changed drastically; she looked neat and respectable. She was struggling with brown paper bags bearing the names of the few good shops that had survived the war.

I put down my cup of very good coffee and hugged Diane. 'Could we have a word in private, please?' I asked meekly. 'Hello, Rosie, how are you?'

'I'm very well, Miss Riana.' This was a Rosie I didn't know: demure, respectful, nicely dressed in a modern full skirt, and with her hair tied up in a ponytail. She looked what she was: a very young girl. Perhaps she'd changed her ways... or maybe it was all an act to fool Diane.

'I'll take the bags upstairs.' She edged towards the door. 'I'll be careful to hang everything up for you, don't worry.'

Diane sat down and took off her gloves. 'I think I'll have a cup of coffee with you,' she said. 'I feel a "telling off" might be on the cards.'

'No,' I said. 'Well, not exactly. I just don't want Justin popping into my house whenever he takes it into his head, that's all. Don't trust him, Diane. Now, tell me, where on earth did you come across Rosie?'

'She just applied for a job, that's all. And as for Justin, he might well have a claim on your house. He is Edwin's son, after all.'

I decided to shelve the matter of Rosie; just now there were more important things to discuss. 'But Justin is not *Beatrice's* son, and she's the one who sold me the house.'

'Just take the document to the solicitor and find out for sure, that's my advice. Justin seems a decent enough young man to me – a little arrogant, maybe, but well intentioned and charming.'

'Did he ever pay you a penny for any of the paintings he's bought?'

'But Riana, he's broke so he never *buys* any paintings. He does some clerical work for me instead. I'm rather sorry for him, really, and if you don't want him I'll have him.' She was smiling, but I could see Justin had charmed her – just as he charmed and fooled everyone except me.

'Well, until everything is sorted I want him to keep out of my way. I don't love him and won't marry him, not even for Aberglasney.'

'Think about it,' Diane said. 'He's handsome and partial to you, and in the old days many women married for expediency.'

'A marriage of convenience, like in books!' I said scathingly. 'Well, I have a career and a house that I've brought to life again. If Justin had a claim, why didn't he come forward when the house was little but a ruin, the gardens overgrown and the Americans stationed at the bottom of the garden?'

Diane lifted her eyebrows. 'At the bottom of the garden? Like *fairies* in books!' She smiled with humour.

'Very funny.' I sighed heavily. 'I know I'm a fool, Diane, but I love Tom. Whatever he's done I can forgive him, if only he loves me as he says he does.'

'Better have one willing suitor who wants to marry you than have a fly-by-night, excuse the pun, like Tom, an American pilot who might well go home as soon as he finds whatever it is he wants here. At the moment, he's conspicuous by his absence, isn't he?'

There was a gentle knock on the door, and Rosie peeped in. 'Anything you want, Mrs Readings?' she asked.

I looked at Diane in surprise, and when the door closed behind Rosie I had to ask, 'She's very polite to you, isn't she?'

'She's a very good help, and I get on with her well enough.' Diane smiled. 'Mind you, she did quote you as a reference.'

I rather took offence at that. 'The cheeky little madam!'

'I like the way she calls me Mrs Readings. She's about the only one who does.'

'Why did you and he never marry before?' I asked.

'I think dear Mr Readings wanted to keep his options open, dear. He had other "ladies" and I knew it, but I didn't question him on it. He would have been defensive, and I know he didn't want me to be possessive, so I pretended to be as unbothered by our arrangement as he was.' She hung her head. 'But I was never content to remain a mistress – and then, at last, he asked me to marry him, and he died making me a widow almost immediately.' She stopped speaking and looked down at her pale long fingers, with her engagement ring and the band of gold sparkling up at her.

'At least he gave you the ring as a promise,' I said comfortingly as I hugged her. Grief and loss were dreadful emotions. I felt them every time Tom walked in and out of my life.

'We will have a quiet day today.' Diane lifted her head. 'I'll rest if you don't mind and then tomorrow I will come with you to the solicitor in Swansea and we'll sort out the matter of the house.'

'I already saw my solicitor,' I told her. 'He told me that Aberglasney was indisputably mine.'

'Best to be sure,' she insisted. 'You know I'm good at business, Riana, and I'll read the bill of sale properly and ask to see Edwin's will as well.'

'I understand Edwin didn't make a will.' I forced a smile. 'Seems he didn't have time after he was accused of murder.'

–

We set out early the next day. Diane drove us with skill and speed through the bombed streets of London and out into the country, both of us quiet with our own thoughts until we reached Swansea.

A cart pulled by an old horse drew in beside us as Diane stopped the car alongside the curb outside the solicitor's office, the man shouting out in a raucous voice, 'Rag and bones!' and handing out pennies and farthings for old rags or pots and pans. Anything he could make use of. As I stepped out of the car I could see the poor overladen horse jerk the cart into movement, the creature's head dipping up and down with the effort of moving the weight until the wheels began to roll freely along the street.

To my agitation, the door of the solicitor's office was locked. A policeman stood outside, and I looked up at him questioningly. 'I had an appointment this morning to see Mr—' I got no further as the policeman held up his hand.

'There's been an unfortunate incident in the building, madam. There are fatalities. You must go away. The building inside is unsafe.'

'Fatalities?' I echoed his words and looked at Diane aghast.

'I shall find out what's happened,' she said firmly. 'I have a friend, a top man in the service. I will speak to him.' She took my arm and propelled me to a small, neat tea shop just around the corner from the solicitor's office, and I sat there stunned, meekly drinking tea and waiting for her to come back.

After my third pot of tea, Diane returned. She was pale, and I quickly called for another cup and poured her some hot tea. 'It's bad,' I said, and she nodded.

'There was an explosion. Several people have been killed. The police think it was an unexploded bomb from the war. I'm sorry, Riana. I should have come with you before now.'

'It's not your responsibility,' I said shakily. 'I saw the lawyer myself and he said everything was legal enough, that Justin was an illegitimate son and had no claim. I wonder how Mr Jeremy is. I do hope he's escaped the explosion.'

'I doubt it,' Diane said. 'It's terrible, they don't know how many people are under the rubble, but as it's a building of offices of legal people, it shouldn't be too hard to make an identification of the deceased.'

'So an unexploded bomb caused all this havoc.' I was quite shaken. 'Poor Mr Jeremy, he was very old. Too old to be working, really.'

Diane gave me a quick look and poured more tea for herself. 'All our young men are still trying to recover from the war. Oh dear, I feel quite shaken. I wish I'd never suggested coming here.'

'Well, you weren't to know there would be an explosion, were you? Look on the bright side, we could have been caught up in it all.'

Diane shivered. 'Don't be so cheerful!' Her tone held a touch of sarcasm, and I smiled to myself. Diane was getting her old spirit back.

–

Diane became weary of the peace and quiet of Aberglasney after a few days, and on the following Monday we had lunch in Swansea and then I waved her off. I waited until I could no longer see her car in the distance, and then turned to look straight into the dear face of Tom.

'Riana.' There was a world of love and sweetness in his voice, and in spite of myself I wanted to sink into his arms.

We stood looking at each for a long moment, and then we both moved and he was kissing me, holding me as though he would never let me go.

He took me for tea in a simple tea shop, and we sat holding hands over our cooling tea. I knew questions could wait, and I went with him willingly for a walk – along the darkening streets, through Victoria Park, along the sea front – holding hands like lovers. Well, we were lovers, even if we'd made love only once.

He booked us a room in a guest house, and I went with him willingly. I decided that if I could only have him sometimes that was better then nothing at all. Did he love me? I was afraid to ask, but he wanted me, I could see it in his eyes, and for now that was enough.

He took me gently, slowly, and I revelled in his touch. Sensations I'd never known before swept my body, tingling my senses and bringing me to a cascade of desire and a tumbling of joy as my body and senses were lost and my mind was bursting with stars. And then, sated, we lay on the bed alongside each other holding hands, his broad chest rising and falling with the breathlessness we were both feeling.

In me there was a wonder that any man could rouse such passion, such burning, melting love. I adored Tom. I loved every shape of his lean body: his fine buttocks, his strong legs, his broad chest. I *loved* him.

Later we showered and shared a bottle of precious red wine in our room. I had no nightclothes with me so I wrapped myself in one of Tom's shirts and sat cross-legged on the bed, holding my glass between my fingers. I had never been so happy in all my life. And then Tom spoke.

'You should marry Justin Mansel-Atherton, you know.' He said it gravely, with no hint of a smile, and my heart almost stopped beating.

'What did you say?'

'For your own good, Riana. He's eligible, young, attractive... He might well have a claim to Aberglasney, you know.'

I was tearful and furious all at once. 'You've just made love to me in the most wonderful way, and now you are telling me to marry another man! Are you mad?'

He took my hand, and though I tried to pull away he held on to me. 'Riana, there are people who want me dead,' he said. 'If I lived with you, even, I'd be putting you at risk, don't you understand that?'

I dragged my hand free and flopped down on the bed. 'I don't understand anything!' I almost screamed at him. 'I love you, Tom, don't you know that? You appear and disappear without a thought for my feelings! I don't know what you are involved with, but I don't care. I just want to be with you!'

'Sleep on it.' Tom spoke abruptly. He tucked himself inside the bedclothes and turned his back on me. I sat up, staring at his hair, which lay in curls on his neck, for a time. I wanted to touch his hair, kiss his neck, but in the end I closed my eyes, turned away from him and cried myself to sleep.

In the morning Tom had gone, and when, shamed, I went to check out, I found he hadn't even paid the bill properly. He'd left a sheaf of notes as if I was little more than a prostitute.

I hurried to the station. I just wanted to get home, shut myself in my room and try to heal my tattered pride. I didn't want to do anything – no painting, no social weekends with the ghost hunters. Perhaps I would just marry Justin and, as a married woman, get a sensible job and let Justin figure out the best way to keep the house in a good state of repair. If Justin *was* the real heir, I presumed he'd inherit whatever money the Mansel-Athertons had hidden away.

It sounded an easy way out – just hand over responsibility to someone else. I sat listening to the *clackety-clack* of the train, closed my eyes and went over every detail of my night of love with Tom in my head.

Chapter Thirty-One

Diane became a frequent visitor to Aberglasney. The trouble was, she always seemed to have Justin in tow – as well as Rosie, who cooed and fussed over Diane as though she were a princess.

Diane enjoyed the ghost weekends and continued to market my paintings, and I thought her respect for Justin and her dreams of him marrying me and making my life easier were sweet but ill placed. The more I saw of Justin, the more I knew I loved Tom, despite everything.

One happy event in my life was that my painting grew in maturity. I put new focus on the house, painted odd corners of the rooms with ghostly images lurking mistily in them. I often painted the old cloisters, which had been built hundreds of years ago, and thought of Tom and me sitting under the arches on a summer's day, when deep shadows and brightly-patterned sunlight had shaped the gardens. I often thought of those days with nostalgia and hurt in my heart.

The grass and flowers had been wild then, and it was because of Tom and his men that the flower beds had begun to have order and shape. Of course, I could afford two gardeners now, who kept the gardens trimmed and neat and weeded, but I knew I would never forget that

Tom was the one who had planted my garden and made it beautiful.

I knew I should be pleased with my life. I had good friends – especially Diane, who had my best interests at heart – and I was becoming a 'name' now in the world of art. I was known as the strange young lady who lived with ghosts, but I didn't mind what folk said about me as long as my work was appreciated. I was even commissioned by a minor royal to paint an ancestor sweeping grandly across the lawn at Aberglasney. In spite of myself and my best efforts, the lady ended up bearing a striking resemblance to Beatrice. The painting was returned with a short letter telling me the likeness to the royal lady was not quite right and would I do more work on the face?

I looked at the painted miniature I'd been allowed to borrow and worked with a focused mind, and at last the likeness was almost perfect. This time the painting was accepted and I was paid a handsome sum, which I immediately took to my bank in Swansea, grateful that I was secure for at least another year if I wasn't too enthusiastic with my spending on the house.

Summer came and went, hot and dry and with visitors galore, who were not only coming to see the house but also to visit the beautiful gardens, making use of the newly-restored drive and entrance archway. I saw Tom only twice during the summer, and each time he told me he loved me, took me to bed and made such beautiful love to me that I cried each time.

Now the summer had gone, there was an autumnal touch to the evenings, and the leaves fell like coloured patterns on to the well-manicured grass lawns. I walked the gardens — shuffling through the crisp leaves and kicking them up in heaps like a child.

And then it suddenly became winter once more. The nights drew in and shadows crept across from the cloister into the garden, and I felt that first summer at Aberglasney was long ago and far away.

The house was almost restored to its former glory now; there was electric lighting all over the house, though we still used oil lamps and candelabras for effect on the ghost weekends. My career was blossoming, and all I needed to make my life complete was Tom. But he continued to be evasive.

Justin came often with Diane and stayed at the house, and I had yet to prove by law that Aberglasney was mine. Justin seemed to have given up the idea that he owned the place, but I soon found out that I was completely wrong about that.

-

I was sitting in the comfort of the drawing room, wondering what to do for a Christmas party this year and enjoying a glass of much needed sherry, when there was a commotion at the door. I stood up abruptly, my senses alert, imagining Tom had arrived to sweep me away.

A flustered Mrs Ward called me into the hallway. 'It's Mr Mansel-Atherton, Riana. He says he's here to stay and that I must take my orders from him.'

Justin stood in the hallway smiling at me, his bags and cases on the floor beside him. 'Sorry, Riana,' he said, grinning. 'I've nowhere else to go, and this house is rightfully mine. So I'm here to stay, whether you like it or not!' He turned to Mrs Ward. 'Make up a room for me, Mrs Ward.'

She hesitated, looking at me uncertainly.

Justin put his hands on his hips in a 'lord of the manor' pose. 'I won't ask again, Mrs Ward.'

She scuttled upstairs, and I could hear her rummaging in the linen cupboard for sheets. I stood there glaring at Justin for a long moment, and then without waiting he strode past me into the sitting room and sat down in the most comfortable armchair! When Mrs Ward returned he ordered a brandy and soda, and she was so frightened by his authoritative manner that she rushed away to do his bidding.

'What do you think you are doing?' I could hardly speak I was so angry. 'How *dare* you come striding in here as if you own the place?'

'Because I *do* own the place! Call the police, if you like. See what *they* say about all this. Just see if they will throw me out!'

'You know they won't be able to do that on the spot. It takes a solicitor and legal papers to determine who really owns Aberglasney,' I stuttered.

'Precisely, and all you own is a pathetic piece of paper signed by a batty old woman. You only got the house because no one contested it. Well, all that is changed now. I'm back, and if I want to live in my house then I have every right to do so. That solicitor chap told me that before he died.'

I shook my head. 'How convenient for you that a bomb killed him before we could sort this out. Well, we'll see about that in the morning! There are other solicitors who deal with wills and that sort of thing.'

'Well, in the meantime, I'll go to my room. And once in, believe me, you won't shift me.'

'We'll see,' I said, overwhelmed by anger. 'I might get someone to throw you out, if I have to.'

'Threats, Miss Evans? Don't overstep the mark or *I* might be the one to do the throwing out.' He bowed to me as though he was a gentleman and left the room.

I could hear him going upstairs, and I stood near the door and shook my fist up the stairs. 'I hope all the ghosts of Aberglasney rise up to haunt you,' I whispered.

Justin must have heard me, because he turned round and smiled spitefully. 'I know the ghosts of Aberglasney much better than you do, Riana darling, and they are not the ones in the spirit world, believe me.'

'What are you talking about, Justin?'

'Past history, Riana. Things you don't understand and don't need to know about.' Justin was as smug as ever. 'Now, I'll say goodnight.'

He disappeared along the corridor, and I went back into the sitting room and refrained from banging the door shut. I sat there and fumed as I heard Justin's footsteps across the landing, wondering if he was attempting to intrude into my studio to look at my unfinished paintings. If he was, he would soon find out that I always kept it locked! It looked as if I was stuck with Justin until I could invoke some legal law that would have him evicted.

In the morning, Justin was seated at the breakfast table with Mrs Ward serving him bacon and eggs and toast as if he was lord of all he surveyed.

'You don't have to wait on Mr Mansel-Atherton,' I said crossly. 'Let him cook his own breakfast, seeing as he's not even paying for board and lodge here.'

'No man pays board and lodge when he owns the house,' Justin said, rebuking me, and Mrs Ward made a hasty retreat to the kitchen.

I followed her. 'When Justin pays your wages you can wait on him as much as you like. Until then, please do what *I* ask.'

'It's difficult for me to take it all in,' she said. 'The Mansel-Atherton family has owned Aberglasney for as long as I can remember.'

'Well, I'm the legal owner now,' I said more gently, 'and I'll prove it. I'll go to a London solicitor if I have to and get Justin thrown out of here.'

'Want breakfast?' Mrs Ward adroitly changed the subject. 'I've just made a fresh pot of tea.'

I sat down. 'I'll have tea and toast,' I said, sulky as a child, 'but I won't eat with that man. I'll stay in here with you.'

'That's all right,' Mrs Ward said, and I felt, churlishly, that she was giving me permission to eat in my own kitchen.

Later, I heard Justin go upstairs, and by the banging and moving of furniture I realised he was searching my house. He wasn't the first one to make a search of Aberglasney; what were they all looking for? Could they *really* all still be looking for Mr Mansel-Atherton's engine designs, after all this time? Of course, I thought, Justin could be looking for proof of his inheritance. My blood ran cold.

I hurried upstairs just as he was going in to the blue room, Beatrice's room. I pushed the door open and there he was on the floor, tapping the boards, a chisel and a hammer lying alongside him.

'What do you think you are doing?' I stared down at him, my hands clenched to my sides, longing to hit him.

'What does it look like?' He sat up and leaned back against the wall. He looked unruffled; Justin always appeared to be in full evening dress, even though he now wore casual trousers and an open-neck shirt. 'I'm searching the old house.'

'But *why*?'

'You must be incredibly stupid, Riana. My father's plans are here somewhere. Designs for a new type of aeroplane engine, so revolutionary and brilliant that I could still make a fortune from them if I discovered them, even now. Everyone wants to get their hands on my father's drawings, from the United States Army Air Forces to the Russians.'

I went cold. Was that why Tom kept returning to me, making love to me, only to learn if I knew about the drawings and where they could be kept? He was in the United States Army Air Forces, after all.

'Sounds as ridiculous as the presence of ghosts to me,' I said 'Now get up from here and get out of my house before I call the police and tell them your intention was to come here and rob me.'

'How would you prove that, Riana my darling? All I would have to do is show the police my birth certificate and they would back off. With my name it would be hard to prove that I am not the rightful owner of the house, wouldn't it?'

'Where's Beatrice when I need her?' I muttered, and Justin turned his back and continued to remove floorboards.

In the kitchen, Mrs Ward was washing the floor, her hair tied up in a scarf and a hint of steel curling pins peeping out over her forehead.

'How can I get rid of that man, Mrs Ward? He's trying to ruin my house! He's busy pulling up floorboards at the moment in the blue room.'

Mrs Ward gave me a quick glance, but remained tight lipped.

I stared at her for a long moment. 'What do you know about these designs that Mr Edwin created? Is it common knowledge that there are lost plans, worth a fortune, hidden in this house?'

She shrugged. 'There was talk when he was taken away by the police, but we villagers didn't know anything about designs and plans and such and no one has ever found anything in the house. If they were to exist though, they'd be worth a mint of money.'

'How do you know that?'

'Just the way that strange men have been here to search. I suspect all this nonsense about lights and ghosts has always been more to do with folks searching the old place than any ghosts.'

I shook my head and tiptoed across the wet floor and went out into the garden to be on my own to think things through. I sat under the cloisters. Could it be true that the mysterious noises in the night, the bumps and crashes, had been made by men searching the place all along? And the flickering lights on the landing, so eerie in darkness, were the candles of burglars come to rob Beatrice of what was rightfully hers? I shivered. It seemed as unlikely an explanation as the ghosts.

It was cold in the garden, and a rim of frost edged the stonework. But in a few weeks spring would be coming and the brave yellow of daffodils would make bright splashes across the borders of the gardens. But I was running ahead of myself. I had to plan for my Christmas party for my ghost hunters. My first job was to get rid of Justin. I would ask Diane if she knew of a good lawyer who could look at all the facts – my bill of sale versus Justin's claim to the house because of his name – and learn exactly what the law was about the ownership of Aberglasney.

I would be desolate if Justin proved to be the owner, but I felt my bill of sale was legitimate and legally binding. However, I knew it would take heaven and earth and the might of the law to move Justin out of my home.

Chapter Thirty-Two

Diane arrived for a visit, but she was in a very funny mood. 'I find Justin very convincing,' she said.

We were sitting on the sofa. It was comfortable and warm in the room, with a glass of good port to keep us company.

'Why on earth are you taking Justin's part?' I was disturbed by Diane's attitude. She seemed to think Justin was the true heir to my house and that I could do worse than to marry him.

'Don't be silly, Riana. I'm thinking of you. He's young, he's ambitious, and as I told you I will be leaving the gallery and all the goodwill of the business to him. He's become very close to me.'

'He's charmed you,' I said bluntly. 'Has he made love to you yet?' As soon as I spoke the words, I regretted them.

'Riana! How could you be so gross? I loved my Mr Readings. You know that the greatest day of my life was when he put a ring on my finger.'

'I'm sorry, that was uncalled for,' I said at once. 'Of course, you wouldn't want a boy like Justin, not after a good man like Mr Readings.' And yet I looked at Diane afresh. She was much younger than Mr Readings, of course. She was a comfortably upholstered but nonetheless attractive widow with lots of money and influence.

But then I was being silly. Why would Justin want me and the house if he'd already settled for Diane and her fortune? I hugged Diane and kissed her cheek and told her again how sorry I was… and yet and yet, was she really my friend? Was anyone really my friend, including Tom, my dear man? And then there was Mrs Ward… She was constantly there at Aberglasney. She had every chance to search the house whenever she cleaned and dusted and changed the linen. Has she discovered any papers? And if so, was she keeping them from me? I was growing paranoid, and I hated it.

Diane persuaded me to go to London, and together we visited her lawyer – who was young and keen and told me my documents regarding Aberglasney were legal and binding. 'Of course, the son has a right to contest the will,' he added, and my spirits sank.

We travelled to the guest house, and once there I sat in a chair my head in my hands. 'You know Justin is forcing himself on me, don't you?' I said miserably.

Diane looked at me sharply. 'You don't mean…' Her words trailed away, but she had a glitter in her eyes that I didn't like to see.

'Not physically, of course,' I replied hurriedly. 'I mean that he insists on living in my house, in spite of my protests. Well, today I've got an appointment with another lawyer, Mr Prentice, a fine London lawyer who specialises in houses and wills and such.'

'Why didn't you tell me?' Diane said. 'I've wasted my time advising you and taking you to see my lawyer. What are you thinking of, Riana? Don't you trust me?'

'I trust you, but I don't trust Justin,' I said. 'No doubt he advised you which firm to visit.' She nodded slowly, and I smiled. 'I thought so. You are too trusting, Diane.'

I went to see Mr Prentice on my own because I knew Diane would put Justin's case to him, even if it was only out of a sense of rightness and fairness. The lawyer had modern premises, very unlike Mr Jeremy's dark offices and book-lined study. Mr Prentice sat in a bright light room with two windows and a warm light over a polished, immaculate desk. His ink tray was spotless, no ink blotches stained the burnished wood, and even the nib of his pen was shining as though it had never been used.

Mr Prentice read the bill of sale in silence, absorbing it all quickly and digesting it in silence. At last he spoke. 'Looks legal and binding to me,' he said, and I breathed a sigh of relief. 'So what is the problem, Miss Evans? I assume there is one, or you wouldn't be here.'

I told him about Justin and his claims, and he leaned back in his chair, adjusted his glasses, and listened carefully.

'I visited Aberglasney once,' Mr Prentice remarked, 'on a business matter concerning putting funds into designs for a new type of aeroplane engine. Unfortunately, I couldn't raise the money, but the plans were brilliant, quite brilliant. We haven't seen their like again. But later, if I remember rightly, Mansel-Atherton was accused of murdering five girls.' He paused and lit a cigar. 'All nonsense, of course, not a real shred of evidence against him. I hear the room had been freshly painted. I always thought that if the chimney had been blocked, the lead paint fumes could have killed all the girls in one night, as they lay sleeping in their beds, but not a man like Edwin Mansel-Atherton. He had no motive, for a start. Still, the case ruined him. He killed himself, I believe. Now back to business.'

He paused and picked up a great tome of a book. 'The point is, did Mr Mansel-Atherton ever acknowledge this son in writing? The man had a wonderfully creative brain, so he would know what he was about. Was the father's name on the birth certificate? These questions I must answer before I know for sure what this young man's claims amount to. I will write to you with my findings, Miss Evans, and in the meantime don't worry too much. I think you are pretty safe. Where may I contact this young man?'

'He's in my house, and he won't be moved,' I said, and Mr Prentice frowned.

'He's going to have to be evicted through the law courts then,' he said. 'Or, and officially I didn't tell you this, you could have friends to literally remove him by force.'

That sounded tempting. I could imagine Justin being thrown out on his ear. How indignant he would be that his arrogant pride had been dented! I put my papers away in my bag and got to my feet. 'Well, thank you, Mr Prentice. I will wait to hear from you then. Please be as quick as you can.'

He rose and shook my hand. 'Of course, Miss Evans. I'd be delighted to act for you at once.' His smile was warm, and his hand held mine a little longer than was necessary.

I drew away, blushing. He was a very attractive man, even though he was of mature years. What a pity I was in love with Tom – who didn't appreciate me at all, who came and went at a whim, and who seemed to get me into danger whenever he was around. And yet my heart ached for him.

I left the office walking on air, however. Aberglasney was almost surely mine, and a good-looking man had found me attractive and showed it. I really felt positive for the first time in ages. Also, Mr Prentice had given me an idea to mull over about the death of the maids.

I turned a corner and stopped walking abruptly. Ahead of me was a couple, arm in arm, and I recognised Diane's fashionable hat. I slowed my pace and kept a discreet distance behind them. The man too looked familiar: the hair, the slant of the shoulders, the cut of the clothes… it was Justin and Diane! She'd lied about their relationship, making me feel disgusting for even suggesting there was something between them, and there they were together! Thank goodness she hadn't come to see Mr Prentice with me; she would have proved to be a thorn in my side.

I took the underground back to Diane's house and packed my bags as quickly as I could. I didn't even leave her a note; I just wanted to get home as quickly as I could.

It seemed an age before I again stood in the roomy hallway of my house, and I sighed with pleasure. It was all mine, and at last I was beginning to learn the real secrets of Aberglasney.

Chapter Thirty-Three

There was no sign of Mrs Ward so I made a cup of tea and sat in the kitchen, drinking it thirstily. I'd thought about what Mr Prentice had told me about the death of the young girls, and I realised what he'd said made sense, even it hadn't been the paint itself that had killed them. Hadn't Mr Jeremy told me that lead poisoning took days, not hours? It would be difficult to kill five people at the same time though, that much was true. Wouldn't they scream, run away, or even overpower a man by sheer numbers? In any case, I believed Beatrice. She knew her husband and common sense told me that she spoke the truth. Perhaps Mr Prentice had the truth of it: perhaps the chimney *had* been blocked, and they had suffocated from the fumes of the fire.

I put down my cup and went upstairs with my case, aware for once that the house was deathly quiet. One by one I searched the rooms, poking a brush up chimneys – bringing down lots of dust, and once a very dead bird, but no sign of plans or papers at all.

Lastly I went to Beatrice's room. It was cold and empty, and when I put my hand near the bars of the electric heater there was no warmth in them; Beatrice had not been home.

I sat cross-legged on the floor and poked dispiritedly a little way up the chimney, thinking I was completely on the wrong track. Nothing but soot fell into the hearth, spattering the carpet and my skirt in the process.

The wall was cold behind me as I leaned back against it, exhausted and disappointed. It seemed so logical that if a blocked chimney had been the cause of the deaths of the girls then the papers would be hidden there – preventing the smoke from finding a way out.

I found a newspaper left on the bedside table – proof that neither Mrs Ward nor Treasure dusted in here too often – and spread it over the floor near the fireplace. I decided I would make a determined effort this time! I leaned halfway up the chimney, feeling soot fall in my hair. The brush handle met resistance this time, and – very excited – I pushed harder, feeling like the chimney sweeps of old must have felt.

Suddenly, a huge parcel fell into the grate, covered in a chunk of soot as big as a brick, followed by sheets and sheets of newspaper. A box wrapped in old newspaper lay in the grate, and I stared at it for a moment, not daring to think I'd found the hidden 'treasure'. Was this box really what all the fuss had been about?

I picked up one of the loose newspapers. It was yellow and crumbling, and when I looked at the date I saw it was over twenty years old. As I looked at it, I knew the truth: Edwin had hidden his designs in the chimney, wrapped in old newspaper, all those years ago. But the box, and the papers, had blocked the chimney, causing the deaths of the young maids, who had all slept in the blue room together...

I cleaned up the grate as best as I could and took the box to my studio. As I suspected, it contained a sheaf of technical drawings. I meticulously copied the drawings – leaving bits I thought vital out and altering complicated arithmetic that I didn't even understand. A couple of hours passed, but when I had finished I put the original drawings into my art folder, hurried to the blue room and stuffed my 'copies' up the chimney. I was confident no one would make sense out of them, even if they found them.

I heard the front door open, and I knew Justin had come back from London as quickly as he could. He and Diane had realised I must have gone home. I heard voices in the hall and realised Justin had brought company.

I changed and went downstairs to greet my guests. I knew I had to keep a cool head and play Justin's game for now, work out just what he and Diane wanted.

Mrs Ward had returned and she nodded her head to me in apology as she carried a tray of drinks through the hall. 'Sorry I was out when you came home, Riana. I didn't expect you till the morning.' She paused. 'I hope you don't mind, but I've invited the colonel to come over for a drink, ahead of the rest of the ghost people.'

'Of course I don't mind.' I was relieved. Whatever Justin planned, he couldn't do any harm while there were guests in the house. Tomorrow was the Christmas ghost-haunting weekend party, so the house would be overrun.

I noticed my visitors had made themselves at home. Diane had kicked off her shoes and was seated next to Justin. She beamed at me as if nothing was amiss and took a drink with a sigh of satisfaction.

'Why did you run off home so suddenly?' Diane said, looking at me over the rim of her glass.

'A whim?' I said. 'Actually, I saw you and Justin together arm in arm and didn't want to play the gooseberry.'

Diane laughed. 'Well, I suppose I'd better tell you my guilty secret then. Justin is my son.' Diane dropped the bombshell without a blink of her eye, and I stared at her in amazement.

'Your son?' I looked at Justin and saw the same features: the dark hair, the slant of the eyes, the upright carriage.

'You and Edwin Mansel-Atherton then?'

'That's right. We were lovers once, and dear Justin is the result.'

'But Edwin never acknowledged him, did he? And that's why you pressed me to marry him! Diane, I thought you were my friend.'

'Of course I'm your friend, but I'm also a mother. I would love you and Justin to run Aberglasney together. What could be better?'

'But I'm not in love with Justin. I could *never* marry him. Sorry, Justin.'

'Excuse me, Riana.' Mrs Ward came into the room with another tray of drinks. 'Don't forget we've got visitors tomorrow,' she hinted.

I got to my feet. 'Well, if you'll all excuse me, I'd better help Mrs Ward get the bedrooms ready. Help yourselves to drinks.'

'Aye.' Mrs Ward spoke wryly. 'I've been upstairs to put the linen out, and it looks as if we've had the chimney sweep in some of the bedrooms.'

Justin and Diane gave each other a quick glance. 'We'd better help then.' Diane was the one to speak. 'Come on, Justin. You can help me clean up for dear Riana's sake. We don't want her weekends ruined, do we?'

I knew at once Diane had realised that the chimneys must be where the papers were hidden, so I decided to speak. 'These plans of Mr Mansel-Atherton's. They might be a lever for you to use against me concerning the owner-ship of Aberglasney, Justin, but I would never marry you. I'm in love with another man.'

'Rubbish!' Diane said softly. 'You haven't started to live yet, Riana.'

'Well, about the designs everyone's making a fuss about. I wondered if they were hidden in the chimneys. I did look, but I found nothing.' I spoke the lie easily, knowing I could be among enemies, not friends.

Diane looked at me for a long time. 'So you've found them then? You're not a very good liar, Riana. Still—' she waved a limp hand at Justin '—we can talk about this later, but perhaps we should just get out of the way for now. We'll take a drive to the village pub, shall we?'

'Later' I took meant as once I was alone and Diane and Justin could bully me into telling the truth.

'I'm so tired,' I said and declined Diane's invitation, but urged them to go on without me. Once they had left, I rubbed my forehead, and Mrs Ward touched my shoulder. 'Shall I make you a cup of cocoa, Riana? You look so pale.' She made me a drink and then took off her apron. 'I've had enough for today,' she said. 'Kitchen is closed.'

Diane and Justin returned from the pub some time later, having had, I suspected, a good chat about the designs. 'Finished tidying the rooms?' Diane yawned.

'One more drink and then I'll retire for the night,' she said. And, true to her word, once she'd drunk the large gin Mrs Ward had poured her – and Justin had done likewise – she kicked off her shoes and, rather unsteadily, asked Justin to take her arm and lead her up to her room.

'Well, our guests will sleep well tonight.' Mrs Ward kicked off her own shoes and put her feet up on her little stool.

'How can you say that?' I knew I sounded weary. 'They might start searching the place once everything is quiet.'

'I don't think so. I slipped some of that laudanum stuff in their drinks. I could see Mrs Diane's eyes beginning to close when she was going upstairs.' Mrs Ward smiled, and I wondered if she had an ulterior motive in keeping my two guests quiet for the night. What was wrong with me? I was suspecting everyone I came in contact with. Was I in even more danger now I'd found the plans?

I went to bed at last, but I couldn't sleep. I tossed and turned and wanted Tom to come to take me away from everything. But then how was I to know if he cared for me, or if he too only wanted poor Edwin's papers, like all the others? Tom was in the United States Army Air Forces, I reminded myself, and the plans for a new engine would probably help his career along well enough. He could even be a spy! Perhaps that was why he'd been abducted.

I fell asleep at last and dreamed of Mrs Ward, all the ghosts of the dead girls, and poor Edwin, along with a smiling Diane and Justin, holding out a wedding veil towards me as they stood round my bed.

I woke sweating. It was dark and silent and I was alone and very afraid, and it took me a very long time to fall asleep again.

Chapter Thirty-Four

There were fewer guests for this year's Christmas ghost-haunting weekend. Colonel Fred, of course, and young William, plump Betty, and most of my 'old faithfuls', as I called them. To my surprise, the handsome lawyer Mr Prentice turned up in a fine shiny car, with a letter and a wink for me. With Diane and Justin, it was a healthy crowd. Almost.

I read the letter quickly and smiled. Mr Prentice had done his research well. Justin had no claim; he was not a Mansel-Atherton at all. The name on the birth certificate read 'Jameson' – Diane's name before she married, I imagined.

I passed the letter to him. He read it and shrugged. 'Ah, well. It was a good try. No hard feelings?' he said airily.

Speechless, I returned to my guests and hid my fears about the designs, about Justin, and about my foolish longing for Tom, and made a show of being happy for my guests. I'd made name cards for everyone, and with good humour everyone pinned them on before we sat down to dinner in the decorated dining room.

The table was graced with a starter of fish and toast. Somehow, with her usual skill, Mrs Ward had managed to acquire some tinned anchovies and a pound of salt butter – the taste was delicious. I knew she'd cooked rabbit and chicken for the main course, with tiny roast potatoes and tinned peas. We'd have tinned fruit and custard for pudding. All in all a good meal, considering the war had not long ended.

After dinner the guests retired to the sitting room where they could relax and smoke and have a drink or two of mulled wine, which I hoped would make them feel more festive, before my little speech and then the ghost hunt would begin. I felt a shiver of apprehension, however. Something was amiss tonight, and though I tried my best to hide it I felt spooked and scared, and I wasn't sure if it was of the living or the dead.

Justin came and sat beside me and put his arm around my shoulders. I looked at him disapprovingly, but it made no difference.

'Where are they?' he said without preamble. 'The drawings, did you find them? I take it from what Mrs Ward said that you've been poking up chimneys here.'

So Justin was my enemy. 'Did you attack me when I first arrived?' I asked, my lips trembling. 'Have you been plotting against me and interfering with my paintings all this time?'

'Hey, hold your horses. I haven't attacked anyone, and no, I haven't done anything to you or your precious paintings. Silly daubs, that's all they are.'

That stung, but I knew he was trying to distract me. 'Go away,' I said. When he did not, I rose and refilled my glass and sat next to the colonel. 'What are you hoping for tonight, Colonel Fred?' I spoke as cheerfully as I could, and he tipped up his glass of brandy and winked at me.

'Who knows, dear lady? I might just make my fortune here tonight.'

'What do you mean?' I asked uneasily.

'Why, I might just capture a ghost on film, Riana. What do you think I mean? Mind you, if anyone gets a good picture it will be young William. He's the clever one here. He's got a very good degree, you know, even though he is a bumbler at times.'

I felt bewildered. I really knew nothing about these people I was accommodating in my house. Who could I trust, and who meant me harm? I wondered if the drawings were safe in my studio, but it wouldn't do to check now; someone would be sure to follow me.

The front doorbell rang out, sounding somehow like the knell of doom. I heard Mrs Ward go to answer it, and then Rosie came into the room, a young child in her arms. His skin had darkened, and his curly hair had also grown darker, and I realised it was her son – hers, and the handsome airman Carl Jenkins.

'I want them, the drawings.' She stood in the middle of the room, her feet planted firmly on the carpet. 'Carl died trying out a version this new engine. Not quite correct, the engine wasn't, because Mr Mansel-Atherton never gave the Americans all the designs, as he promised. My Carl crashed his plane because of the mistakes, so by rights my son should have any money coming from the designs.'

Justin jumped to his feet. 'The drawings might not even still exist.' He sounded angry. 'My father might have destroyed them. Have you thought of that?'

'Carl told me about them. They exist all right, and as for her—' she nodded in my direction '—doing the place up, she must have found the drawings by now.'

'Who are you working with, Rosie?' Justin demanded. 'Just who is pulling your strings? Is it that other yank, Tom Maybury?'

I went cold. 'Excuse me,' I interrupted them both. 'Rosie, there are no drawings, no plans. Not any more. Wise up, it's all a story. If such plans still existed, the house would have been saved. It wouldn't have been sold to me in the first place.'

'Riana's making sense,' the colonel said. 'I don't know what these drawings are, but they are obviously worth a considerable amount of money or folk wouldn't be so eager to find them.'

'What do you know, you silly old man?' Rosie sank into a chair. She had tears in her eyes — were they genuine?

I looked at her baby's sweet face. His eyes were huge and dark, and he clung to his mother as if he would never let her go. Rosie clearly took good care of him, so she couldn't be all bad. And her man had given his life to trial Edwin's designs — only without the originals, the Americans had evidently got the new engine wrong. 'You might as well stay Rosie,' I said. 'I'll make you up a bed.'

'I can't go anywhere anyway,' Rosie said. 'There's no inn or hotel that will take me in — not with a black American child, they won't.'

'You shouldn't have come here,' Mrs Ward interjected. 'Wherever you go there's trouble.'

'Oh, look, little Carl—' Rosie's tone was mocking '—there's your loving grandmother. Want to hold him, Mother? He's quite civilised. He won't bite or anything.'

'That's enough, Rosie,' I said sharply. 'No one here is prejudiced against you or your son.

'You kidding?' Rosie said. 'I've been shunned by the villagers. No one would put me up, not even for one night.'

'No wonder, calling on good people at this time of night. Where's your sense, girl?' Mrs Ward's tone had softened. 'Come into the kitchen. I'll make you a cup of tea and a bite to eat.'

'I'm so tired, Mum,' Rosie said softly. 'A cup of cocoa in bed would be lovely, thanks.'

'Rosie can have my room, Mrs Ward,' I said. 'The bed is big enough for her and the baby in there.'

'But where will you sleep, Riana?' Mrs Ward asked.

'I'll take the blue room. Beatrice has gone away visiting relatives again.'

'But my dear,' the colonel said, 'that is the room that is most haunted! That's the room we all want to visit!'

'That's fine.' I felt doubtful and superstitiously frightened at the thought of sleeping in what was supposed to be a haunted room, but Beatrice seemed to manage all right when she was here. 'I'll be going to bed later than everyone else, anyway. I always do when I have guests.'

'I'll sleep in the haunted room,' Justin said.

Then young William volunteered. 'Please, Miss Evans, let me sleep in there. I might just get a good picture — a reward for all the weekends I've spent here — and I haven't had a good picture yet.'

There was a clamour of voices, and I held up my hand. 'William wins the prize,' I said. 'He's the youngest and the keenest ghost hunter. He can have the blue room, and I'll take his room.'

William beamed. 'Oh good! I'll stay awake all night with my camera at the ready, just so I don't miss anything.'

'William—' Diane was staring at William suspiciously '—what is it you actually do for a living? I don't think you've ever mentioned it.'

'It doesn't really matter, Diane,' I interrupted. 'I have a policy of allowing guests to keep their private lives just that.'

'I'm not very good at my job, so I've taken up part-time photography – weddings and such. Perhaps I'll make my mark with that.'

I glared at Diane. 'Happy now? What William does is *his* business.'

–

It was the early hours of the morning when at last I went to bed. I lay in an uneasy state of mind, wondering who intended to do what harm to me and my house. It was clear Edwin's drawings were at the root of all the mysterious comings and goings, the strange abductions, the threats on my life... And what part did Tom have in it all? That was the main reason for my uneasiness.

I went over the facts against him yet again. He was a military man, an airman... the drawings would have some significance for him. I turned over on my back and then sat up sharply. I could smell smoke!

I was alert now, and I realised the smoke was curling down the servants' staircase. I ran to the blue room, calling out, 'Fire!'

When I reached the blue room I opened the door gingerly, knowing from the wartime bombing that when air hit flames they could leap and burgeon. To my horror, I could see William kneeling by the blazing fire in the grate, apparently unconscious and overcome with fumes.

The fake drawings had fallen from the chimney and begun to burn, setting the room itself alight.

Guilt engulfed me. I'd taken the electric heater out of the room to put in my room, and William must have tried to light the fire. The false drawings were pushed into the chimney, blocking it, and now poor innocent William was suffering the same fate that the five young maids had — suffocated by fumes!

But then William groaned. He was still alive!

Coughing, I dragged William to the door and on to the landing. 'Help, fire!' I shouted loudly. 'Everyone get out of the house!' I managed to pull William's inert body to the stairs and somehow bumped him down them into the hall below. Guests were already coming out of their rooms.

'I'll phone the fire brigade.' The colonel was in his dressing gown, a ruffled Mrs Ward at his side. She too was in her dressing gown, with her hair awry. In other circumstances I would have been amused by her embarrassment — but not now.

'I'll phone,' Mrs Ward said. 'Fred, you help Riana with the young lad.'

Soon we were all on the lawn, shivering against the early morning mist. Rosie cuddled her little boy; his dark eyes were wide with lights glowing in them as he looked up to the house, where the flames were beginning to take hold.

And then the fire brigade arrived, bells clanging, and the police had sent a car which screeched to a halt in the drive. A woman in uniform came towards me. 'I've come because of a suspicious fire, but my intent is also to investigate the death of Mr Mansel-Atherton.'

I knew that voice. I looked up. 'Miss Grist!'

She held a badge towards me. 'I'm Detective Delia Grist as it happens,' she said. 'And we've been observing matters here at Aberglasney for some time. You, with your blundering ways, almost ruined things for us.'

'But why were you posing as a librarian?' I asked.

'It was a cover. I was there merely to observe what you were up to,' Miss Grist said, 'and taking the chance to research the old newspapers. And at the same time, *you* were coming in to do the same research!' She actually smiled. 'To be frank, you were nothing but a pain in the neck. Ah, look, the fire is out. An isolated little fire, I'd say. Now, let's all go into the undamaged part of the house where I can question you all in relative comfort.'

I ushered all my guests into the sitting room and realised the damage had been confined to the top of the floor, where the blue room had been. I realised then that the only guest missing from the room was young William. The ambulance was still outside so he hadn't gone to hospital.

I hurried back to the garden. I could hear coughing from under the yew tree tunnel, and I walked timidly into the darkness, fearing I knew not what. There was a creeping sensation along my scalp, as if all my hairs were standing on end, like those of a frightened cat. I heard soft footfalls behind me, but when I turned no one was there. Gasping with unnamed fear, I stood back against the branches of the yew tree, trying not to breathe too heavily.

I saw a dark shadow then, coming slowly, inexorably towards me. A misshapen figure in the dark. A limping, heavy-breathing figure as if from some nightmare world.

And then a glimmer of light illuminated his face. It was twisted and blackened by smoke, and he looked like a monster... not the familiar young William I'd always known.

'William, I thought someone had called an ambulance for you.' I spoke nervously as he came to stand inches from my face. He smelt of smoke and dust, and he was like a stranger to me.

'I sent the ambulance away. I didn't want to go to hospital, you interfering witch!'

'But William, I saved your life. I dragged you out of the room and into the fresh air.'

'And you let the designs burn to ashes, you stupid woman. You denied me the chance to make a name for myself. I could kill you!'

He hit me. The blow was so hard that I fell back on to the dew wet grass. I saw William kneeling over me, his strong hands around my throat. My mind refused to accept the sense of it. I couldn't believe it. Young William was the one who had attacked me. He had been my enemy all along.

'You silly bitch.' His tone was venomous. 'Why did you have to buy the house and invite folk in to prance round the place at will? If you hadn't come here, I could have searched in peace.'

He shook me fiercely, his hands tightening around my neck. I was beginning to see sparkles of lights I couldn't draw in any breath.

'You've finished me off,' William growled. 'My career is over. I'm an engineer, and I was writing a paper on Edwin Mansel-Atherton. I could have made my name if it wasn't for your interference! Why didn't you go when I tried to make you? Now I'm going to have to kill you!'

I was beginning to lose consciousness as his fist slammed into my cheek. I was barely able to see, when a dark figure leapt on William dragging him away from me. And then Tom was there, beating the life out of William!

My head started spinning with all the chaos and the smoke and the shocks I suffered and I blacked out…

When I came to, the police were taking William away before Tom killed him. Tom knelt beside me and touched my face. 'All right, Riana my darling?'

I thought he was going to propose or at least declare his unending love. Instead he said, 'Where are the designs? Edwin's designs? Tell me, Riana. It's very important.'

My heart sank. 'They are in my studio, in my folder. Does it matter now?'

Tom was running like a deer across the lawn and into the house, and I put my hands over my mouth, unaware that my eye was swelling and turning black. My head was aching with the smoke and fumes, and my throat closing up so much that each breath was an agony. The worst of the whole horrible episode was that I now knew, without doubt, that Tom only wanted me for what he could get out of the designs.

I felt hands lift me to my feet, which helped me to drag more air into my lungs.

Eventually, I was led indoors by the faithful Mrs Ward, who'd come looking for me. 'My poor house,' I croaked.

'Aberglasney isn't badly damaged, Riana, so don't worry about the house. Just worry about your poor little face.'

As we got into the hall, Tom was coming down the staircase, my folder clutched awkwardly to his chest. He flung it open and, discarding my precious sketches, found the papers. 'These are the originals?' He waved them in my face.

'Yes. I did copies and stuffed them back up the chimney in the maids' room,' I said hoarsely. 'Those are the ones that burned.'

'You clever darling!' He kissed me soundly, and I winced as his fingers touched my bruised cheek. He helped me move, rather shakily, to a chair, and Miss Grist came to my side just as I was about to accuse Tom of being a spy and a traitor. In truth, I didn't care about any of those things though. All that mattered was that he'd played fast and loose with my feelings to get the damned designs for a stupid engine design, which were probably useless now anyway.

'There will be an investigation, of course, but if I'm right then the discovery of these papers up the chimney proves Edwin Mansel-Atherton is an innocent man,' Miss Grist said. 'The maids died because the chimney was blocked. They would have died from carbon-monoxide poisoning,' she explained. But then she added, self-importantly, 'All this should have been reported to the police, of course.'

'The police were here plenty of times – including you, Miss Grist.' I was very aware of Tom standing beside me with the plans in his hands. 'You even tried to ruin my business – so you could search for the plans all the better, I presume?'

'Luckily for you I *was* here,' Miss Grist said, ignoring my accusation, 'or you might not be alive now.' Her tone implied I was stupid and interfering and if I had been strangled then it would have been better for everyone. She sniffed and added cattily, 'It's well known that carbon-monoxide poisoning causes visions and hallucinations, by the way, Miss Evans. Ghosts indeed!'

At this, everyone – including Justin and Diane, the colonel and Mrs Ward, and all my other guests – gathered around me in support, and I felt ashamed of mistrusting any of them. I looked up at Tom. 'And what is your part in all this?' My tone was hostile. 'Are the designs that important to your precious American air force? More important than I am?'

'I had to get them, honey, don't you see? Even though searching for them myself put me in danger from my own colleagues. The designs make Carl's death the responsibility of the United States Army Air Force, you see. These plans – the originals – prove that the plane Carl was testing wasn't built correctly. The engineers didn't have Mr Mansel-Atherton's complete designs, and so they screwed it up.'

He kissed me, and I stared at him, breathless with love and bewilderment.

'There will be compensation due for his child.' Tom looked at Rosie as she stood, holding the baby close. 'You, Rosie, and your little one, will be cared for always.'

He put both his arms around me and kissed me again. I saw the colonel wink at Mrs Ward, and she had a smile on her thin face.

'More importantly,' Tom drew my attention, 'with the designs out of the way, I knew you would be safe, Riana my love. Not only British and American soldiers, but also an independent searcher wanted the plans badly

– someone who wasn't afraid to kill. Until the drawings were found, you stood in the way. You were in danger all the time!'

'That independent someone being William, but why?'

'He'd taken an engineering degree, but he never really made the grade. He'd heard and read a little about the missing designs in an engineering magazine, and he wanted a good look at them. He probably photographed them before he put them in the chimney and lit a fire.'

'But they were the false ones I drew anyway. What good were they?'

'William wouldn't have known that. Not until he'd studied them in detail. He would have plagiarised the bits that he'd thought valuable so he could write a paper on it himself.'

I glanced at stony-faced Miss Grist. 'And this lady?' I asked Tom.

'We worked together on this case, that's all,' he said. 'We did it so we wouldn't blow Detective Grist's cover. Didn't she explain things when she took you to a police safe-house that night of your art exhibition? I knew that some soldiers had plans to search your house, and I wanted you out of the way and safe while they did so, so I asked Detective Grist and her colleagues to take care of you.' He folded me close to him again, and I saw Miss Grist's sneer. I remembered events rather differently. So it had been Miss Grist that night who had interrogated me about my relationship with Tom and threatened me with starvation! She had wanted Tom for herself, but like a man he never saw it. I snuggled into Tom, but Rosie's voice interrupted my delight and relief.

'Look, there's a ghost! There's really a ghost!' Rosie gasped with fear.

I turned in Tom's arms, still holding on to him, and laughed. 'That's only Beatrice,' I said. And then Beatrice walked towards the big stone wall that surrounded the garden leading to the graveyard beyond. She waved her little hand and then walked right through a solid stone wall.

'She's gone home,' I said softly. 'Beatrice has at last been able to join her dear Edwin.' And I felt a moment's grief at losing her, but strangely no shock.

Then Tom turned my bruised and battered face gently towards him and possessed my lips gently but commandingly. And as tears of happiness came to my eyes, my ghost hunters – my true friends – cheered and clapped, and I knew there was no need any more for words.